To Keller ✳

*For keeping me company as I write and
reminding me every day of courage, kindness,
and God's eternal grace.*

Chasing Rome

A Novel

John Gray

author of _Manchester Christmas_

PARACLETE PRESS

Brewster, Massachusetts

2022 First Printing

Chasing Rome: A Novel

Copyright © 2022 by John Gray

ISBN 978-1-64060-778-1

The Paraclete Press name and logo (dove on cross) are trademarks of
Paraclete Press

LIBRARY OF CONGRESS CATALOGING-IN-PUBLICATION DATA

Names: Gray, John (John Joseph), 1962- author.
Title: Chasing Rome : a novel / John Gray.
Description: Brewster, Massachusetts : Paraclete Press, 2022. | Summary:
"The third book about Chase Harrington and Gavin whose adventures take
them to Rome. Join them as they make new friends, solve a mystery, and
in the end surprise you"-- Provided by publisher.
Identifiers: LCCN 2022015943 (print) | LCCN 2022015944 (ebook) | ISBN
9781640607781 (hardcover) | ISBN 9781640607798 (epub) | ISBN
9781640607804 (pdf)
Subjects: BISAC: FICTION / Christian / Romance / Suspense | FICTION /
Romance / Action & Adventure | LCGFT: Romance fiction. | Christian
fiction. | Novels.
Classification: LCC PS3607.R3948 C49 2022 (print) | LCC PS3607.R3948
(ebook) | DDC 813/.6--dc23/eng/20220408
LC record available at https://lccn.loc.gov/2022015943
LC ebook record available at https://lccn.loc.gov/2022015944

10 9 8 7 6 5 4 3 2 1

Published by Paraclete Press
Brewster, Massachusetts
www.paracletepress.com

Printed in India

Chasing Rome

CHAPTER 1

You Take the Biscuit

There are more than six thousand languages spoken in the world and Chase Harrington was proficient in exactly one: English. Yet, no translation was needed to understand the snarky look she was getting from the neatly dressed barista at the Sciascia Caffè in the Prati neighborhood of Rome.

Chase and her fiancé, Gavin, boarded a flight out of JFK the evening before, just as *Jeopardy* was coming on the television at the airport bar. After nine sleepless hours on the plane, a six-hour time change, and a bumpy cab ride into Italy's capital city, she needed an immediate influx of caffeine to make this day possible.

It was two in the afternoon on a crisp December day when faded brown floorboards that no doubt had been cut and nailed in place more than a century ago were creaking and whispering secrets under Chase's light feet. She noticed, the moment she walked in, that this coffee house was nicer than the ones back home, with its ornate wood molding, an exposed brick wall, and large chunky furniture that dared you to sit.

"Did I pronounce it wrong? Do you call a cappuccino something else here?" Chase asked politely.

The barista remained still as a statue, his frozen gaze fixed on Chase's lovely, albeit tired face.

Just then, a different voice chimed in, "He won't give it to you, luv."

The words, in an alluring accent, came from an attractive young woman with long red hair who was seated at a small table to Chase's left.

Chase turned to the lady with the charming brogue and asked, "Why not?"

The redhead put her newspaper down now and replied, "Cappuccino is never served this late in the day in Rome. Better to get a coffee."

Before Chase could change her order, the front door to the café flung open and a tall, handsome man stepped halfway in.

"Are you good, babe?" he said, turning every head in the place.

It was Chase's fiancé, Gavin Bennett, holding a brown leather leash that led to her Australian shepherd, Scooter.

"Yes," Chase replied, a bit flustered. "Just trying to get the hang of ordering something to drink in Italy. We've been here less than an hour and I've already broken a rule."

She could see Gavin's confusion but waved him away with her hand, saying, "I'm fine. Be right out."

Gavin flashed that broad, disarming smile and replied, "Sounds good. Hey, can you grab me a coffee, hon?"

Chase turned back to the waiting barista and said, "Forget the cappuccino. Two coffees, please."

The man immediately smiled, then turned his back to Chase and got busy working at a large silver machine with enough shiny knobs to launch a space satellite. There were hissing and banging noises that for some reason reminded Chase of *Charlie and the Chocolate Factory.* The *Oompa Loompa* spun back around and placed two small cups on the counter in front of Chase.

"Here we are, that is two euros," the barista said in perfect English.

"Oh, so we do speak American, eh?" Chase said with a hint of mischief in her voice.

The barista didn't crack a smile but gave Chase a quick wink with his right eye.

Chase reached into her jacket pocket and pulled out a fistful of strange-looking coins and currency.

"They gave me this at the exchange counter after we landed," she said, hoping the man in the apron could offer some assistance.

Chase looked at the redhead, who was enjoying the show from her table, and said, "I'm a shopkeeper's dream, the silly American who doesn't know what anything costs and will probably pay fifty bucks for a drink."

The woman replied, "Not to worry, Antonio is very honest."

Chase looked back to the barista and said, "So, you're Antonio. Nice to meet you."

The barista plucked coins from her open hands and said to Chase, "These are each worth one euro. I'm taking two."

Chase smiled, answering, "Thank you, Antonio. Let me give you a tip."

The barista stepped back as if she had offered him poison, raising both hands in front of him.

"Not allowed," he said firmly.

Chase, then mumbling to herself, "Wow, okay. So, no cappuccino after noon and no tipping, got it."

As Chase was about to go outside with her two coffees, she turned to the redhead and said, "Thank you for the help earlier. I'm Chase."

The woman, wearing a white knit sweater and jeans, rose from her seat and extended her hand to shake, answering, "Riley, and you're welcome, luv."

Chase smiled, asking, "Is that an Irish or Scottish accent?"

Riley feigned a shocked expression and raising her voice, "Oh, St. Francis on a bicycle, my poor granda must be spinning in his grave back in County Cork. That's Ireland, dear."

"Gran-what?" Chase replied.

"Da, Gran-Da, that's my grandfather," Riley explained.

Chase nodded, "Gotcha. Well, I love the accent and your name, very pretty."

Riley folded her arms and replied, "You wouldn't think so if you knew the rest of it."

Chase had to ask, "The rest? "

"O'Reilly, is me last name, believe it or not, as you Americans say."

Chase trying not to smile, then said, "So, your name is Riley O'Reilly?"

"It's worse than that," she answered. "My full name is Ophelia Riley O'Reilly.

Chase chuckled, then said, "So, if we use your first initial?"

"That's right," she replied. "My name is O. Riley O'Reilly. My da had a sense of humor."

The thought of it made both women share a laugh.

Chase liked this stranger and smiled warmly, saying, "I have to run, but it was really nice meeting you, Riley."

Just then the door opened, and Gavin poked his head back in again. "Not to be a bug, but it's chilly out here."

Chase set down the coffees, ran to the door, and grabbed Gavin by the hand. "This is my fiancé, Gavin. And Gavin, this is Riley."

Gavin extended his hand to shake hers, saying to Chase, "We just landed and you're already making friends."

Riley grasped Gavin's hand with both of hers and exclaimed, "Stop it, now. I've seen some dingers in my day, but you take the biscuit."

Gavin couldn't help but laugh out loud, "I'm sorry. What?"

"The biscuit, what you'd call *the cake*," Riley explained, adding, "And dinger means good-looking."

Chase intervened, saying, "I think she's calling you a stud muffin, babe."

Riley laughed and replied, "I don't know that expression, but she sounds about right."

Riley's eyes then darted down to the floor looking at Chase's dog. "And who have we here? Is he Irish? He looks a wee bit Irish."

Gavin answered, "Australian, actually. His name is Scooter."

Riley bent down on one knee to see the pup's face and rub his head, saying, "Sorry your gal is leaving you out in the cold, Scooter. I could talk the hind leg off a donkey if you let me."

Gavin looked at Chase, then whispered, "A donkey?"

Riley rose and looked at the happy couple, explaining, "Old Irish saying. Just means I'm a chatterbox."

Gavin picked up the small drinks Chase had just purchased, asking, "What's this?"

The cups were much smaller than a normal cup of coffee and filled with a dark black liquid.

Riley, again in her thick Irish accent, explained: "I saw the whole thing, Gavin. She tried, but ordering drinks in Italy can be a bit tricky if you don't know the lingo."

Gavin and Chase just stared at Riley, enjoying her accent and personality.

Riley continued. "Here you can only get cappuccino in the morning, and if you ask for coffee you get espresso."

Chase looked at Gavin and said sarcastically, "You read ten books on life in Italy and somehow you missed that chapter?"

Riley poked her red head in between them and whispered, "What you want to order is a Caffè Americano."

"And that's coffee?" Gavin asked.

"Not exactly," Riley answered. "But close."

Gavin looked at his watch. "Hon, we should, you know?"

Chase agreed. "I didn't realize it was that late."

Riley, curious now, asked, "What hotel you staying in? Is this your honeymoon?"

Chase held up her left ring finger to reveal the Tiffany's diamond Gavin had given her the year before. "Engaged, but that's why we're here, to be married."

Riley gave Chase and Gavin an unexpected hug, "Well, good on you both then."

Gavin explained, "We're actually not staying at a hotel. Chase thought it would be more fun to stay with a family for a few weeks and learn the culture. So, we'll be in a home in the Monti neighborhood of Rome."

Riley lit up. "Very nice indeed, and not so far from the Vatican, if you fancy a chat with the Pope."

Chase finished her strong drink in one gulp, put the cup down on the table, then said, "It was so nice to meet you, Riley. I hope I see you again."

Riley returned to her seat and replied, "This is my spot most afternoons at two."

Riley sipped her own drink, then added, "And it was nice to meet you both."

Outside the café, Chase and Gavin spied a large orange taxi sign on a metal pole at the corner. They didn't stand more than two minutes before a car arrived and a stout man in a wool cap stepped out to open the door for Chase.

Gavin fished a small piece of crumpled yellow paper from his jacket pocket. Speaking slowly, he read aloud, "Via dei Capocci, number eleven."

The driver didn't respond. Instead, he returned to the front seat, put the car in gear, and off they went.

A few blocks into the trip the driver turned and said in almost perfect English, "Three minutes. You weren't too far."

Chase smiled at the driver and asked, "Do most people in Rome speak English?"

She saw him nod his head up and down in the rearview mirror, before answering, "Sì. I mean yes. Most."

Both Gavin and Chase were mesmerized by the beauty of the architecture as they slowly made their way down the streets of Rome. Some Gothic, most with a Greek vibe. Occasionally they'd come to an abrupt halt and the driver would gently tap on the horn to get someone's attention.

Double-parking was common on Rome's narrow streets, and the two of them swallowed hard as the cab squeezed through passages that appeared too small to fit.

When three minutes were up, the driver double-parked himself and said, "Eleven on Via dei Capocci."

Chase paid him in euros and the pair emerged from the cab holding hands.

The building looked like many of the brownstones back in Manhattan, with a red brick façade and a thick tile roof, serving, now anyway, as a landing pad for a half-dozen noisy birds.

"Tell me again what we're doing here?" Gavin asked facetiously, as he looked up at the building.

Chase turned to meet his eyes, "Come on, anyone can stay at the Marriott. I want to feel like we're a part of it."

Gavin, answered back: "By staying with strangers in a strange place?"

Chase sighed now, asking, "Since when are you NOT up for an adventure?"

Gavin could see disappointment in her face and quickly snapped out of his funk, answering, "You're right. You're always right. This could be fun."

Chase then shifted to a more serious tone, saying, "And remember, Mr. Bennett, you have the most important assignment of all."

Gavin smiled. "I know, you want me to plan a month of romantic adventures."

Chase then spun in a circle on the cobblestone sidewalk with her arms extended to each side, saying, "And with all of Italy to choose from, the options are endless."

Gavin looked up at the building again, asking, "You sure about this place? The lady of the house barely spoke English on the phone, and she sounded—"

"Rude?" Chase finished his thought.

"I was going to say, um, what's the word?" Gavin added. "Joyless."

Chase took his hand again. "Perhaps we can bring her some joy then. Besides, if we want real Rome, this is the place—I can feel it."

Gavin replied, "And she's okay with Scooter staying?"

Chase answered, "I told her about him, and she said fine."

Just then, the two of them heard an older woman clear her throat from above. Both sets of eyes traveled up the front of the building to a tiny balcony where a woman in a modest house dress stood with her arms folded like a proctor giving an exam.

"Are you two going to talk all day or get in here?" the woman called down with a heavy Italian accent.

Curly gray hair framed her wrinkled face and dark, sad eyes.

"Not too late for the Marriott," Gavin mumbled to Chase, as he looked up at the woman hovering above like a hawk on a tree branch.

Then a different voice called out from behind, "Ignore her, she's just mad that I didn't clean up after breakfast."

Gavin and Chase turned to find a beautiful woman a bit older than Chase with long dark hair, full lips, and dusty brown eyes.

She said in a welcoming tone, "I'm Francesca. That's my mother-in-law barking at you. Let's go in before she dumps water on the three of us."

Chase squeezed Gavin's hand, and with Scooter in tow the three began their Italian adventure. They didn't know that the moment they stepped through that door, they'd be walking into a mystery filled with hope, loss, and endless love.

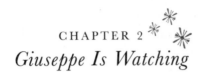

CHAPTER 2
Giuseppe Is Watching

It took fourteen steps to reach the second-floor apartment that Chase and Gavin would call home for the next twenty-eight days. Before Francesca reached for the faded brass doorknob, the door opened on its own and Gavin and Chase were greeted by a teenage boy and his dog. Scooter stepped in front of Chase protectively. The dogs gave each other a quick sniff, and soon both tails were wagging.

"Good boy, Giuseppe," the young man said, extending his hand to shake Gavin's like a gentleman.

"Welcome," he said. "I'm Giovanni. Everyone calls me Gio. It's spelled G-i-o, but in Italian it's pronounced like 'Joe' in English."

Gavin, who towered over the boy, gave him a firm shake back. "I'm Gavin. This is Chase, my fiancée."

Gio shook Chase's hand as well, adding, "Wow, you're pretty."

"Giovanni Michael," Francesca scolded from the hallway. "Forgive my son's boldness."

Gio turned a light shade of red, looked down and said, "Sorry. Sometimes I just say things."

Chase intervened, "Hey, if compliments are thrown at me, I'm happy to catch them."

"You all speak English so well," Gavin observed.

Francesca answered, "If you live and work in a place popular with tourists, it helps."

All conversation stopped then as an older woman standing just inside the large apartment cleared her throat, securing everyone's attention.

"Did you say fiancé?" she asked.

Chase answered, "Yes ma'am. We are here in Italy to be married."

Francesca, sensing what was coming next, spoke, "Mamma. It's okay."

Chase looked at Gavin, confused as to what was wrong.

The old woman answered their doubt in slightly broken English, "A fiancé is not a husband. So, until you are married, *due camere.*"

Gavin looked at Francesca for a translation.

"Two rooms, she's saying. Until you're married you must be in two rooms," Francesca explained.

Chase smiled wide. "Oh, ma'am, that's fine. We feel the same way. We have forever to be together."

"Nonna," the old woman replied.

Gavin then: "I'm sorry?"

The woman smiled for the first time since they lay eyes on her, "Call me Nonna."

Gio explained, "It means grandma. Everyone calls her Nonna."

Gio started toward the back of the apartment, calling back over his shoulder, "If you need two rooms, I need to move my exercise stuff out of the way in the spare bedroom."

Chase looked around the simple, yet spacious apartment and said to Francesca, "So we've met you, Gio and Nonna. Does your husband live here as well?"

The moment the question left her lips Chase regretted it, as she watched the smile drain from Francesca's face. The woman bit down on her lip as if searching for something to say.

Francesca then responded, "Matteo, my husband, died recently."

Gavin wanted to take hold and support the poor woman; her posture seemed to grow frail before his very eyes.

All he could was offer a soft, "We're so sorry."

Neither Chase nor Gavin wanted to ask what how the man died. Judging from the widow's age and her son Gio, he would have likely been in his early forties. *Cancer?* That's where the mind automatically goes when someone so young passes. As both Chase and Gavin learned long ago, some loose threads need not be pulled, so they left the matter alone.

Chase reached over to touch Francesca's arm instead, saying, "I didn't mean to pry. Forgive me."

Francesca nodded and managed a small smile, when Gio returned, asking, "Forgive you for what?"

Nonna intervened, "Nothing. Not for your ears."

Gio looked to his grandmother, answering, "Okay, grumpy."

Francesca then let out a deep breath, as if merely mentioning her late husband took something out of her.

She then hugged her son, Gio, and said, *"Ti voglio bene."*

Gio hugged his mother back, saying, "I love you too."

Gavin broke up the tender moment, asking, "So, two rooms. Is there one I should take?"

Francesca answered, "The one to the right is prettier, with a view of the street. Why don't we give that one to Chase."

Chase grabbed her bag from the floor and said, "Sounds good to me."

Francesca then said to Gavin, "And we'll put you in the room to the far left. I'm sorry if it smells like a teenage boy."

Gavin flashed his country-boy smile, "No worries, Francesca, I'm accustomed to the smell, having once been one of those myself."

As they started toward their rooms, Chase stopped, saying, "I just realized something. Nonna, when we agreed on a price to stay here it was for one room, not two. We should pay more."

Nonna, looking confused, turned to her daughter Francesca, and they shared a quick exchange in Italian.

Francesca then turned to her guests, saying, "Nonna says one, two, doesn't matter. She's happy you are here."

Chase smiled at the older woman, answering, *"Grazie."*

Gio lit up when he heard Chase say thank you, asking, "You speak Italian?"

Chase giggled, "Me? Gosh no. I only know about ten words."

Francesca and Gio both smiled, letting Chase know they appreciated the effort just the same.

Chase's room was, as advertised, the prettier of the two, with rose-colored wallpaper and a soft, queen-size bed. A set of beige doors creaked open to a small balcony that looked down on the busy street below.

Chase swept her eyes left to right, taking in more than a dozen shops and restaurants she'd have to explore. Off in the distance, a short walk away, she spied the top of a church. It was faded tan stone, with an old cross peeking over the building tops, like a child looking over a fence.

Scooter nuzzled up next to Chase's leg, taking in the view himself. Suddenly Scooter's body went stiff, his eyes focusing on something down on the street.

"What's wrong? What do you see?" Chase inquired.

She looked out herself and spotted an orange tabby cat snaking his way through the chairs of an outdoor café. The customers, busy eating and chatting, didn't seem to notice him.

Scooter let out a low growl as his head shifted left, causing Chase's eyes to follow. Another cat. No, wait, two more. Then three and four. What was going on? Who owned all these stray cats?

Chase and Scooter emerged from the room to find the welcoming family all sitting at the kitchen table enjoying a late-in-the-day snack of bread and cheese.

"Sit, sit, please," Francesca motioned to Chase.

Gavin entered the room and joined them.

"Hey Gav, I can see the whole city from my room," Chase said. "How's your view?"

Gio put his hand over his mouth, trying not to laugh.

"Um, well." Gavin began. "I'm looking out at a stone wall. I'm guessing the building next door."

Francesca explained, "It is. Sorry about that, Gavin. But hey, take three steps out the front door and you'll have plenty to see in every direction."

Gavin took a bite of the cheese and said, "Oh my God, this is so good."

Nonna turned to him, saying, "Italy is known for three things: romance, wine, and cheese."

Gio intervened, "Not to mention the Vatican, Venice, the shopping, and about a million other things."

Chase smiled at the boy, saying, "You really do live right in the middle of a history book here. It's so cool."

Francesca then asked, "Where are you two from? In America, I mean."

Gavin with his mouth half-full of cheese, tried to answer, "She's from Seattle and I'm from Manchumstum."

Chase laughed, "Gavin, really? He said Manchester. It's in Vermont. That's a little state where—"

Francesca interrupted: "I know Vermont. They have the pretty orange trees and those funny bridges."

Chase was curious, asking, "Funny bridges?"

Francesca stood up from the table, and using her hands, explained, "Yeah, they're kind of short and fat and have a roof on them."

Gavin jumped in, saying to Chase, "She means covered bridges. Yes, Vermont has lots of those."

Chase then asked, "Speaking of architecture, outside my window, over the buildings, I could see the top of a beautiful church."

Nonna, listening quietly, finally spoke, "Santa Maria dei Monti. Sì. It is beautiful. That's my church."

Gavin then, to Nonna: "We'll have to check it out. We have lots of places to visit and not much time, really."

Francesca asked, "What do you mean?"

Chase took Gavin's hand across the table, "We decided to get married in Italy, but we wanted to spend a few weeks here meeting people, seeing the sights, figuring out the best place to say *I do*."

Gavin added, "You know, kick the tires first."

Nonna asked, "Tires?"

Chase turned to Gavin, saying, "Honey, they don't understand what that means."

She then turned to the others, explaining, "What Gavin means is, he wants to look around Italy before he decides where we should get married. Capish?"

The three nodded in agreement, as Gio asked with a smile, "Is that another one of the ten Italian words you know?"

Chase chuckled at the boy. "I guess it is."

As Gavin devoured another piece of thick bread, Chase inquired, "Can I ask you for advice on getting around? We can take a taxi, but, um—"

"Nonsense," Francesca jumped in. "My brother, Giuliano, is like a taxi, only better."

"Better?" Gavin asked.

"Yeah," Francesca continued. "Giuliano—we call him Jules when we speak English—can drive you, and he's fun and cheap."

Gavin smiled, then asked, "Do you think you could call him and see if he's available? Does he speak English too?"

Nonna answered, "Sì, yes, he does. Francesca will call."

Chase then mentioned, "We don't need him right away. We both want to walk the neighborhood with Scooter first."

"Speaking of which," Gavin said, "are we okay bringing a dog through the streets of Rome? I don't know if there are any rules against it."

"Rules no, but cats, yes," Gio cautioned.

Chase then, "I meant to ask you, what is it with all the cats? I saw four of them out my window.

Francesca explained, "There are three hundred thousand stray cats in Rome."

"Wow," Gavin exclaimed.

Francesca continued, "You mentioned on the phone that you lived in New York City?"

"Yes, for a year," Chase replied.

"Well, you have pigeons, we have cats," Francesca replied.

Gavin nodded his head, answering, "I guess you do."

Francesca then said, "I will talk to Jules and put the two of you together."

Chase nodded, saying, "Thank you so much, for everything."

Gavin put his fourth piece of cheese back down on the plate and said, "I'd better stop, or I'll have no room for dinner."

Gio looked at his watch and said, "Dinner? It's barely five o'clock."

Francesca could see their American guests looked a bit confused again, so she explained, "Nobody eats dinner in Rome until after seven."

Gavin asked, "Since we're in Italy, is there a place nearby you'd recommend spaghetti and meatballs?"

Gio covered his mouth, laughing again.

"What?" Gavin asked.

Francesca explained, "That's an American thing. Here you get pasta with delicious things mixed in."

"But not meatballs?" Gavin asked, smiling.

Gio patted Gavin on the shoulder like a big brother, answering, "Not so much."

Chase laughed at Gavin and said, "This sounds like my cappuccino I tried to order today."

The Italians at the table all turned, giving Chase their undivided attention, curious about what she meant.

Chase explained, "I was in this really nice coffee shop and asked for a cappuccino at three in the afternoon."

Nonna mumbled something under her breath in Italian and made the sign of the cross on her forehead and chest.

"I know," Chase said to Nonna, enthusiastically. "They totally freaked out."

Gavin then said, "So no cappuccino after noon and don't order the spaghetti and meatballs like you're at the Olive Garden."

Gio curious, asked, "What olive garden?"

Chase laughed, "No, not an actual—"

She patted Gio's hand across the table, explaining, "That's the name of a restaurant chain in America. It's supposed to be authentic Italian food but it's not."

Gavin interrupted, saying, "The breadsticks are good, though."

Francesca then said to Gavin, "You certainly like bread."

The five of them all shared a laugh as Chase said, "Well, I've got jetlag from the long trip, so I'm going to grab a quick nap and then we can go find a place to eat."

Francesca answered, "La Taverna is a great spot, just a two-minute walk."

Gavin rose from the table and said, "A nap before dinner does sound good."

As the two slowly made their way to their respective bedrooms, Nonna called out in her fractured English, "Just reminder, fiancé is not a married. So, we stay in our rooms all night. *Capite*—you understand?"

Gavin saluted and replied, "You have my word, ma'am."

Chase then, "Once we turn in later, you won't see us until morning."

Nonna reached down to pet their dog, Giuseppe, and said, "He's old and a little deaf but he sleeps in the hallway, and if anyone comes out of their room, Giuseppe barks."

Gavin smiled, answering, "He sounds like a great watchdog."

Nonna looked Gavin in the eye and said, "You're a nice young man and I can tell you honest."

"Thank you, Nonna," Gavin replied.

Her face took a serious turn now, as she added, "Just know, Giuseppe is watching."

Gavin smiled and looked to Chase, silently mouthing the words, *Giuseppe is watching!*

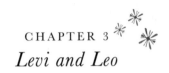

CHAPTER 3

Levi and Leo

There are roughly 450 islands off the coast of Italy, some large, while on others you could toss a Frisbee from one side to the other. As the sun rose on Chase and Gavin's first full day in Rome, two hundred miles away, a quiet, gentle man named Levi rose to begin a very long day on one of those islands. The small stone structure he called home housed a dozen men with a singular dedication to their faith.

Levi opened the closet door in his room to reveal a half-dozen brown hooded robes, neatly pressed, lined up like soldiers on hangers. Despite their all looking identical, Levi paused to consider his choice for the day, saying to himself, "This one, I think."

He pulled the robe over a T-shirt and matching brown slacks, leaving just his footwear to choose. Many at this religious retreat preferred sandals, but Levi felt a touch of rebel in him today, opting instead for a pair of bright red running shoes.

Once dressed, Levi made his way down a long corridor, finding the others in the house already up and sipping coffee in the large kitchen.

"Good morning," Levi said. "I'm heading inland, to Rome, if anyone needs anything."

A man in his eighties raised his hand, but before he could speak, Levi said, "Your favorite wine from that shop near the Tiber?"

The old man nodded in agreement.

A younger man in a robe matching Levi's then asked, "Has it been a month already?"

Levi responded, "Just about."

Another of the half dozen men at the table then inquired, "How is the game going?"

Levi, busy taking down a box of cereal from the cupboard, answered, "Good, I think I've got him on the run."

The older man who wanted Levi to get him wine then asked, "Game?"

Levi turned to him, speaking louder now, "My CHESS GAME against my brother. Remember? Once a month, after I shop, I sit with my brother at his church, and we play chess."

The older man scratched his bald head and nodded, "Yes, of course. I remember now."

Levi then turned to the newest member of their religious retreat and said, "Anything for you, Tommaso?"

The man with dark hair and a noticeable scar above his left eye shook his head no.

Levi touched his own forehead, still looking at the man, asking, "How are the headaches?"

Tommaso, in barely a whisper, answered, "I'm fine."

"Good," the kindly monk answered, sitting down to eat his bran flakes.

After breakfast, Levi took a short walk from the house down to an aging dock where a small boat was waiting. The man behind the wheel was dressed in mustard-colored overalls, a thick wool sweater, and a black seaman's cap.

"How's the game going? Did you get his queen yet?" the salty-looking sea captain asked.

"Not yet, but I'm closing in," Levi replied with a wink.

It would seem everyone on this island knew of Levi's year-long chess match with his brother. Once a month, at least, he'd travel from the island to Italy's mainland, making his way to Rome.

The captain untethered the rope from the dock, then said, "Hold tight, Levi, the sea is talking today, and she has plenty to say."

Miles away in Rome, Gavin and Chase awoke to the smell of fresh rolls baking in Nonna's kitchen. Gavin was wearing a pair of white sweat-pants he picked up cheap at T.J. Maxx back in New York and smiled when he saw Chase shuffle into the kitchen in one of his old Boston University T-shirts that stretched down to her knees.

"Something smells amazing," Chase said.

Francesca was at the counter pouring fresh coffee into two mugs, replying, "Every day Nonna makes homemade rolls."

Gio emerged from his room, adding, "There's also biscotti and pastry in the fridge if you'd rather that."

Gavin replied, "If we eat like this every day the plane won't be able to fly us back home."

Nonna, Gio, and Francesca looked him, puzzled, causing Gavin to explain his joke, "Too heavy. We'd be too heavy for the plane to get off the ground."

Nonna, still confused, replied, "From one roll?"

Francesca explained, "He's joking, Nonna."

Chase's eyes were fixed on something that was right in front of their noses last night, but she'd failed to notice until now.

"We had those on my house growing up," Chase said.

Gavin turned to see she was talking about and saw, stuck to the front of the refrigerator, were dozens of cheap plastic magnetic letters—A, B, C . . . the whole alphabet.

Francesca walked over to touch the scrambled letters, and replied, "Oh, these? We use them to leave notes for each other."

"Notes?" Chase asked.

Gio explained, "Let's say we are out of eggs. You write the word EGGS on the refrigerator with these letters, and it tells anyone who is going near a store to pick them up."

"Ah, clever," Gavin replied.

Francesca then said to Gio, "Tell them about the game we play."

"Game?" Chase asked.

Gio answered, "Every time you open and close the refrigerator door the letters move around. After a few days you'll see a clump of letters together and we try to make words out of them."

· Chase looked at Gavin and immediately thought of a board game they played when they lived in a mansion in Briarcliff Manor, outside of New York City. Sometimes those Scrabble letters revealed words as well.

Reading Gavin's face, she shook her head no, agreeing, without words, that they should leave the past where it was and not mention it. Besides, she was anxious to eat breakfast and start exploring Rome.

The boat ride for Levi to the mainland took less than a half hour. What came next for the monk was a three-hour car ride through the winding hills of Follonica, Grosseto, and Tuscania. If all roads lead to Rome, this was a bumpy one.

Once in Rome, Levi made his way on foot through the charming streets, stopping at his favorite stores, making certain to grab wine for his friend as promised. The brand he liked was easy to spot because of the beige-colored label with a small cross on the top. The name of the vineyard was printed in black letters below: Paraclete.

Being from a monastery, of sorts, and having a priest for an older brother, Levi knew the term *Paraclete* was from the Greek word *advocate*, but in the world of Christianity it usually meant *Holy Spirit*. He wasn't sure if the old monk from the house liked it for the taste or the religious roots. Either way, it was a bargain at just twenty euros.

His early start from the island assured Levi would reach Santa Maria church in Rome shortly before 11 a.m. His best friend in the world, his brother, Leo, celebrated a short Catholic mass in Latin at 10 a.m., followed by the hearing of confessions.

On days like this, when Levi was early, he took a seat in his favorite pew positioned directly in front of the church's west wall and the *stations of the cross.* Levi looked up at the ninth station depicting the third time that Jesus fell under the weight of the cross. Levi was transfixed by the detail in the statue's face showing the determination in Jesus's eyes to rise again despite all the torment and pain.

There were several elderly Italian woman clutching rosaries waiting their turn to spill their sins to Father Leo, so Levi rested his tired feet on the red velvet pad of the kneeler in the pew, knowing it might be a while before he played chess with his brother.

Three blocks away, Gavin and Chase emerged from the well-appointed home where they were staying, with Scooter on his leash ready to greet the day.

"Left, or right?" Gavin asked with a smile.

"Surprise me," Chase said as she squeezed his hand tight.

Before they made the trip to Italy, Chase and Gavin spent hours looking at photographs of the places they planned to visit. None of those pictures came close to capturing the true beauty of this ancient city, now that it was before their very eyes.

Each building they strolled past was straining to get their attention, heralding stories of war and love, chariots, and mystery. Chase was careful to hold tightly to Scooter's leash, as cats of every stripe darted in and out of the shadows along their walk.

Monti, the neighborhood where they were staying, was a well-heeled section of Rome, and the stores that lined both sides of the street reflected it with exotic names like Shiva, Kaja, and Eventi.

Gavin waited on the sidewalk with Scooter as Chase ducked into a store that sold a variety of tea. Once inside, Chase was struck by the decor, which looked more like an art museum in Paris than a store in Rome. Each box of tea was thoughtfully presented and lit. When that perfect lighting illuminated the prices however, Chase quickly did an about-face and was back outside in the fresh air.

As Chase reached Gavin on the sidewalk, he said, "Hold this a second," attempting to hand her Scooter's leash.

Unfortunately, the leash fell to the ground just as a cat darted out from behind a parked car, and Scooter took off like a rocket.

Both Gavin and Chase ran after Scooter, but with each step the dog seemed to double the distance between them.

A block away at Santa Maria church, confessions were complete, and Levi rose to give his brother a hug hello.

"I trust it was a safe journey, little brother?" Father Leo asked.

Levi, thinking of the choppy seas, answered, "Safe enough."

To the left of the church's altar, in an area where they performed baptisms on the first Sunday of the month, sat a small table with two folding chairs. On the table rested a chess board with a game already in progress, a bottle of wine, and two empty glasses.

"Shall we?" Leo asked, turning to take his seat for the battle to come.

As Levi walked by a large statue of Mary holding the baby Jesus, he spied a young man with tan skin kneeling and praying by himself.

"He looks intense," Levi said to his brother.

Father Leo looked to see who Levi was speaking of, then whispered, "Four times a week, for the last few months."

Levi noticed the boy looked thin, and said, "Perhaps he's sick. Things like that drive people to prayer."

"Perhaps," Leo replied, adding no more to the conversation.

The sudden silence caused Levi to ask, "Even if you knew something about that young man, you wouldn't tell me, would you?"

Leo nodded slowly, "No I wouldn't."

Levi mocked him a bit now, adding, "You don't trust your only brother. Tsk, tsk."

The priest shot back, "Oh and you tell me you everything that you and the others at your monk house are up to?"

"Excuse me, sir," Levi replied. "We call it a hermitage, not a *monk house*."

Leo adored his brother, so he just smiled and said, "Remind me again, is it my move? This frail old mind forgets things."

"Oh, nonsense," Levi replied. "You know it's my turn, and don't try sneaking any of your players back on the board."

As Leo leaned in, watching for the next move, he asked, "You mentioned a while back, you had some secret project on the island. Can you elaborate?"

Levi shook his head from side to side, "You keep your secrets, I'll keep mine."

As Father Leo poured wine, the young man who had been praying alone rose and started toward the church's door. Just as he pulled it open, a black cat running as if the devil himself was after him, dashed into the church and hid under a marble pedestal that held holy water.

Right on the cat's heels came Chase's dog, Scooter, barking as he pushed through the door and zeroed in on his prey.

"What in heaven's name?" Father Leo called out. "Somebody grab that dog!"

The young man, without hesitation, let go of the door and moved quickly to snatch Scooter's leash.

No sooner did he have it in hand than the church doors opened again, this time with a beautiful woman and her fiancé in hot pursuit.

"Jesus, he's fast," Gavin said out loud.

Chase, realizing where they were standing, turned to Gavin, saying sharply, "Gav, language!"

Gavin saw the church was empty, except for two men dressed like clergy and the young man holding Scooter's leash.

"Sorry, fathers, about screaming *Jesus*," Gavin called out to Levi and Leo.

Father Leo smiled and replied, "Oh, we're used to hearing that name in here, son."

Chase turned her attention to the boy holding her dog and tried to meet his eyes to say thank you. Instead, he quickly shoved the leash in Chase's hands and scurried toward the church door. As he pushed by Chase, she noticed he was wearing a yellow hooded sweatshirt with a red emblem on the front and an animal at the center. It was all so quick; she couldn't make it out.

"*Grazie*," Chase called out to the teen.

His only answer was the door slamming behind him.

Gavin realized the two men at the chess board were still watching, so he said, "Apologies, fathers, the dog got away from us when he saw the cat."

"Occupational hazard for dog walkers in our fine city," Father Leo replied. "And we're both not fathers. I'm a priest, he's a brother. Brother Levi."

Chase saw the chess game and the two glasses of red wine waiting, and said, "I can see we disturbed you. We'll be going."

As Gavin, Chase, and Scooter opened the church door to go, Gavin called back to the men, "Hey, don't forget you've got a cat loose in here."

Levi answered, with a twinkle in his eye, "This is Rome; there's a cat loose everywhere."

Chase smiled and gave Scooter a firm tug as the three stepped back onto the street.

"Shall we continue our tour of the neighborhood?" Gavin asked.

There was silence as Chase just stood and stared at nothing.

"What?" Gavin inquired. "Is something wrong?"

Chase answered, "Nothing. Something about that boy."

Gavin was silent now, looking at his fiancée, waiting for more.

Finally, Chase said, "It's nothing. Let's finish our walk."

Every few steps Gavin looked up at Chase for more, wondering if their morning adventure was as random as it seemed, or if something besides a cat had led them to that church.

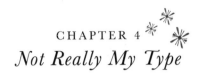

CHAPTER 4

Not Really My Type

Day three in Rome began with a knock on the front door of the apartment where Chase and Gavin were guests.

"I've got it," Gio called out, stomping his feet across the room.

"Go easy, Giovanni, we have people below us," his mother scolded.

"*Mi scusi,*" Gio called back.

Chase noted quietly to Gavin, "That means *sorry.*"

Gio flung open the door and was immediately picked up by a bear of a man with wavy dark hair and arms the size tree trunks.

"*Gio, nipote,*" he said with glee. "*Come stai?*"

"I'm good, Uncle Jules," Gio replied in English.

After his feet hit the floor again, Gio pointed to Gavin and Chase, saying to his uncle, "These are the Americans staying with us. We're trying to use English as much as we can for them."

Jules's face lit up as he sauntered toward them, saying in a strong accent, "I love America. Especially your movies. *Toto, we not in Kansas anymore. You can't a handle the truth. Houston we gots a problem.* Sì? Is good?"

Gavin and Chase instantly broke into laughter at the man's gregarious nature.

"WOW," Gavin answered. "It's as if Tom Hanks was standing right in front of us."

Jules, recognizing the name, responded, "Tom Hanks, yes, the castaway on the island. *WILSON, you come back my silly ball.* I cried at that movie."

Chase extended her hand to shake Jules's. "I think we all did. Hi, I'm Chase."

Gavin followed with a handshake of his own. "I'm Gavin."

With that, Jules took Chase's shoulders in his hulking hands and planted a kiss on both of her cheeks, saying, "Welcome to Rome."

Gavin wasn't offended by the personal gesture but was taken off guard when Jules turned and did the same to him, a kiss on both cheeks.

"Alrighty then," Gavin said, blushing a bit. "We don't get much of that in Manchester."

Jules got excited again, asking, "Football? Manchester United. Sì?"

Chase stopped him there. "No, no. He means Manchester, Vermont. It's a place, in America."

"Ah, my bad, as you say," he replied. "So, you need a driver?"

"We do, thank you," Gavin shot back.

Chase then said, "We walked around the neighborhood, but we want to see more."

Jules then spoke to Francesca and Nonna in Italian, they responded the same, and he turned his attention back to Chase and Gavin.

"Twenty euros for the hour. You want more hours, more euros. To drive you around Italy, yes?" he said.

Gavin nodded and smiled, "Sounds fair, let us both grab our coats."

Rome is the capital of Italy and the largest tourist attraction in a country full of them. While the city itself is less than 500 square miles in size, it packs three million people.

In doing her research, Chase learned that much like Manhattan, Rome is not one city but a collection of neighborhoods, each with its own personality. Jules deliberately drove slowly so they wouldn't miss a thing.

"Here is the Pantheon," Jules called out, pointing to his right.

He then drove by the Vatican, the famous Trevi Fountain, and a half dozen other places Chase had either read about or seen in movies.

When Chase spotted a store she wanted to visit, Jules double-parked and waited patiently as other drivers beeped their horns and attempted to squeeze by.

They stopped for lunch at a place called Cipasso Bistro, the second-floor balcony offering a lovely view of the Tiber River. The early December air had some bite to it, but heat lamps worked nicely to keep the diners toasty.

After a few hours of food, driving, and shopping, the happy couple was on their way back home, when Chase looked out the car window and said, "Wait, I know this block."

Sure enough, it was the coffee shop where she and Gavin had stopped two days prior, when she tried to order a cappuccino.

"Quick, what time is it?" Chase asked Gavin.

He raised the smartphone and said, "A little after two."

"STOP," Chase called out to her driver.

Jules stopped and turned his head to see what the fuss was about.

She explained, "I made a friend the other day in that coffee shop, and she told me she's here most days at two. I want to say hi."

Chase jumped out of the car, then called back to Gavin and said, "I won't sit or anything. I just want to see if she's here."

Before Gavin could answer, Chase had gone through the coffee house door.

Chase's eyes went to the table where her friend Riley had been sitting before, but there was an old man working on a crossword puzzle in her place.

Chase quickly scanned the property, then called out, "There she is, Riley O'Reilly!"

The tangle of thick, untamed red hair flipped up from the book she was reading on a small couch, as Riley searched for the person calling her name.

When her eyes found Chase, she shouted back, "Oh, strike up the band and cue the craic, if my American girl isn't here."

Chase giggled, then replied, "I don't have a clue what that means, but hi, how are you?"

Riley dashed over to Chase, giving her a hug, answering, "If I were any better, they'd lock me away."

Chase was about to speak when Riley cut her off. "Where's the side of beef you had with you the other day? I'd love to get me mitts on him again—Gavin, was it?"

Chase was a bit taken aback by the description, but managed a smile before answering, "Gavin, yes. He's in the car."

Riley then, "What brings you here, luv? More coffee?"

Chase smiled, "No, we were out with our driver discovering the city and I saw the café and just wanted to say hello."

Riley looked at her watch, then grabbed her book and handbag off the table, saying, "That's sweet of you. Hey, I have to meet a friend, might you and Gavin give me a ride? It's not far."

"Of course," Chase replied.

As Chase started toward the door, she saw the same barista that she encountered her last time in.

When the man looked up and met Chase's eyes, she wagged her finger back and forth and said to him, "No cappuccino after noon."

The man couldn't help but grin, before nodding his head out of respect for the lovely American who handled his prior rebuke with such grace.

Jules saw the ladies coming and was already out of the car and around to open the backdoor for them.

"That's some red hair you got on you there," Jules said, with a smile to Riley.

She grabbed it with both fists and replied in her Irish accent, "Terrible to wash and dry, but it keeps me neck warm in the winter."

The car door now open, Chase was about to get in and sit next to Gavin, when Riley inexplicably jumped in first, putting Chase on the outside.

"Ooo-kay," Chase said to herself under her breath, clearly annoyed that her new friend took the spot next to *her* guy.

Riley told Jules where to take them, and, the entire ride over, the Irish lass never took her eyes off Gavin, asking questions about his life and home.

Chase was used to women breaking their necks whenever Gavin walked by; he was six-foot-two, in perfect shape, and had those deep-blue eyes. She was usually not the jealous type, but Riley's instant infatuation with Gavin was starting to annoy her.

Do I say something? she thought to herself, *or just let this overt flirtation slide?*

As the car pulled up in front of a high-end clothing store, Jules announced, "Here we are, ladies and Gavin."

Before Chase could open the door, she saw a striking young woman with short dark hair, smokey eye liner, and plump, full lips waiting in front of the store. She seemed to be waving and trying to get their attention.

Chase heard a low giggle from Gavin and turned her attention back to Riley, who had her hand on top of his and gave it a squeeze, saying, "It was so great to see you again, Gavin."

Chase's blood pressure shot up fifty points in two seconds and she was about to scream when Jules opened the back door and said, "Watch your step, ladies."

Chase got out first and Riley right after.

As Gavin slid over to leave the backseat, Chase put her hand on his chest, stopping him, and said firmly, "Give me a moment, love."

The attractive woman with the short hair, still standing just outside the store, smiled as Riley waved back to her. The Irish redhead was about to leave Chase and greet her friend when she felt a hand latch on to her elbow, like talons from an angry hawk.

"Hold up, sister," Chase said.

Riley turned and could see in Chase's face that something was wrong.

Before Riley could even ask, Chase began, "I get that Gavin is a handsome guy and you're not the first woman I've been around who gets a little handsy."

Riley looked genuinely shocked, saying, "Handsy? Excuse me?"

Chase then, "No, I don't think I will. It was rude for you to jump in ahead of me and sit next to Gavin when I'm his fiancée, and it was rude to be patting his hand like he's your little puppy dog while I'm literally two feet away."

Riley looked annoyed now, folding her arms, saying only, "Go on."

"You probably don't mean any harm," Chase continued. "But where I come from, you don't poach other people's . . . ya know."

"Men?" Riley offered right back, with a sharp tone.

Chase nodded, "Exactly. And if I'm coming off as a bit protective of my guy, well—"

Chase didn't finish that thought before the beautiful young lady with the short dark hair and sexy eyes dashed over to join Riley and Chase by the curb.

Riley reached out immediately and locked fingers with the woman, brought her hand up to her face, and gave it a loving rub on her cheek. Chase was confused as to what was happening.

Riley remedied that quickly when she said, "This is my girlfriend, Tessa."

Chase's mouth went wide, and all she could muster was, "Girlfriend? I see."

Chase then looked into Riley's eyes and added, "So that means you're . . ."

"Gay. Yes, Chase, I'm gay." Riley answered. "So, when I tell you, as cute as Gavin is, he's not really my type."

Chase, looking embarrassed now, replied, "I'm so sorry. I missed that entirely, didn't I?"

Riley rubbed Chase's arm now, letting her off the hook. "It's alright, dear. As long as you don't think I'm after your fiancé."

Chase looked at Gavin, who was still in the car and watching all this from behind a closed window, then turned back to Riley and said, "Nope, I think we're good."

Chase then crinkled her face, showing embarrassment, and extended her hand. "Hi, Tessa, I'm Chase, Riley's stupid friend."

Tessa took her hand and shook it, replying, "She's always causing a commotion, Chase, don't worry about it."

Riley then asked, with a smile, "Now that we know who is gay and who is straight, we were about to grab a bite to eat on Tessa's lunch break. Do you want to come along?"

Chase looked at the car with Jules and Gavin waiting, then said, "That's kind of you, but we just ate. Let's exchange phone numbers and hang out soon, though."

Riley typed her number into Chase's phone, saying as she punched the digits, "I'd love that. We can make it a double date."

Chase returned to the backseat of the car, prompting Gavin to ask, "Who is Riley's cute friend?"

Chase let out a loud laugh and replied, "Trust me, she's not your type. If you were single, I mean, which you are most certainly not."

Gavin gave Chase a hug and a peck on the lips, "No I am not. Speaking of which, I have to get busy planning some romantic excursions for us here in Italy. Hey, Jules, you got any suggestions on romantic things to do?"

Jules thought a moment, then said, "People love to stroll the grand canal in Venice. Lake Como is romantic too."

Gavin smirked a bit, "Yeah, I read about those. I'm looking for something more adventurous."

Jules pondered some more, then said, "It's not romantic, but if you like adventure you should see the Colosseum."

Gavin smiled and looked at Chase, but it was clear she was not convinced.

"Oh, come on, babe, remember watching *Gladiator* together? *Are you NOT entertained?*" Gavin said, doing his best Russell Crowe imitation.

As Gavin made a pouty face, Chase said, "I can't resist you when you do that. Sure, we can put the romance on hold and see the Colosseum first."

Gavin clapped and Jules smiled, as he slowly drove back to the apartment. What none of them knew, however, was the key to romance for Chase and Gavin in Italy was indeed waiting inside the famed Colosseum. It stood five foot two, had paint on its shoes, and was leaning on an easel.

CHAPTER 5

He Was Just There

When Chase opened her eyes on her fourth morning in Rome, a familiar sound greeted her. Rain. The heavy drops pinging off the stone window ledge reminded her of the apartment on Manhattan's Upper East Side. The aroma of fresh coffee made her question, for a blink, whether she was still in Italy or back above the coffee shop in New York.

A hard knock shook her back to reality, as Nonna opened the bedroom door and said in slightly broken English, "The rolls, they getting cold."

Chase smiled because in this home this older Italian woman seemed to be everyone's grandmother, including, it would seem, hers.

Gavin was already at the kitchen table and was finishing his second roll before Chase arrived in festive red pajamas that had tiny Christmas trees printed on them.

"I see we're getting into the holiday spirit?" Gavin observed.

"Ho, Ho, Ho," Chase replied, with a giggle.

Francesca and Gio came through the front door, carrying a bottle of orange juice and the morning newspaper. Watching the teenage boy smile, Gavin and Chase could feel the love in this home.

Chase's mind wandered to the sad news that was shared the day they arrived, that Francesca's husband, Matteo, Gio's father, had died recently. Chase was curious about what happened, but seeing them so happy in this moment, she let the question fall from her mind.

"What are you up to today?" Francesca asked Chase and Gavin.

Francesca snapped her fingers in front of Chase's nose to secure her attention. "Today? Hello? Plans today?"

Chase buttered a roll as Gavin poured her a cup of coffee, and replied, "I think we're going to the Colosseum. Right, Gav?"

Before her fiancé could answer, Francesca said, "I asked because I have to work and if you wanted to see the art gallery I manage, you could tag along."

Chase lit up and said, "That sounds like fun. We can hit the gallery first and then the Colosseum."

Gavin then pointed out, "We also have to get Scooter out for a walk, don't forget."

Gio went over to Scooter, who was on the floor next to Giuseppe, saying, "Giuseppe needs a walk too. Why don't I take them to mom's gallery with you guys and then bring them home afterward?"

Francesca saw everyone waiting for her approval, so she took a bite of bacon and said, "Sounds good to me."

The walk over to the gallery only took ten minutes. The small structure was wedged between a candle shop and a shoe store in the expensive Monti neighborhood. Scooter and Giuseppe matched strides and occasionally bumped bodies, like a couple of kids on the way to the park playfully shoving each other.

Even though the gallery had only been open a few minutes, there were already a half-dozen customers inside, pointing and reacting to the artwork on the walls.

An older Canadian couple raised their hands as if in a classroom, waiting for Francesca or someone to call on them.

"Yes, may I help you?" Francesca said.

"Everything we see is for sale?" they asked.

"Yes," Francesca replied. "This is a store, not a museum."

The couple then asked, "And the price we see is the actual price? There's no sale today or coupon or something?"

Francesca took a deep breath and reminded herself that tourists were eighty percent of her business, then responded calmly, "No, I'm sorry. We don't do coupons here."

It was then that Gavin heard a loud bark in the distance. His eyes immediately went down to Giuseppe and Scooter on the floor, only to realize Scooter was missing.

"Scooter?" he called out to the busy store. Everyone in the gallery looked around, but there was no sign of the dog.

Then came a second bark, followed by a third, causing Chase to say, "He's back there somewhere."

The group of them walked to the very back of the gallery, turned a tight corner and found Scooter sitting in front of a single painting.

"SCOOTER," Chase said firmly now, patting her leg hard, "COME HERE."

The loyal dog hated to disobey Chase, but after giving her a quick look, his eyes went back to the painting, and the barking commenced.

"I'm sorry," Chase said, taking Scooter by the neck, before dragging him away.

Gavin looked at the painting for a moment. It depicted a typical street you'd find in Italy, with shops on both sides and a man sitting on a bench peeling an apple. That was it, nothing more. Before turning to go he noticed something else, scribbled at the bottom right corner of the painting: in bold gold lettering was the name *Alexander*. It was obviously the artist's signature.

When Gavin returned to the front of the gallery, Chase and Francesca were discussing whether it was better to get married in a church or something less formal.

"I guess it all depends on what you want," Francesca said to Chase.

Gavin turned to Gio, "Would you mind holding him for me? He's being weird today."

As Gio took the leash, Chase leaned into Gavin's ear and said, "You see him barking like that, so fixated. Not good."

Gavin knew exactly what Chase was implying, since it was Scooter that had led them to so many clues and mysteries in the past.

Gavin gave her a hug and whispered, "Don't even go there. He's fine."

Chase pushed her mind to something else, and then asked Gavin, "So, you wanna get to the Colosseum, my little gladiator?"

Gavin teased her, saying, "You know, I could dress up in one of those outfits."

As they were giggling with each other, Francesca held up her phone and said, "I just texted Jules. He'll be here in a few minutes."

"Shoot," came out of Gio's mouth.

Everyone turned to see Scooter running away from the group, back toward the rear of the gallery again.

"I'm sorry," Gio said, "I guess I wasn't holding the leash tight enough."

Gavin told Chase and Francesca to stay put, as he calmly took those long strides of his across the floor of the gallery, back to the area where he had retrieved Scooter just moments earlier.

Sure enough, he turned the corner in the back, finding Scooter sitting in front of the same painting with the street scene and the man peeling an apple. Only this time, Scooter wasn't barking. He just sat and stared.

Given Scooter's past, Gavin decided to take a seat right next to the dog on the hard floor.

"So? What do we see?" he asked the pup.

Gio was surprised, watching Gavin and this dog both studying the painting so carefully.

Finally, Gio asked Gavin, "Why is he doing this?"

"That's the million-dollar question," Gavin answered.

"Maybe he's hungry and wants the apple," a voice from behind said.

It was Francesca, standing with Chase. Scooter looked up at all of them, then walked in a circle twice, collapsed to the floor and closed his eyes for a quick siesta right in front of the painting.

Chase moved over to get a better view of the painting and saw nothing of interest. Just a boring city scene, with a guy having a healthy snack, that's it.

She did notice that name *Alexander* in the bottom right corner.

Realizing that Francesca and Gio were watching all of this, Chase finally said, "He's a strange dog sometimes. Maybe he does like the apple in the painting. Who knows?"

Gavin took up Scooter's leash, waking him from his slumber, and as they started back toward the front of the gallery, Chase asked Francesca, "Is that a special painting? You know, from a famous artist?"

Francesca shook her head and said, "No, that's why it's hiding in the back of the gallery. Nobody wants it."

The entire group went back to the front door and could see the side-walk alive with people, couples mostly, off in search of love and pasta. Just then, Jules's familiar car pulled up to the curb, signaling it was time to go.

The rain finally stopped, but the drive to the Colosseum still took longer than usual because of the holiday traffic. Gavin and Chase would soon learn they were fortunate to have Jules as their driver.

"I'm assuming you two don't have tickets to get in and plan to stand in line when you get there?" Jules asked.

Gavin shrugged his shoulders, looked at Chase and replied, "We didn't really think about that part."

Jules tapped the steering wheel and responded, "Well, Jules has you covered."

Chase leaned her chin on the top of the seat separating them from the back, asking, "Has us covered, how?"

"My friend Marco runs security there and is meeting us at the north entrance. He'll take you in for free," Jules replied.

"Awesome, thank you," Chase said back, tapping the kind driver on the shoulder.

December was not the busiest time of the year for tourist attractions in Rome, but the 2,000-year-old Colosseum was the exception. As Jules drove by the amazing structure, they could see a long line had already formed outside.

After being dropped off, Chase and Gavin found Marco, who was wearing a sharp blue security uniform, and, true to his word, he waved them right in.

There were guided tours everywhere, and while some were being given in Italian, a few were in English, so Chase and Gavin would stop and eavesdrop on whatever the guide was saying. They made their way around the large structure and even saw a secret compartment down below where the gladiators once waited before they fought in the arena.

Feeling they had seen everything worth seeing, Gavin started toward the exit, when Chase said, "Before we go, I have to find a bathroom."

There were security guards every fifty feet, so Chase asked one where the restrooms were, and he pointed toward a door about a hundred yards away.

Gavin was studying some of the architecture, so Chase said, "You stay here, and I'll be back in five."

Gavin did as he was instructed, snapping a few pictures as he waited. He'd seen photographs in books but none of them did the Colosseum justice. You could feel the gravity of this place just standing here.

Just then, the crowd thinned, and Gavin noticed a short older man with cocoa brown skin, in a long black coat, standing before an easel and canvas. He was wearing a heavy workman's belt like a carpenter might have, but instead of tools hanging off, he had tiny paint cans with dozens of colors. He was dipping a paintbrush and creating his own masterpiece.

Gavin quietly approached from behind and could see the man was only half finished.

"Very nice," Gavin said, not knowing if the man even spoke English.

Without taking his eyes off the painting, the man said in Caribbean accent, "American—East Coast, perhaps?"

Gavin smiled, "Pretty good. Vermont."

Then Gavin got playful, trying to copy the man's accent, adding, "And you sound like you are from Jamaica, mon."

Again, without turning to look at Gavin, the man laughed and said, "Bahamas, which is much more fun."

Gavin, now in his normal voice: "Oh yeah, why is that?"

The man dipped his brush in the water, shaking it to clear off some red paint, turned to face Gavin, and replied, "Because we have pirates. In Nassau."

Gavin nodded, saying, "You're right, pirates are more fun."

The man kept painting, then asked, "You here alone?"

Gavin looked to his left and right, answering, "No, I'm here with my fiancée."

The man continued, "Hitting all the tourist spots?"

Gavin looked down the corridor for Chase but could see she wasn't coming yet. Finally he answered, "Yeah, I suppose. We're actually in Italy to be married."

"Congratulations," the painter replied. "So, this is a trip for romance?"

Gavin smiled. "That it is. In fact, I'm in charge of finding romantic things for us to do."

The man continued painting, silently working on his project.

Gavin then said, "Well, I should probably go find my fiancée. Nice to meet you."

The man stopped painting, turned to Gavin, and said, "If you want to see true romance, I can help you find it."

Gavin, wondering why Chase was taking so long, looked back to the man, "You can? Um, okay, sure, if you have suggestions."

The man looked at Gavin, catching his eyes this time. "Do you like riddles?"

"Me?" Gavin shot back. "Sure, I guess."

He then said, "A lock, a kiss, a letter, a puzzle."

Gavin, obviously confused, replied, "What about them?"

The old man returned to his painting. "You want to see true romance for you and Chase? That's the answer."

Gavin counted out on his fingers, trying to remember them, saying out loud, "A lock, a kiss, a letter—and what was the last one?"

The artist smiled, answering, "A puzzle. Good luck."

Gavin, getting a little worried about Chase now, then said, "Thanks. You too."

With that, Gavin dashed off in the direction of the bathroom Chase went to. As he got closer, he let out a sigh of relief when he saw her walking toward him.

"I'm so sorry, the line was ridiculous," Chase explained.

Gavin gave her a quick hug and said, "No worries. I just met the most interesting man."

"Interesting how?" Chase inquired.

Gavin replied, "He was doing a painting, so I said hello and mentioned I was looking for romantic places in Italy."

"And?" Chase replied.

Gavin, then more animated, said, "And he says to me, I'll give you four clues."

"Clues?" Chased replied.

"Well, he called them riddles," Gavin continued. "They were a lock, a kiss, a letter, and a puzzle."

Chase pondered a moment and said, "Are those supposed to be four different things or all together?"

Gavin scratched his head, "He said it like they were all different."

"Interesting," Chase said.

Then Gavin recalled, "He said to me, if you want romance for Chase those are the, um . . ."

Gavin stopped talking, his voice drifting off before finishing the thought.

"Gav?" Chase asked, "What's the matter?"

"Chase," Gavin answered.

"What?" she asked.

"No, I'm not calling you. He said *Chase*," Gavin said.

Chase paused a moment and said, "So?"

Gavin answered back, "I never told him your name."

Chase shrugged, confused, replying, "You must have, hon. How else would he know?'

Gavin thought a moment and said, "Let's go find out."

He took Chase by the hand and what started as a walk turned into a light jog back to the area where Gavin had spoken to the old man.

Gavin's eyes scanned right, then left, then right again, before he said, "I don't get it."

"What?" Chase inquired.

Gavin then, "I swear he was just there."

Chase looked at the crowd going in every direction, then said, "Maybe he left."

Gavin scratched his head and looked around, before saying, "At his age and with that easel and big canvas. No way."

Chase didn't know what to say, but then Gavin suddenly dashed off. She assumed he'd spotted the man, but it was a security guard leaning against the wall Gavin was after.

"Excuse me, sir, do you speak English?" Gavin asked, partially out of breath.

The guard took off his hat, showing respect, and replied, "Of course. How may I help you?"

Gavin turned and pointed, "There was an old man painting, over there, like two minutes ago? Did you see where he went?"

The guard looked bewildered. "Man? Painting? I don't recall that, sir."

Gavin took a beat before saying, "Did you just come on duty? 'Cause you would have seen him; he was right there."

The guard shook his head no. "I'm sorry, sir, I've been here since we opened. I remember seeing you, but no man."

Gavin looked around, confused, causing Chase to take his hand and say, "There's a million people here, Gavin. The guard just didn't see him."

Gavin looked around again and then up at the sky and said, "I guess you're right."

Chase then explained to Gavin, "And you probably mentioned my name and didn't realize it. I'm always on the tip of your tongue."

That comment made Gavin laugh, as he gave Chase a hug. Holding hands, they made their way out of the famed Colosseum with Gavin counting on his fingers and mumbling something under his breath.

"What did you say? Chase asked.

Gavin turned to her, repeating it louder this time, "Lock, kiss, letter, puzzle: the clues from my vanishing friend."

There truly was romance and adventure tied to those four words, as Chase and Gavin would soon find out.

Peroni Gran Riserva," Gavin said to himself, as Jules drove them back home to the apartment.

"Did you just speak Italian?" Chase asked. "What does it mean?"

Before Gavin could answer, Jules did: "Beer."

Chase looked at Gavin for confirmation, and he said, "Francesca asked if I wanted anything at the store and I gave her twenty euros to pick me up some Peroni Gran Ree-serv-ah."

Chase said, "And I thought you only drank Sam Adams."

Gavin replied, "If we're going to learn the culture here, I should try their favorite beer, right?"

Chase raised an eyebrow and replied, "So this is strictly research, huh?"

Gavin laughed. "Of course."

Once home, the two found Nonna watching a small television in a room off the kitchen.

"Hey Nonna, what's on TV?" Chase asked.

The older woman stood up, gave a silver knob on the front of the television a whack, shutting it off, and then answered, "Silly stories. Beautiful people fighting, making up."

Chase thought a moment, then said, "It sounds like the soap operas we have back in America."

Nonna nodded, responding, "Sì. *The Young and the Reckless*, yes?"

Gavin laughed, gently correcting her, "You mean *restless*. *The Young and the Restless*. Although if you watch those shows they can be reckless."

Nonna didn't follow the joke but nodded, then asked in her best English, "How was the gallery? You were gone long time."

Gavin looked at Chase, remembering how odd Scooter was acting at the gallery with that one painting, but there was no point sharing that with Nonna.

Instead, Chase took off her coat and said, "The gallery was great. Then we went to the Colosseum."

Gavin was about to sit when, Nonna pointed at him and said, "Francesca got your beer."

It was a bit early for Gavin to drink alcohol, but seeing Francesca had gone to the trouble, he smiled and gave Nonna a thumbs up.

As Gavin approached the refrigerator, he saw the plastic letters with magnets attached to the door, all lumped together except for four, UOVA.

It looked like gibberish, yet because they were lined up perfectly, Gavin turned to ask, "Is this a word?"

Nonna strained her eyes to see, and then said in English, "Eggs. We need eggs."

Chase commented to her, "That's so clever, leaving notes for each other that way."

Nonna just nodded in agreement before picking up an old broom and sweeping the day's dirt. Scooter and Giuseppe suddenly appeared. The two of them had been taking a nap in the back bedroom and only now realized Chase and Gavin were home.

Gavin cracked open a beer and excused himself to his room, leaving Chase alone with Nonna for the first time since they met. Chase was silent, watching Nonna tend to the floors, and couldn't help but notice there was a sadness in her eyes.

"You okay, Nonna?" Chase asked softly.

Nonna stopped sweeping, her eyes now watery with tears, but didn't seem capable of speaking at that moment. She just shook her head, indicating she was not.

Chase rose and put her hands on top of the old woman's as she held the broom, stopping her from sweeping any further.

"Come sit with me a moment," Chase said. "The dust can wait."

Nonna leaned the broom upright in the corner of the room and went to the stove where a small pot had been resting on a low flame. She took two white porcelain cups down from the second shelf of the cabinet, put a tea bag in each and poured the hot water.

"Sugar, milk?" Nonna asked, as she placed the cup in front of Chase at the table.

"No, thank you, just the tea is fine," Chase replied.

Neither woman spoke for what seemed like a half hour, the two of them sipping the tea and enjoying the quiet. Sometimes silence can work like medicine for the soul.

Finally, Nonna spoke, "I miss this."

Chase didn't answer, she just waited for more.

"With my husband and son," Nonna said.

Chase then asked, "Sitting with tea?"

Nonna smiled now, answering, "Yes. Ordinary things."

Chase thought for a moment about her own life and instantly understood what Nonna meant. Back when she lived in Manchester, Vermont, not long after she met Gavin, they'd get up some mornings and rush to a local bakery for fresh rolls. If the weather was warm enough, they'd take the hot rolls and coffee over to East Arlington and sit on the banks of the Battenkill River. There they'd relax, hold hands, and watch the water carry all their troubles away.

Chase reached and gave Nonna's hand a squeeze, saying, "Ordinary things."

Then she took a leap of faith with the woman she barely knew, asking, "Tell me about your husband."

Nonna wiped her eyes and said, "His name was Alessandro. He was proud of his name because it belonged to his father and his father before him."

Chase looked up to a shelf on the wall and a small black and white photo with a handsome-looking man, his arm around a beautiful young woman.

"Alessandro?" Chase asked, at the frame photo.

"Sì," she replied.

Nonna continued. "We met when I was only sixteen. When I came of proper age, he asked me on a date, and we were never apart after that."

Chase could sense there was something Nonna wasn't saying. Then she did.

"Well, that's not true," Nonna added. "During the war he was away for nearly a year."

Chase thought of being separated from Gavin for that long and her heart sank. She responded, "That had to be so hard."

Nonna rose from her chair and went to retrieve the photo from the shelf, replying, "It was. I wrote him letters, but he never wrote back."

Chase didn't know what to think of that, then Nonna explained, "He couldn't, you see. They move around so much. It was impossible to get a letter home."

Chase imagined this young Italian man off fighting a war, when Nonna said, "I'm not even sure he got half the letters I sent."

Nonna went to the stove to pour another cup of tea, asking Chase, "More?"

She smiled and handed her nearly empty cup to Nonna, answering, "Sure, it's wonderful."

Nonna then laughed to herself.

"What?" Chase asked.

Nonna poured the tea and sat again, resting the photo of her departed husband face up on the table between them.

"We always talked of traveling someday," Nonna said.

Chase asked, "But you didn't?"

"No," she answered. "Not enough money and time. Never enough time."

Chase thought a moment and said, "I'm sure he showed his love in other ways."

Nonna lit up now. "Oh yes, he did. He was a carpenter, and sometimes if he worked at a house in the country and there was a flower garden, he'd borrow a few and bring them home to me."

Nonna was looking at the window above the kitchen sink now, adding, "I'd put them in a tiny vase on this windowsill, so they'd get sunlight."

Chase could picture the flowers right now, bathing in the afternoon sun, then said to Nonna, "Well, that sounds very romantic to me."

Nonna looked sad again, and responded, "What I wouldn't give to have a letter from him back then. I could hold it and read it again and again."

Chase was imagining Nonna younger with Alessandro on her arm, when Nonna said, "We had a special way of saying goodbye."

Chase smiled. "What did you do?"

Nonna was smiling now. "He'd say, 'Take care of my favorite girl,' and I'd say, 'Take care of my favorite guy.'"

"That's really sweet," Chase said to her.

"How about you?" Nonna asked. "Do you have a special thing between you and Gavin?"

Chase almost blushed, before answering, "We do. I say *I love you now*. And he replies, *I love you always*."

Chase let the silence hang there, before asking, "Nonna, how did he die?"

Nonna, without flinching, answered, "Stroke. Working in the garden behind the house. He never woke up."

Chase reached for her hand a second time. "I'm so sorry."

"I wish I could hear his voice once last time," Nonna said. "Or sit with him here and have tea."

Chase's eyes were filling with tears, as she said, "Ordinary things."

Nonna squeezed Chase's hand back. "Sì. You understand."

Gavin returned to the room and put his empty bottle in the recycling bin next to the trash.

He felt something heavy lingering in the air, so he turned to both women, asking, "You ladies okay?"

Chase rose and gave Gavin a big hug, whispering in his ear, "Yes, and I love you."

Gavin was confused but squeezed his fiancée tight and said, "I love you too."

Nonna rose. "Gavin, I have a job for you."

"Me?" he answered back.

"Sì," she replied. "We have some Christmas decorations up in the attic in a big box. Can you get it for me?"

"Sure," Gavin said, leaving the room immediately to complete his task.

Even though Gavin had only lived in the apartment a few days, he knew where the attic was because in the far hallway you couldn't miss the small pull-string hanging down from the trapdoor ceiling.

A careful tug and the door opened, dropping a ladder down for Gavin to climb. His size twelve feet overwhelmed the small rungs, so he was cautious not to slip as he ascended the rickety ladder.

Gavin had to crouch a bit, to avoid slamming his head on the low ceiling up there. He saw old furniture, a crib that Gio had no doubt used years earlier, and what looked like a pool table with no legs, splat on the floor.

His eyes swept the attic searching for the elusive Christmas box and finally he spotted it in the corner. Gold tinsel spilling out gave the contents away. As he moved toward the box, Gavin tripped and fell face first on the dusty floor. He hit so hard, Chase and Nonna heard the bang from the kitchen.

"Are you alright, cowboy?" Chase called up to the ceiling.

Gavin rose, coughed a bit, then shouted back, "I fell."

Chase walked out of the kitchen toward the trap door and ladder, yelling up, "Are you hurt?"

"Just my pride," Gavin said.

Gavin looked back to see what had sent him tumbling and found an antique oak box. It was roughly the size of two phone books, with a latch and a large keyhole. Gavin tugged at the latch to see if it would open, but the sturdy lock held firm. He then gave the box a quick shake and could hear things banging around inside.

Gavin set the mystery box aside and finished what he came to do: retrieve the Christmas decorations.

"Chase? Let me hand this down to you," he called.

Chase appeared beneath the ladder and Gavin slowly lowered the cardboard container.

"It's filthy," he said.

After dusting off the front of his shirt and pants, Gavin climbed down, pushing the ladder back up where it belonged.

"So, are we decorating?" Chase asked Nonna.

"Me? No. It's for Francesca and Gio," she answered.

Chase had déjà vu of an elderly man she met years earlier in Vermont. He'd lost his daughter and stopped decorating his home or celebrating Christmas. Chase wondered if Nonna, having lost her husband and son in the same year, might be feeling the same way, and if she was, who could blame her?

The silence of the moment was broken when the front door swung open and Francesca and Gio bounced in, singing an old Italian song that was playing on the radio, *Ti Amo, Ti Amo*.

Francesca stopped singing and called out, "How was the Colosseum?"

Gavin pause, then replied, "Strange."

Gio stopped in his tracks and asked, "Strange how?"

Gavin looked at Chase, not certain how to explain it.

Finally, Chase threw her hands in the air and said, "Go ahead, tell them."

"Well," Gavin began. "I met a man who wasn't there, and he said he could help me find the greatest romance in all of Italy."

Gio asked, "Wasn't there?"

Chase intervened, "There and then gone, he means."

Francesca, then asked, "Help you how?"

Gavin smiled, "By giving me four riddles to solve."

Chase added, "Each word, or riddle, leading us to something amazingly, stupendously, romantic."

Francesca in dramatic fashion went over to the kitchen table, pulled out a chair, and tapped the seat for Gavin to sit next to her, saying, "Well, park yourself and give us the first clue."

CHAPTER 7

Get an Old One

During the eight-hour flight from JFK to the Leonardo da Vinci International in Rome, Chase and Gavin had taken turns thumbing through a travel book they'd purchased at a small bookstore in SOHO, mapping out the best places to see and eat in Italy. For pizza, everyone worth their salt knew that Naples had the most authentic pie, but tonight they were in Rome, so the next best bet, according to their travel book, was a place called Emma.

Jules, their driver, made the short run over to get two pies, as Nonna lay out plates and the good silverware. Chase picked up a fork and gave Gavin a confused look, wondering why they'd need utensils to eat pizza.

When dinner arrived and was placed at the center of the table, they noticed it wasn't cut into eight slices like back in America; it was one big solid pie. Francesca produced a stainless-steel wheel cutter and sliced the still hot pizza into more manageable chunks.

Gavin would typically take a slice of the thin New York style pizza, fold it onto itself and eat it like a sandwich. Here the pie was thicker, and Chase soon realized why they needed the knives and forks: they'd be cutting it up like steak.

With a mouth full of pizza, Francesca asked, "So, tell me about these clues."

Gavin explained, "As we said earlier, Chase and I went to the Colosseum to look around."

Gio interrupted, asking, "And that's when you saw the man who wasn't there?"

Gavin corrected him: "Oh, he was there, I just couldn't find him after."

Francesca then asked, "So, this gentleman gave you clues or riddles, as he called them?"

Gavin nodded and smiled, "Exactly."

Gio looked from his mom's face back to Gavin's, saying, "Well? Give us the first one."

"Lock," Gavin said flatly.

Nonna, not following, said, "Look? At what?"

Chase then explained: "Not *look*, Nonna, LOCK. The man told Gavin if he wanted romance, the first riddle was lock."

Francesca asked, "Like a lock on a door? What's romantic about that?"

Gavin nodded in agreement, saying, "Not a thing."

The five of them sat there, letting the pizza get cold, thinking about this silly clue from what must have been a senile old man. That's when they heard the toilet flush and Jules emerge from the bathroom.

"What about a lock?" he asked.

Gavin said what everyone was thinking at that moment, "I thought you left."

Jules smiled a big toothy grin, "And miss out on Emma's pizza? Not a chance. I had to clean up a bit."

Nonna rose and grabbed another plate from the cupboard for Jules, pointed at an empty chair, and told him, "*Siediti.*"

Gio, not wanting to leave Gavin and Chase in the dark, said, "That means sit."

Jules took a seat and a huge slice of the pizza, ignoring the knife and fork and raising it up for a big bite, exclaiming, "So good."

He poured himself a glass of wine, and before taking a gulp, asked again, "What about a lock?"

Chase answered, "A mystery man told Gavin if he wanted to find the most romantic things to show me in Rome—"

"Italy," Gavin interrupted.

Chase then, "Excuse me?"

"He said in all of Italy, not just Rome," Gavin corrected her.

Chase responded, "Right, Italy."

She then turned back to Jules, "He said in all of Italy there are four romantic things and then gave four clues to find them."

Jules, following along, then asked, "And one of them was lock?"

Gavin answered, "Yes."

Jules finished his slice of pizza, then said, "I know all of Italy from my job as a driver, so let me think a minute."

Gavin was spying another slice of pepperoni, as Chase poured herself a small glass of water from the bottle on the table.

Jules finished his glass of wine in one swallow, looked around with a grin and didn't speak. He didn't need to; his eyes made it clear he knew something they didn't.

"What?" Francesca asked her brother.

Jules got up and went to the fridge, and opening the freezer, said, "Do we have any dessert?

Francesca took her napkin and threw it at her brother playfully, raising her voice, "Forget the ice cream and speak!"

Jules took out some frozen chocolate gelato and replied, "You'll kick yourself when I tell you."

Gio rose from his chair, pointed at his uncle, and yelled, "Ponte Milvio!"

Jules pointed right back at his smart nephew and said, "Correct."

"What's that?" Gavin asked.

Francesca then, realizing she should have known this before, replied, "*That* is a bridge only a few miles from here, over the Tiber River."

Nonna understood as well, added, "Sì, the locks of love."

Chase rose from her chair, "Wait, locks on a bridge, I've heard of it, but I think you're confused; that bridge with the locks is in Paris."

Francesca agreed, saying, "They have one, that's true, but so does Rome."

Gavin then added, "I looked at the brochures on Italy and they didn't mention this Ponte whatever bridge."

"That's because the locks became a problem and the city ended the romantic practice years ago," Francesca explained.

Gavin, still a bit confused, asked, "Romantic how?"

Chase took his hand, "You've never heard of this, hon?"

She could see in his face he had not, so she explained, "Couples go to the bridge to pledge their love and place a padlock on the bridge and throw away the key."

Gio took his mother's hands in his and started dancing with her around the kitchen, saying in an exaggerated Italian accent, "Then your love, she live on forever!"

His silliness caused everyone to laugh.

Gavin, finally understanding, then asked, "So if they stopped doing this on the, what did you call the bridge?"

Jules replied, "Ponte Milvio."

"Right, Ponte Milvio," Gavin answered back. "If they stopped doing this lock thing, why would the old man give it to me as a clue?"

Chase leaned back in her chair, saying, "Good question."

Jules then surprised them when he said, "Because they've started it again. The locks."

All eyes on Jules now, as he continued, "Sort of, I mean. They installed these sturdy lampposts at the bridge, and you can put locks on those. This way it doesn't hurt the structure."

"And it's legal?" Gavin asked.

Jules shrugged his shoulders and said, "Yes and no. Mostly yes."

Chase smiled at Gavin and gave him a look that said, *So? What do you say, cowboy?*

Gavin took one look into Chase's eyes and asked, "So how do you get to this bridge?"

Gio clapped his hands and said, "Yeah, we're going on an adventure."

"We?" his mother, Francesca, asked. "*We* have schoolwork and chores to do."

Gio frowned and grabbed a tennis ball off the floor, getting both dogs, Giuseppe and Scooter, excited to play.

"Oh, all right," he said to his mother, before tossing the ball across the floor and sending both dogs scurrying.

At that moment, Chase's phone rang. She looked down at the name on the screen and said, "I'm going to take this."

As Chase stepped away, Gavin grabbed a third slice of pizza and said, "So where do we get a lock to put on the bridge? Do you guys have Home Depot around here?"

"What's that?" Jules asked.

"Gosh, how do I describe it?" Gavin replied. "They sell things you'd need to fix things around the house."

Francesca looked at her brother, Jules, saying to him, "Sounds like Bricofer."

Jules agreed, saying to Gavin, "Bricofer is a store that sells toilets, flooring, cabinets, locks. They're all over Italy."

Gavin, taking another bite of the pizza, replied, "Just like Home Depot."

With that, Chase came back in the room looking happier than when she left, saying, "That was Riley."

Gavin, addressing the others, explained, "Her new Italian friend."

"She's Irish, ding-dong," Chase shot back playfully.

Gavin responded, "Italian, Irish, Martian, so?"

Chase, realizing everyone was looking at her, said very quickly, "She wanted to get together and do something and I was like what do you wanna do and she was like, I dunno, what do you wanna do, so then I told her about the old man with the clues and the lock and the bridge—"

Francesca interrupted, asking Gavin, "How many cups of espresso has she had today?"

Francesca smiled at Chase, then said, "I'm just teasing. Go on."

Chase laughed at the joke, then replied, "About twenty, to answer your question."

She then winked at Francesca, saying, "Kidding. Anyway, Riley and her girlfriend Tessa are bored, so I suggested we all get locks and go to the bridge and lock our love forever."

Jules put his wine glass down, still half-full, saying, "Sounds like I'll be driving, so we won't be finishing that."

Nonna rose from her chair and said to Jules, "I'll make coffee."

Gavin crossed the room to put his arm around Chase, saying, "This is going to be fun."

Chase snapped her fingers, then said, "Wait. We'll need a lock."

Gavin answered her, "We were just discussing that while you were on the phone, they have a big hardware store like back home. We can get one there."

Nonna, busy putting fresh coffee in the machine, then said, "The lock for the bridge? Don't go to Bricofer."

"Why?" Chased asked sincerely.

Nonna turned to look at Chase and explained, "The legend of this bridge is very old. If you want to lock your love, you need an old lock."

Gio, listening to his grandmother, then asked, "You mean, like an antique, Nonna?"

Gavin ran his fingers through his thick hair, asking, "Where on earth can we find an antique lock in Rome?"

Jules laughed, then said, "This city was founded 753 years before Christ was born. I'm pretty sure we can find an antique store with locks."

From just behind them the sound of barking began. Everyone assumed instantly that Scooter and Giuseppe were fighting over the ball, but Giuseppe was curled up in the corner resting. All eyes then went to Scooter, who was standing at attention in front of the refrigerator, staring and barking at the closed door.

"Does he want a snack?" Gio asked, moving toward the fridge.

"Wait," Chase said firmly, causing the boy to stop. "Just wait."

As they inched closer to the refrigerator everyone noticed a handful of letters were separated from the rest.

O S T I A.

Gavin, realizing what Chase might be thinking—*First the painting at the gallery and now this*—tried to pronounce it out loud, "Oh-Sty-Uh?"

He then asked the group, "Is that a word for something? Did one of you leave that on the fridge?"

Gio, Francesca, Jules, and Nonna all looked at each other, but no one acknowledged doing it.

Chase then said, "It's probably just nonsense then. You guys said when you slam the door the letters move around."

Francesca looked more closely and said, "It is a word. It's pronounced O-Stee-Ah, and it means *host*."

Gavin then asked, "Like someone who hosts a party?"

Nonna corrected him, "No. Host like what the priest gives you at Mass. The Eucharist, the host."

"Oh, that host," Gavin replied.

Francesca shrugged it off, saying, "It happens all the time. We get letters and find words, but they don't mean anything."

Chase grabbed her phone and said, "I'll call Riley and tell her first thing in the morning we're going to find an antique store and then go to the Ponte Milvio bridge together."

She then looked at Nonna and said, "I promise we'll get an old one."

As everyone went about their business that evening, Scooter was down on the tile floor looking up at that word OSTIA. His light blue eyes traced each letter, before he let out a deep sigh.

Francesca was right: it was a word, but not the one they thought. More important was this simple truth: what had happened to Chase twice before, first in Vermont and then again near New York City, was indeed happening again.

Scooter knew it, and soon enough, so would everyone.

CHAPTER 8

That's When I Knew

A cold December wind swept through Rome as the sun lifted over the historic buildings to the east, signaling another day had begun. Despite the chill, a kitchen window was being held partially open by a hardcover book, letting fresh air into the apartment.

Chase was up early and thought she'd be the first to brew coffee, but Francesca was already enjoying a cup by that open window.

"Interesting way to use a book," Chase said, as she entered the room.

Francesca looked to the window where the thick novel was acting like a stick.

"One of Dumas's tales, I suspect," Francesca replied. "My husband loved swashbuckling adventures."

"Are you a big reader?" Chase asked.

Francesca shook her head no, and replied, "I find real life more challenging than fiction."

Francesca's eyes drifted to a shelf and a framed photo of her, her husband, Matteo, and Gio, who was barely three at the time.

Chase saw any happiness drain from Francesca's face, as the recent widow stared at the memory, forever preserved behind glass.

"You must miss him," Chase said quietly.

Francesca looked away from the picture, raised the coffee cup to her lips, and answered, "More than you could know."

Chase poured herself coffee and took a seat opposite Francesca at the table and asked, "Do you mind if I . . . ? What I mean to say is—"

She stopped herself mid-sentence.

"How did he die?" Francesca asked, engaging Chase's eyes.

Chase didn't answer; she just took a deep breath and waited.

"It was an accident, six months ago, out working a job. Just a horrible, stupid accident," Francesca replied.

Chase responded, "Can I ask what he did?"

Francesca replied, "He was a mechanic. A good one. He could fix anything, especially engines, motors, that kind of thing."

Chase looked back at the photo of the man: handsome, chiseled face, big strong hands wrapped about his wife and little boy. Instantly, she could see him as a mechanic, coming home with grease on his face, his beautiful wife, Francesca, wiping it off with a wet cloth before giving him a loving kiss hello.

"Chase?" Francesca asked. "Where'd you go?"

Chase smiled, a bit embarrassed, answering, "Sorry, I do that sometimes. What did you ask me?"

Francesca smiled; she liked this beautiful American with the kind eyes who was sharing time with her family.

"I said, when did you know, with Gavin?" Francesca replied. "That he was the one?"

Chase leaned back in her chair and was quiet a moment. Whenever she got this question from her mom or one of her girlfriends back home, she'd give different answers because there were many times Gavin did something so selfless it stopped her heart with wonder. But this moment, this question from Francesca, a woman who clearly had lost so much and was raising a child on her own—she deserved the truth. So, Chase shared a memory she'd never told another soul.

"You know Gavin grew up on a farm, right?" Chase began.

Francesca nodded, "Yes, he told us."

"About a year after we started dating, I was walking on his farm when I noticed up beyond the hayfields, was a tall hill," Chase said. "And way up top was an odd rock formation, something that didn't look natural."

Francesca considered what Chase said, then asked, "What did it look like?"

"It was stones, piled on top of each other, almost like a pyramid," Chase explained.

"Okay," Francesca replied.

"So," Chase continued. "I asked him what it was, and he told me a story about something that happened when he was only twelve years old."

Chase got up and grabbed the pot of coffee, saying, "It's kind of a long story, so we should refill these mugs."

After the cups were brimming with hot coffee, Chase continued. "When you live on a working farm everything you have is for sale or put to use. On Gavin's farm, his father had livestock, chicken, goats, horses, and sheep."

"Sheep?" Francesca asked, then jokingly said, "Like, BAAAAAA."

Chase giggled. "Exactly. The one rule Gavin's parents had was, he was not allowed to name any of the animals or think of them as pets—"

Francesca interrupted, "Because they may have to sell them or even eat them?"

Chase nodded, "Correct. I don't think they ate them, but they would get a dozen lambs, fatten them up, and sell them for a profit."

"So, what does this have to do with the rocks on the hill?" Francesca asked.

"Well, when Gavin was twelve his father bought ten baby lambs for the farm. As they took them off the wagon, they noticed there were eleven."

"Okay," Francesca replied.

"The delivery man said it was too much trouble to take the extra lamb back so Gavin's family could keep it for free," Chase explained.

Francesca just leaned in, dying to know what would happen next.

"Well, Gavin flashed those blue eyes at his parents, and they said, since the lamb didn't cost them anything—"

Francesca blurted out, "Gavin could keep it!"

Chase smiled, "That's right, as a pet. He called it Lucky, because it certainly was the lucky sheep, and he raised it with the others that year."

Francesca then observed, "Thinking about those rocks now, I'm worried this story doesn't have a happy ending."

Chase didn't respond to her comment, instead pressing on, "Later that fall, the latch on the gate wasn't fastened and all the sheep got out. Gavin and the others went to round them up and they found ten."

"So, one was missing?" Francesca said.

"Yes," Chase answered, "Then it got dark, and it wasn't safe to keep looking at night."

Francesca waited for the rest, as Chase continued the story. "The next day Gavin and his father went to the top of that hill and to the edge of a cliff up there. They looked down and sure enough, there was the lost sheep, way down below."

"Was it still alive?" Francesca asked, concern in his voice.

Chase took a deep breath, "No. The fall killed it. They figure it got lost and went right over the edge in the dark."

Francesca seemed upset now, "His poor sheep."

Chase then got to the most important part of the story, "Gavin's father said it was alright to just leave it there, but Gavin refused. He tied a long rope to a maple tree, tossing it over the edge. He then walked the long way down to safely reach the dead sheep a hundred feet below."

"What did he do?" Francesca wondered.

"He tied a lasso and used it as a harness for the sheep. Then once he was back up top, he slowly pulled that heavy sheep up until it reached him."

Francesca could imagine a younger Gavin, strong for his age, doing just that.

"Go on," Francesca said.

"He buried the sheep at the top of the hill and marked the grave with the stones. He even took a small piece of wood and wrote the name on it in red paint as a kind of headstone."

There was a long pause, then Francesca finally spoke, "I asked you earlier when you knew Gavin was the one. Are you telling me you loved him because his pet died, and he buried it?"

Chase smiled and said, "No, there's a part you don't understand."

Francesca waited for the final piece.

Chase then, "I went up to the stones and looked down at the name on the marker, and even though it had been twenty years, you could still make out the red letters. It said *Sheep*."

"Sheep?" Francesca asked, "I don't get it; wasn't its name Lucky?"

Chase picked up her cup of coffee again and smiled. "That's what I thought too. Turns out Lucky was fine; he was found when they rounded up the original ten sheep that were lost."

Francesca pondered a moment, then said, "So he went after the lost sheep, even though it wasn't his favorite."

"Correct," Chase replied, "And—"

"He gave it a proper burial as if its life mattered," Francesca said, finishing Chase's sentence.

Chase nodded, then said, "Because it did. Even though that sheep was destined for slaughter someday, on that day he was in Gavin's care, he was Gavin's family, and his life mattered very much."

Francesca let out a sigh, as if the story took her breath away.

"That's my Gavin," Chase said. "That's when I knew."

"That's when you knew what?" a voice asked from the corridor.

It was Gavin rubbing the sleep out of his eyes, crossing the room to give Chase a gentle kiss good morning.

Chase looked at Francesca, hoping she wouldn't spill the beans of what they were just discussing, and was pleasantly surprised when Francesca answered Gavin, "Just girls trading stories, nothing important."

Gavin had no clue what that meant, so he smiled and said, "Cool. Is there more coffee?"

After breakfast, as if on cue, Chase's phone let out a *ding* telling her Riley and her girlfriend Tessa were downstairs and ready for the day's lock-hunting adventure.

Chase went to the small balcony that looked down on the street and shouted, "We'll be down in a minute."

"THE COLD—close that door," Nonna shouted at Chase. "Who are you yelling to?"

Chase, a bit embarrassed, replied, "Sorry, Nonna, my friend Riley, she's going with us today."

Nonna flung opened the door and stepped onto the balcony, looking down at Riley and Tessa, saying, "You two, come up now. Breakfast."

Riley looked at Tessa, then back up to Nonna, and said in her Irish accent, "We already ate there, luv, but thank you just the same."

Nonna shot Riley her best Italian grandmother look and replied, "Is not a request. UP!"

Thirty seconds later, Riley was standing in the doorway of the flat, wearing a black leather jacket, torn designer jeans, and brown boots that went above the knee. She looked fashionable, with a wild edge to her. Tessa, in contrast, was wearing black leather pants and a lilac-colored sweater that brought out her pretty eyes.

"Nonna, Francesca, Gio," Chase began. "This is Riley, who is obviously from Ireland."

"Excuse me?" Riley joked in her Irish accent. "What exactly makes it obvious?"

Gio smiled and said to this redheaded stranger in his doorway, "Everything."

Gavin added, "You practically come with a box of Lucky Charms."

"And?" Nonna asked, pointing to Tessa, who was standing at Riley's side.

Chase answered, "That is Riley's friend Tessa."

Riley reached down and locked fingers with Tessa, making it clear they were more than just friends. Chase and Gavin weren't sure how Nonna might respond, being from an earlier generation.

Nonna glanced at their hands locked together, looked up to the attractive couple, and said, "Good for you."

With that a car horn sounded, causing Nonna to throw her hands in the air and return to the balcony, looking down at Jules double-parked out front.

"What's the matter?" Nonna called to him. "You no come up anymore?"

Jules stuck his head out of the driver's side window and answered, "I already ate, and your coffee tastes like motor oil."

Nonna picked up a pot which was empty, returned to the balcony as if she were about to toss it, causing Jules to laugh and say, "You know I love you, Nonna."

Chase and Gavin grabbed their jackets to fend off the cold wind that snaked through Rome's endless streets, turning toward the door to go. Scooter, her faithful pup, ran to the door and nudged the leash that was hanging there.

Chase made a pained face and said, "I'm sorry buddy, not today."

Seeing Chase felt guilty leaving him, Gio said, "How about I take him for a walk with Giuseppe? They can bark at cats and visit my mom at the gallery."

Gavin looked at Francesca and Gio and said, "That would be great, thank you."

Jules beeped again, causing Francesca to say, "You'd better go before Nonna dumps hot coffee on his head."

As Chase locked hands with Gavin and turned to leave, Francesca tugged the elbow of her jacket, getting her attention.

"Thank you for sharing that story," she said to Chase.

Her eyes now glistening with silent tears, Francesca looked into Chase's, adding, "Next time I'll share mine."

Chase gave Francesca a hug and whispered in her ear, "I look forward to it."

With that, they were off to find an antique lock, not knowing the surprises awaiting them.

CHAPTER 9

It Always Belonged to You

"You'll need a jacket if you plan to walk the island today, Tommaso," Levi said.

The man with dark eyes and hair to match shook his head no.

"No to the coat or no you're not going for a walk?" Levi asked.

Tommaso stared out the window and uttered just one word, "Both."

"Are you feeling better? You certainly are looking stronger," Levi added.

Tommaso didn't answer. He just continued looking out the window toward the sea. The large stone building was a religious retreat, known for silence, so this man who answered questions with one word fit right in. Although, in truth, he didn't really fit in here at all.

Levi had so many questions for Tommaso, but something told him not to push, so he didn't. He let the man be and went about his duties on the island.

Some two hundred miles away, his brother, Leo, was unlocking the church door to Santa Maria parish, allowing the faithful few in for morning Mass. Father Leo noticed a young man that he'd seen at least thirty times previous, making his way toward the same pew, where he'd kneel and pray. He was easy to spot because he always wore the same yellow hooded sweatshirt with the image of a red bull on the front. The priest knew if someone came into church this frequently, bad news was often their silent partner, prayer being the last rung on the ladder.

Seeing the young man so often, always alone, the priest wanted to ask if he needed spiritual guidance, but like his brother, Levi, Leo didn't like to push people. In matters of faith, they both believed people must walk their own path and find their way to the light.

Father Leo wasn't worried about Levi today, just curious about a secret he'd been keeping several months now. They used to share everything, but this was different.

One of the other priests in Rome suggested to Leo, "Maybe your brother has a secret girlfriend."

That thought just made Leo laugh. Girls, fast cars, a crazy life, none of it ever interested his little brother. A quiet life on an island suited him just fine.

"Father, isn't it time for Mass?" a woman asked Leo.

It was Nonna, out of the apartment and finally back to church.

"Yes, Nonna, thank you for keeping me on task," the priest replied.

As he stepped onto the altar to ready his tools of the trade—vestments, chalice, Eucharist—his mind shifted from his brother to Nonna. How awful, he thought, that she lost her husband to a stroke and then her son in an accident just weeks apart.

He watched her take a seat in her favorite pew, the rosary clutched in her wrinkled right hand. Father Leo hadn't seen her much lately, but it was understandable, losing her son and husband in the same year and now helping to take care of a grandchild. Nonna was sorely missed at the parish's fun events, especially now, being Christmastime.

Father Leo wanted to help her and say just the right thing to make it all better, but what would that be? People think priests have all the answers, a direct dial to the Almighty, but they struggle just like the rest of us.

Before he began the Mass, Father Leo called out, "Nonna, before I get started, your daughter, Francesca, told me she wanted to donate a piece of artwork from her gallery to our Christmas auction. Would you remind her, please?"

Nonna didn't speak, she just looked up and nodded yes.

A few blocks away Chase and Gavin were squished in the backseat of Jules's sedan, excited about their romantic adventure. First stop: Carlucci's Antiques, a shop that Riley knew well because she had sold her grandmother's brooch there when she first arrived in Rome and needed money.

"I don't know if the same man will be there, but he gave me a fair deal," Riley said with a smile.

Tessa looked sad, saying to Riley, "I wish I had known you then. I could have loaned you the money and you wouldn't have parted with a family heirloom."

Riley just patted her hand, "Thanks, luv, but I'm alright."

Gavin asked, "And you think this antique store may sell old locks?"

Riley looked out the window at the passing buildings, answering, "He has a little of everything in that place, so yeah, I think he might."

It was a tight street with merchants on both sides, causing Jules to say, "I can't park here, so I'll circle back in ten minutes."

Chase patted his shoulder and said, "Sounds great, Jules, thank you."

As they got out of the car, Riley said, "I know you're paying him to drive us today, so let us split the bill."

Gavin waved her off, answering, "No way. You're doing us a favor coming along. The ride is on us."

With that, Gavin gave a hard pull on the heavy black door with its red lettering that read CARLUCCI, and a small cowbell hanging above it announced their arrival.

The store had long glass cases, the kind you'd see in an American jewelry store, lining both sides of the room. Hanging on the walls were various pieces of art and other odds and ends. They saw an assortment of antique glass doorknobs, oak mantles that once resided in nineteenth-century homes, and, hanging off a thick pine post, a large steel key ring with at least two hundred antique keys dangling from it.

Inside the glass cases were hundreds of pieces of jewelry, some the cheap costume variety, the rest real diamonds, emeralds, and pearls.

An older gentleman appeared from an office and said, "*Buongiorno, posso aiutarvi?*"

Tessa, who was from Italy and therefore spoke Italian, answered the shopkeeper, "They only speak English."

"Apologies then, and welcome to Carlucci's," the man said.

Chase extended her hand to shake, saying, "Hi, I'm Chase, and this is Gavin, Riley, and Tessa."

Gavin jumped right in, adding, "We're hoping you sell antique locks; you know, the kind you'd use to keep something secure."

The man rubbed his chin a moment, then said, "I have one safe in the back I could sell you, but it's very heavy."

Chase corrected the confusion, "No, no. We don't need a safe, just a lock, the kind that clicks and has a key. The older, the better."

"Oh, sì, sì. Over here," the man replied.

In the corner there was shelf with three antique locks, but only one had a key.

"If you want one that can open and close," the man explained, "This is the one."

The lock looked very old, the brass faded and dark from age. And the key didn't go into the bottom, like a lock you'd buy today; it inserted into the front in a hidden keyhole. Covering the hole was a tiny brass door you'd slide out of the way to reveal the key slot. There were initials on the sliding door: W & C.

As Chase held the lock, rubbing her thumb along the smooth weathered brass, she was impressed at how heavy it was.

Gavin then asked the storekeeper, "What does W and C stand for?"

The old man turned and took a leather-bound book down from the highest shelf, dropping it on the glass counter, hard enough to make dust take flight.

"Sorry about that," the man said.

He then took his reading glasses from the front pocket of his red flannel shirt, and started turning pages and tracing his finger up and down in the ancient-looking tome.

"There it is," he said happily. "W and C stands for Wilcox and Company. That's the lock's maker. According to the book, this lock was produced in America and dates to the Civil War."

Tessa, curious now, asked, "How on earth did it get here?"

The man took off his glasses, resting them on the still open book. "You'd be surprised what walks through the door, young lady."

Chase looked at Gavin and then back at the man. "How much is it, sir?"

There was no price on the lock, which was typical for a shop like this, where bartering was an art form.

"Well," he began. "If this were a re-creation, not an antique, it might cost you fifty euros."

Gavin interrupted, "But that's the real thing, right?"

"It is, so I'm thinking, oh, two hundred," the man estimated.

Chase made a face, "Eek, that's out of our price range."

Gavin agreed, "It really is. Thank you, sir, just the same."

Tessa then said, to a disappointed Chase, "I know you wanted an old lock for the bridge, but we can get a new one at the store for ten euros."

As the four turned to go, the man asked, "Wait a moment, please. Did you say bridge?"

All four nodded their heads, causing him to ask, "Ponte Milvio?"

"Yes," Chase answered, "We are going there today to—"

"Lock your love at the bridge," the man finished with a warm smile. "Why didn't you tell me that earlier?"

Chase was silent as the old man closed the book and put it back on the shelf.

He turned and said, "Tell you what. I was just about to announce my big Christmas sale."

Chase smiled, "You were?"

"I was," he continued. "And today we are taking fifty percent off any lock that is being used in the pursuit of everlasting love."

Chase was touched by the kind gesture, but before she could reach for her wallet, he said, "In fact, I think seventy-five euros is going to be the price."

Gavin reached out and shook the man's hand. "Sold, and thank you."

As Chase peeled out the currency, Riley was off to the side, looking closely into one of the glass cases. Suddenly she stopped and brought her hand to her chest.

"What is it?" Tessa asked.

"My brooch, it's still here," Riley said, sounding shocked.

She then looked over at the man and said, "Are you Mr. Carlucci? The owner?"

The old man smiled and said, "I am. And you're the young woman who sold me the brooch you're looking at."

Riley got emotional, "I am."

"Had to be five years ago, yes?" Carlucci asked.

"At least five," Riley answered.

"You'll think I'm lying, but I remember your red hair and that accent," the shopkeeper added.

Riley looked at the others, her eyes filling with tears now, the sudden swell of emotions catching her off guard.

"I'm so sorry to get like this," Riley said. "But when I came to Italy, I had such grand plans, and everything fell flat. I had to make some tough choices and one of them . . ." Her voice trailed off.

Chase finished her thought, "One of them was selling things you care about in order to survive."

Riley looked at Chase, a bit embarrassed, answering, "It was."

No one spoke, then Riley said, "I'm fine now. Got a good job and Tessa in my life."

She looked back into the case at the brooch, explaining, "It belonged to my grandmother in Glandore, Ireland. I wore it over my heart."

As Riley gently touched her own chest where the brooch once sat, she added, "I never thought I'd see it again."

Tessa looked at Mr. Carlucci, "How much is it, sir?"

He crossed the room to the case and said, "If memory serves, I gave you a hundred euros for it."

Riley nodded in agreement, "That sounds about right."

Mr. Carlucci then said, "Before we continue our negotiations, can I tell you a secret about jewelry?"

Riley looked at the kind man's face and answered, "Sure."

Carlucci continued, saying, "Some jewelry can be worn by anyone. But other pieces, special pieces, insist on having one owner."

He then reached into the case, taking it gently out of the satin pouch it had been resting on all these years.

Gavin asked, "What do you mean, one owner?"

Mr. Carlucci looked at him and said, "Gavin, was it? Your name?"

"Yes, sir," Gavin responded.

"Well, Gavin," the old man continued. "This brooch belonged to Riley, and I tried to sell it. I tell you, a hundred people must have looked at it over the years, some trying it on. But they always put it back. Something told them not to buy it because—"

With that he handed the brooch to Riley, saying, "It always belonged to you."

Riley took it in her hands and the tears returned, falling gently down her cheeks.

Tessa snapped open her purse to retrieve her wallet, causing Mr. Carlucci to say, "I wouldn't think of it. My gift. Merry Christmas."

Riley stepped around the counter, and without saying a word gave Mr. Carlucci a hug.

As she pulled back to see his face, she said, "God bless you."

Suddenly there was a loud clang from the cowbell above the door.

"I've circled three times—are you almost ready?" Jules asked.

He then looked from Chase, Tessa, and over to Riley and said, "Why is everyone crying? Are the prices that high?"

Gavin laughed out loud and said, "We'll be right out."

Jules vanished back into the street, as the old man said, "Go and lock your love at the bridge. It was nice to meet you all."

As everyone moved toward the door to go, Chase stood motionless, her face blank.

Gavin stopped and turned but didn't speak because he knew that look. Chase was off somewhere in her mind, an occupational hazard for writers.

Finally, he said, "You okay, hon?"

Chase broke the stare, turned to Gavin, and said, "Sorry. Just got a weird feeling something was happening."

"What, Chase?" Riley asked.

She looked at her friend and answered, "Wish I knew."

Across the city, at that very moment, in the gallery where Francesca worked, Gio had stopped by with Scooter and Giuseppe for a visit.

Normally, just a couple weeks before Christmas, the gallery would be filled with tourists, spread throughout the store. Today, however, every customer was in the back, watching a dog they didn't know barking at a painting.

Scooter was staring at the same piece of artwork that had troubled him before, looking intensely at the artist's name scribbled in gold lettering at the bottom: ALEXANDER.

Francesca, the gallery's owner, turned to the assistant manager and said, "Gianna, do me a favor and track down where this painting came from. I want to know everything there is to know about this artist ALEXANDER."

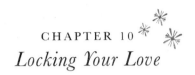

CHAPTER 10

Locking Your Love

There is a three-year waiting list to secure a slot at the prestigious Le Cordon Bleu culinary school in Paris. Despite those daunting odds, for Marie LaFleur a slot was guaranteed, seeing her uncle was an esteemed alumnus and owned a chain of successful restaurants across France. Marie spent weekends by his side learning the art of fine cuisine, and her perfect scores in preparatory school made her an easy early selection.

Willy Klaus, on the other hand, from the seaside village of Binz, Germany, was the longest of long shots. He did not come from money but learned to cook in a high-end resort nestled on the shores of the Baltic Sea. The head chef, an American who went by the nickname Cutty, was trained at the esteemed Culinary Institute in Hyde Park, New York. Taking a liking to Willy the moment the boy was hired to wash dishes, he immediately called him *Billy*. Willy loved the nickname, and it stuck.

When the plates were spotless, Cutty would wave Billy over to the stove and share the secrets to creating the divine dishes that drew tourists by the thousands to the restaurant each year.

Billy wanted to be a chef, like Cutty, and *the* place to train was Le Cordon Bleu in Paris. Billy had little hope of getting in, until Cutty talked to the president of the culinary school and wrote a recommendation letter to the selection committee on his behalf. Billy's financial situation, what some would call poverty, also helped him, since the school had a policy of admitting several *hard luck* cases each year.

Soon enough, Marie, the beautiful, wealthy French girl and Billy, the sweet but poor German boy, were pushed together by fate at the same school at the same time. They were even paired together in a course called *pastry arts* their very first day. Was it any surprise they fell in love within a short time?

Months had passed since that day, and their young romance burned hotter than the stoves they trained on. However, when Marie and Billy announced plans to marry after graduation, both sets of parents were opposed. Dating someone at culinary school was one thing, but marriage this young? The parents were clear: that merger was off the table.

Billy insisted their parents would warm to the idea, but Marie had a different concern. Her family had the financial means to move her right out of Billy's life should she press ahead with plans to marry a destitute German boy.

Billy's intention was to hold fast and reason with their parents, while Marie had a far blunter solution: just elope. Her wealthy parents couldn't stop Marie from marrying the man of her dreams if the deed was already done.

When Billy learned of this, he suggested a trip to Rome and the perfect place to say *I do*. Little did they know, they'd be meeting up on the very same day with another couple deeply in love.

The train ride from Paris to Italy took a little more than ten hours, with multiple stops along the way. Time flew for the lovebirds as they talked about taking their vows by a romantic bridge in Rome that Billy had heard about from a friend. Young lovers dream big, and these two were no exception. They'd get married, graduate, then open a restaurant in in some quaint little village in the south of France.

Yet young love, like champagne, is both intoxicating and dangerous when shaken, and that was Marie and Billy at this moment. They checked their watches and saw they were less than an hour from their destination; the Ponte Milvio bridge.

For Chase, Gavin, Riley, and Tessa, the trip to the same bridge on the same day was a short drive. The Ponte Milvio dated back to the Roman Empire and then, as now, was of strategic importance, giving thousands of pedestrians a way to cross the Tiber River.

Chase had read that the tradition of the *locks on the bridge* began after the publication of a popular novel *I Want You* by author Federico Moccia in 2006. It inspired lovestruck teens to place locks there, and soon the idea spread to other bridges around Europe.

Eventually, the sheer weight of the locks at Ponte Milvio, just as they saw in Paris, forced town officials to cut them away and forbid the practice. When lovers ignored the warnings, officials in Rome relented, placing reinforced lampposts along the bridge that could withstand the weight of the locks. While the practice was technically illegal, many lovers still came to *lock their love*, and people in charge of Ponte Milvio learned to look the other way.

Cafés line the streets near the bridge, along with several fine shops. All are forbidden from selling locks by city ordinance, an effort to discourage the practice. As Jules pulled up a short distance from the bridge, Chase, seated comfortably in the backseat between Gavin and Riley, looked down at the antique lock in her hands. She rubbed her thumb on the little latch that revealed the hidden keyhole and noticed the initials of the locksmith, W & C.

"I'll bet whoever made that lock a hundred years ago in America never imagined it would end up on a bridge in Italy," Gavin said.

Chase met his deep blue eyes, and answered, "I'll bet you're right, cowboy."

Chase then looked at the sun sinking low in the sky, the red glow splattered like spilled paint across the horizon, and said, "Is it me or is this kind of exciting?"

Riley gave Tessa a hug and said, "It's bloody romantic, if you ask me."

It was then Chase realized neither Tessa nor Riley had a lock with them.

Chase pointed toward the beautiful old bridge and asked the ladies, "Didn't you two want to . . . ya know?"

The suggestion caused Tessa to giggle like a schoolgirl with a crush, as Riley said, "Oh no, sweetie, today is about you and Gavin. Tessa and I have forever for things like this."

Gavin interrupted the moment, saying, "We're losing the light—we'd better get going."

As everyone exited the car, Riley said, "I'm not entirely sure this is legal, so watch out for the nine-o."

Gavin laughed, causing Riley to ask, "Didn't I say that right? I learned that word watching American crime shows. Nine-O? The police?"

Chase tapped Gavin's arm to make him stop laughing, saying, "You were close, Riley. It's five-o, the cops. Five-o."

Gavin then said, teasing her, "I looked around for nine-o. I think we're in the clear, but thanks for watching out, Riley."

Riley pushed back her long, curly red hair, revealing her pretty face, answering in that strong Irish accent, "You've got it, mate."

As Gavin and Chase crossed the street to approach the bridge, an older gentleman dressed like a priest in a traditional black cassock approached them.

"Are you my couple?" he asked.

"I'm sorry," Gavin replied.

The priest answered back, "I'm Father Miguel; we spoke on the phone."

Chase replied, "I think you have us mixed up with someone else, father."

The man of the cloth opened a small leather Bible that was in his right hand, took out of a small piece of paper with writing on it, and said, "You're not Marie and Billy?"

Gavin answered, "No, Gavin and Chase. Wrong couple."

Riley, watching and hearing all this from the curb, called over to Chase, "Maybe it's a sign you're supposed to get married."

Chase shot back, "Here? Today? No, I'm waiting until Christmas Eve."

Before the priest could turn and go, they heard a commotion coming down the sidewalk. A young couple, barely into their twenties, were dashing toward the group, breathless and determined to reach them.

"ARE YOU FATHER MIGUEL?" Billy shouted at the priest.

"Sì, I am Miguel," he answered, pointing at Gavin now and adding, "I thought they were you."

Billy and Marie reached them, their eyes took in Chase and Gavin, then both paused a moment to catch their breath.

"The train was late," Marie explained. "Sorry, Father."

It seemed clear Chase and Gavin were not needed for the rest of this conversation, whatever it was, so they both stepped away and started again toward the bridge.

"WAIT," Riley called out.

Everyone looked over at the redhead to see what was wrong.

Riley then dramatically nodded her head to the right, and Chase and Gavin saw a police officer parking his car outside of a bakery.

Once the officer was out of the vehicle and inside the shop, Riley called out again, "Go."

Gavin laughed at the notion of Riley playing lookout, as if they were pulling off some diamond heist.

Before Chase and Gavin could reach the bridge, they heard a young woman raising her voice and getting upset.

"What do you mean you can't? We came all this way," she said.

It was the college student Marie, on the verge of tears.

Chase and Gavin stopped to listen.

"I'm sorry, young lady, but I thought you knew. I cannot marry anyone without the proper documents," the priest explained.

"What documents? We're in love, isn't that enough?" Billy asked, his voice shaky with frustration.

The priest put his hand on Billy's shoulder, trying to comfort him, "You must have a marriage license to get married. It's the law."

Billy looked at his sweetheart now, bit his bottom lip, and said, "I'm so sorry, I didn't know. I should have asked when I called the priest to come."

Marie adored Billy and couldn't stand to see him upset, reaching out to squeeze his hand now.

"It's okay," she said, "I love you, married or not."

"Now," the priest explained, "If you two can wait a day or two and apply for one, I'm sure we can come back here and um—"

"A day or two?" Marie interrupted, "We both have classes and tests. This had to be right now," Marie said.

"I am sorry then," the priest said, before excusing himself and walking away.

Chase then, forgetting why she was here, motioned to Gavin to wait a moment and walked over to the young lovers.

"Is everything alright?" Chase asked.

Billy, protective of his privacy and his girlfriend, raised his hand as if to stop her, "Yes, we're fine. I just messed up."

Gavin joined Chase now at her side, saying, "You two were going to get married today, at the bridge? Was that the plan?"

Marie nodded, her eyes looking a bit lost in that moment. A look that said, *What are we going to do now?*

Chase then, trying to help, said, "Can I tell you both a secret?"

The young couple looked at Chase, waiting.

"As romantic as Rome can be," she began. "This bridge, the Ponte Milvio, is not the place for a wedding."

Marie, wiping a single tear from her eye and seeming more composed now, responded, "It's not?"

Chase looked to Gavin for a little help now, and he joined right in saying, "No, it's not. I've become a sort of expert on romantic things in Italy, and this bridge is no good for marriage."

Billy looked over to the bridge and noticed some locks were attached to the lamppost, asking, "What are those?"

"Those are the locks of love," Gavin answered right back.

Marie, looking confused, commented, "I thought that was the bridge in Paris?"

Chase replied, "Me too, but it turns out the tradition started here in Rome."

The young couple were processing this new piece of information when Gavin said, "So, if you two really want to celebrate your love, you don't want to get married today, you want to put a lock on the bridge."

Marie smiled at the notion and looked to Billy, saying, "What do you think?"

Billy smiled at the girl he clearly adored, answering, "I think when we get married, and we *will* be married someday, Catherine Marie LaFleur. I think we should have our families and friends at our side."

Marie was crying again, just hearing Billy's promise, as she replied, "Me too."

Billy then looked around, taking in the village and shops for a moment, before saying, "Until then, why don't we . . . what did you call it, sir? The thing with the bridge?"

Gavin smiled, answering, "Locking your love. They call it locking your love."

Billy threw his shoulders back, like a man on a mission, before saying to Marie, "Let's get a lock and do that. Would that make you happy?"

Marie hugged him and replied, "Very much."

Riley and Tessa were eavesdropping on the whole conversation before Riley said, "Not to ruin this perfect moment, but you can't get a lock here."

Marie looked at the dozens of shops and restaurants and said, "Surely somebody sells them."

Gavin replied, "Riley is right. I read online that to discourage people from placing locks on the bridge they forbid the stores here from selling them."

Billy put his arm around Marie and said, "I can't believe we took a ten-hour train ride, all for nothing."

Gavin looked at the young man and said, "I'm sorry, brother, that stinks. Doesn't it, Chase?"

There was silence.

"Chase?" Gavin called again, with no response.

Riley then, seeing Chase's blank face, asked her, "Chase, darlin', what's wrong?"

All eyes were on Chase now as she was staring stone silent at the antique lock resting in her hands. She rubbed her fingers on the latch with the initials W & C. Her eyes were intense, as if she were a child putting a puzzle together.

"What was the name of the manufacturer that made this lock?" Chase asked Gavin.

He thought a moment and said, "Wilcox and Company, back in America. Why?"

Chase was silent another twenty seconds, making everyone a little uncomfortable.

Gavin knew Chase was on to something, finally asking, "What is it?"

Chase's expression suddenly changed, the way one's does when they've solved a riddle.

She looked up at the college girl and asked, "What's your name again?"

"Marie," she answered quickly.

"But that's not what he just called you when he said your full name," Chase replied.

Marie, confused for a moment, then said, "Oh, right. Everyone calls me Marie, but that's my middle name. My first name is actually Catherine— but since my mother's first name is also Catherine, I've always been called by my middle name."

Billy asked, "What's this about?"

Chase smiled and turned to the boy, "Oh, I'm onto you next. She calls you Billy. Is that your birth name or short for something else?"

Billy looked at Marie, then answered, "My formal name is Wilhelm. Why?

Chase looked back at the lock and said, "Wilhelm and Catherine."

Gavin then, "What?"

Chase held up the lock and showed everyone the front with the tiny latch and letters etched in, then said, "Wilhelm and Catherine, W and C."

Riley shoved Tessa playfully and said, "Shut the front door."

Marie, looking completely lost, said, "I don't understand what's happening."

Gavin took the lock from Chase's hands and said, "I'll be damned."

Chase turned to the very confused college couple, and explained, "We went to an antique shop earlier today and of all the locks the man sold, this is the one I chose."

She handed it to Billy to hold, adding, "It was made more than a hundred years ago, thousands of miles away. Yet somehow that's the one I find and buy."

Gavin added to her explanation: "And of all the days to come to this bridge to lock our love, we meet you two, Wilhelm and Catherine."

Billy then, starting to understand, looked down at the initials on the lock and said, "W and C."

Chase smiled at him, echoing his words, "W and C."

Chase turned to Gavin now, and said, "I don't think this lock is for us, hon."

His eyes went from her face to the young couple, as Chase added, "It's for them."

Tessa walked over and asked, "Why don't the two of you seem surprised by this?"

Chase looked at Gavin, then he replied, "Because this isn't our first rodeo."

Tessa, not sure how to respond, finally said, "I don't understand."

Chase replied softly, "Neither do I most of the time. I just know, in my heart, something led us to that shop and this lock, and now, this young couple. I'm supposed to give it to them."

Marie, realizing they were gifting her the lock, in her French accent said, "We couldn't. You came to lock *your* love."

Chase took Gavin's hand in hers and said, "I have my love right here. Please, take it."

With that, Marie held the lock and turned to Billy.

He nodded to her and replied, "I think we should do what she says."

Marie gave Chase an unexpected hug and the college students walked hand in hand onto the bridge. Just as they reached the center and opened the latch on the lock, the police officer Riley saw earlier joined them on the sidewalk and looked on as Marie and Billy locked their love.

Gavin said to the officer, "You're not going to stop them?"

The policeman took a bite of his fresh gingerbread biscotti, then shrugged his shoulders and answered, "*Non si può fermare l'amore.*"

As the officer strolled away, Tessa translated, "He says you can't stop love."

CHAPTER 11

Wrap It to Go

Two days had passed since Chase and Gavin helped the young couple on the bridge. While slightly disappointed they didn't lock their own love, something felt right about how things played out.

"Don't worry," Chase teased Gavin. "You still have three more clues to solve where we pledge our love forever."

Gavin smiled and asked, "Do we dive right into the second riddle, or should we pace ourselves?"

Francesca, listening to the lovebirds talk from an adjacent room, called out, "I say dive right in."

Gavin chuckled, "Oh, you think so, huh? Well, grab Nonna and see if we can figure out the next clue."

Francesca walked into the living room and smirked as if she already knew something they didn't.

"What?" Chase asked.

Francesca took a seat on the couch and crisscrossed her legs the way children do, answering, "The old man at the Colosseum told you four clues would lead to romance. Yes?"

Gavin answered, "That's right."

"The first clue was *lock*, and that led you to the bridge, right?" she said.

Chase answered, "Yes."

Francesca continued, "And the second clue or word was *kiss*."

"Correct," Gavin replied, "which seems kind of vague. I mean, people kiss all the time."

Francesca smiled, "What if it was a special kiss in a special place at a special time."

Both Gavin and Chase waited silently for Francesca to explain.

"In Venice, where you find the beautiful canals and gondola rides, there is something called the Bridge of Sighs," Francesca said.

"Size?" Gavin asked.

Francesca shook her head, "Not size like how big something is, but sighs like . . ."

She then let out an exaggerated exhale, sighing as if she were sad.

Chase caught on, "OH, *sighs*. And why do you think this place is the second clue?"

Francesca tossed her hair back behind her head and, using a small tie, put it into a ponytail, asking, "You guys didn't learn this in your travel books?"

Both shrugged their shoulders, so Francesca explained, "Legend says that if a couple kisses under the Bridge of Sighs at sunset, at exactly the moment the bells from the nearby church are ringing—"

"What?" Chase asked eagerly, "What happens?"

"Your love will last forever," Francesca finished.

Chase looked at Gavin and smiled, "I love this. I absolutely LOVE it."

Then turning to Francesca, Chase asked, "And is there a certain day or time of the year?"

"Not according to the legend," Francesca replied. "But the kiss must be under the bridge, as the sun sets and with the bells chiming. If even one of those three is off, you're destined for a life of misery."

Gavin laughed, "Misery, WOW, okay. Well let's hope the sun decides to set that day and the bells work."

Chase turned to Gavin, asking, "What day?"

He then gave her a hug and answered, "The day we drive to Venice and do this baby."

Gio entered the room holding a cell phone, saying, "Mom, did you put this on silent? There are a bunch of messages and calls for you, most from Gianna at the gallery."

As Francesca took the phone from her son, she said, "This might be about the painting that Scooter was barking at."

Chase asked, curious, "What about a painting?"

Francesca let out another sigh, then said, "I didn't want to cause you alarm, but do you remember your dog barking at a painting in the gallery?"

Chase leaned in. "Of course, why?"

Gio replied, "Because he did it again."

Gavin asked then, "When? We haven't been back there."

Gio explained, "I took Giuseppe and Scooter for a walk while you guys were at the bridge with your lock, and we stopped by the gallery."

Chase interrupted him. "And that's when Scooter started barking at the same painting, the one in the back?"

Gio pointed at Chase, "Exactly. He had everyone in the gallery watching him."

Francesca raised her phone to her ear and walked out of the room for a moment, talking quietly into it.

Gio, trying to explain the dog's strange behavior, commented, "Maybe he just doesn't like that painting. You think?"

Chase, given Scooter's track record back in Manchester, Vermont, and again at Briarcliff Manor outside of New York City, knew in her bones this was something more. But trying not to alarm the boy she responded, "Yeah, could be, Gio."

With that, Francesca came back in the room with the phone still to her ear, saying into it, "Okay then, we'll be over in ten minutes."

She hung up the call and looked to Chase and Gavin with wide eyes.

Before she could speak, Chase said, "Are we going to the gallery?"

Francesca replied, "Gianna has some information about the man who did the painting—you know, the one your dog doesn't like."

Gavin, trying to sound silly, piped in, "Should I bring a flashlight? Sounds like we're going on a mystery hunt."

Gio clapped his hands. "I like the sound of that. Let me get my coat."

Giuseppe and Scooter walked toward the front door as if they were part of this adventure.

"Oh, no you don't, troublemaker, you stay here," Chase said, while wagging her finger at Scooter.

The Australian shepherd almost seemed to frown, then spun quickly before tossing himself to the floor.

"And the Oscar for most dramatic dog goes to . . ." Gavin said sarcastically.

Gio returned with a coat for himself and his mother, Francesca.

"Jules?" Chase asked, wondering if they'd need a ride.

Francesca shook her head and said, "Nah, ten-minute walk, tops."

Gio added, "Plus, in this cold, the feet move faster."

Gavin patted the boy on the back, as he opened the front door and said, "Yes they do, Gio."

Anyone on the streets of Rome would have thought there was a fire, as three adults and a teenage boy zipped and maneuvered their way through the thick holiday crowd.

Gio was right. The ten-minute walk took them only seven.

Gianna was watching by the front window and scooted everyone to the back office where she shut the door and turned to Chase and the others with anticipation.

"Well," she began. "I have good news and bad news."

Francesca frowned and said, "I always like the bad news first."

"Right," Giana replied. "Mario, the art distributor, called me back and said that there were a couple of paintings from the last batch that came from another broker named Carlo Valeriano."

"Alright," Francesca said. "So?"

"So, this Carlo," Giana continued, "is on a buying trip somewhere in Spain and can't be reached. Which means, I don't know anything specific about the painting with the big ALEXANDER written in gold lettering."

Francesca, looking frustrated, asked, "So, what's the good news?"

"Well," Gianna replied, "Mario has a catalogue of artists whose work is sold all over Europe and he looked up the name."

"And?" Chase asked.

"And he found two artists with the last name Alexander," Giana continued. "One specialized in portraits only, so this painting of a street scene and a man peeling fruit couldn't be one of his."

Gavin then asked, "And the other artist?"

Giana smiled and said, "He was Greek. Titos Leonidas Alexander. He was fond of painting a kind of a Norman Rockwell style, which included street scenes."

Curious, Francesca asked, "And did he sign his paintings with big gold letters?"

"That I don't know," Gianna replied. "I looked through some catalogues, but I can't find any of his work. Honestly, he's an insignificant artist."

Gavin replied, "Well, it sounds like this is him. But that doesn't answer the larger question—"

Chase finished Gavin's thought: "Why is Scooter so infatuated with his painting?"

Gavin then added, "Why bark at this one thing?"

Gio pondered a moment, then said, "Two things."

"I'm sorry?" Gavin asked.

Gio answered, "He barked at two things. The painting and the letters on the fridge at home, remember?"

Francesca then said, "Yeah, but that was gibberish, just some jumbled letters."

Chase then asked, "What were they again?"

"Ostia," Francesca answered. "It means host."

Gavin then thinking out loud, said, "So, Alexander and Ostia. Is there any connection?"

Francesca looked at Gianna, a young woman who, like Francesca, had spent her entire life in Rome. Gianna just shook her head no.

Francesca looked at Chase and said, "I'm not seeing it, sorry."

Gavin then said, "I hate to throw water on this magical mystery tour, but I think we should consider the obvious."

Chase replied, "That there's no connection, and Scooter is just acting strange?"

Francesca considered the explanation, then said, "He is a long way from home in a new place."

Gio looked at Chase and watched her eyes. She looked as if she was trying to solve a difficult math equation.

Gio asked her directly, "You don't believe that, do you, Chase?"

She broke her stare and turned to the teen. "Me? I'm not sure what to believe anymore, Gio. But, for now, let's just leave it be."

In a strong tone, Francesca said, "Oh no, I want that painting out of here. Your dog isn't the only one who doesn't like it."

Giana frowned and said, "But nobody wants to buy it, Francesca."

Francesca pulled her cell phone out of her pocket, hit some buttons, and said, "Watch this."

She then raised the phone to her ear, and after two rings said, "Father Leo? It's Francesca, Nonna's daughter-in-law. (pause) Thank you for saying that. It has been a tough year for us."

There was another pause where the others could hear the priest's voice on the other end of the phone.

Finally, when he stopped, Francesca said, "The reason I'm calling is I promised you something for the Christmas auction. How about a framed piece of art that's worth five hundred euros?"

There was more talk on the other end, then Francesca said, "Absolutely. I can drop it at the church today."

After another pause, Francesca said, "See you soon, Father Leo."

Francesca flung open the office door and walked the twenty paces to the piece of art that was causing such a commotion.

She pointed at it and said, "You, Mr. Alexander, are outta here."

As Gianna taped brown paper around the 12 x 36 painting, Francesca turned to Chase and Gavin, and said, "You two want to keep me company as I take this to the church?"

Gavin and Chase answered in unison, "Sure."

What none of them knew was that removing the painting would not make what was happening go away. And a big piece of a much larger puzzle was kneeling in a pew at the Santa Maria church six blocks away.

CHAPTER 12

You'll See

B uilt in the year 523, the Chiesa di Santa Maria church was a place of worship dedicated to the Virgin Mary. Legend says that when the plague swept through Rome, a statue of Mary taken from the church was carried through the streets, protecting all those souls who gazed upon it.

At first glance, the stone structure looks like a bank you'd find in Chicago in the early 1900s. Inside, private altars, impressive columns, and gorgeous paintings adorn the ceiling. It's small for a church by Rome's standards, but that was out of necessity, since it's tucked neatly on a street filled with hotels, shops, and restaurants.

The doors were only locked from midnight until six a.m., when the pastor, Father Leo, would rise, slip into a heavy wool robe, and take the passageway from the rectory into the church to unlock them. The large deadbolt made a loud *clang*, causing the stray cats gathered on the church steps for warmth to scatter.

While Rome was filled with wealth, the parishioners of Santa Maria came from the poorest families in the community. That is why, each December, the church held a Christmas auction, raising money to help the less fortunate.

Frequently, the items for the auction were gift certificates from local stores. The most valuable donation, however, came from Nonna: an Italian dessert known as Torta Barozzi. There was something special about the way she made it.

Her creation usually sold for hundreds of dollars, but Father Leo was worried he might not have it this year, given what the old woman had been through, losing her husband and son.

When Francesca, Gio, Chase, and Gavin arrived at the church, a familiar-looking young man pushed open the door, threw up the hood on his yellow sweatshirt, and disappeared into the crowd.

Chase caught a glimpse, turned to Gavin and asked, "Is that the kid who grabbed Scooter when he got loose the other day?"

Gavin looked back toward the street but missed him, so he asked Chase, "Who?"

"Never mind," Chase replied, as the four of them entered the church looking for the pastor.

"There he is," Gio said, pointing to the altar.

Father Leo was replacing a large candle that had burned out.

"Father Leo," Francesca called, "I have your painting."

Father Leo, dressed in jeans and a black sweater, dusted off his hands and came down from the altar to greet them.

"*Buone Feste,*" he said.

Francesca answered, "Seasons greetings to you as well."

"You know, without the whole get-up on, you almost look like a regular person," Gio observed.

The priest laughed and said, "Almost? Good to know, Giovanni."

The group was smiling now, as the priest asked, "Is that the donation, hiding under all that paper?"

He was pointing to the painting that was resting against Gavin's leg.

Raising it up, Gavin said, "This is it."

The priest took the painting, and peeling back the paper, he read the artist's name and said, "Alexander. I don't think I know him."

"He's a nobody," Gio replied. "His work is hated by dogs."

Father Leo looked at Gio and replied, "Dogs? I don't under—"

Francesca cut him off. "He's teasing, father. My son thinks he's a comedian sometimes."

The priest put the painting to the side and then stood there in awkward silence.

Finally, Francesca said, "We should probably get going, then."

This prompted Father Leo to ask, "How is your mother-in-law, Francesca—your grandmother, Gio? How is Nonna?"

Francesca looked at the floor, unsure how to answer that, when Gio did.

"Terrible, father." the boy said.

Chase looked at Gavin, uncertain if they should continue standing there or slowly back out of this private conversation.

Francesca then answered the priest, "Truth is, father, she's not great. First her husband died and then we lost her son, my husband, Matteo. It's been an awful year."

Francesca stopped talking, and silence filled the church.

The priest then said, "I understand. Just know, we miss Nonna here at Santa Maria. I mean, she still comes in, but not like before."

Francesca ran her hand along the top of the pew, looked up at the empty altar, and replied, "I'm sure she misses you too. She just needs time."

Gavin broke the awkwardness of the moment then, saying, "We should probably get going."

As the group said their goodbyes and turned to go, Father Leo called out, "Do you know if she's baking the Torta Barozzi? For the auction, I mean?"

Francesca threw her hands up and called back, "Hard to say. Probably not, father. Not this year."

"I understand," the priest said.

As Francesca put her hand on the large wooden door to go, she turned back and said, "It's a shame, too, because I've never seen her happier than when she's baking for others."

Father Leo smiled and said, "We can't set a clock to our healing."

Francesca considered his words, nodded silently, and out the door they went.

Once they hit the church's stone steps, the cold took a bite out of everyone, prompting Gavin to ask, "Does anyone want hot chocolate? My treat."

Francesca was still thinking about the priest's last words and the absence of Nonna from church. Was she helping herself by staying away? Or making things worse? Francesca knew for certain that Nonna's late husband Alessandro would be furious with her moping around because of his death.

"Can we, Mamma?" Gio asked.

"Can we what?" Francesca asked.

Gavin pointed at a small café two doors down from the church and trying to speak Italian said, ¿*Cómo estás chocolate?*

Francesca and Gio laughed, causing Gavin to ask, "What?"

Chase replied, "You just said *How are you chocolate?* in Spanish."

Gavin laughed, saying, "Whoops."

Francesca looked at him with kind eyes and said, "I'd love some, Gavin, and the café you're pointing at makes the best."

The hot cocoa in Italy was like nothing Gavin or Chase had ever tasted. Rather than mix hot water with some packet of brown powder, the barista in the café took a tin down from the shelf and carefully spooned out a portion of real cocoa. It was bitter and strong in aroma; Chase could smell it as he dished it into a small cup. He then added hot milk with a dash of heavy cream and just a hint of pure cane sugar. A sterling silver rod was inserted into the drink and twirled around several times, and the fresh cocoa, with steam rising from the top, was gently handed to Chase.

"This is amazing," Chase said, being careful not to burn her lips on the white porcelain cup.

"So," Francesca asked, "are you two going to pursue that second clue and go to the Bridge of Sighs to kiss at sunset?"

Chase replied, "You mean, if the bells from the church are ringing?"

"That's right," Francesca answered.

Chase looked at Gavin, and said, "I think we should, first thing tomorrow."

After nodding in agreement, Gavin surprised everyone at the table when he blurted out, "How did Nonna's husband die?"

Chase shot Gavin a look, then said, "That's a bit direct, hon."

Gavin started turning a light shade of red, saying, "I'm sorry."

Francesca put her hand on Gavin's arm and replied, "No, it's alright."

Gavin and Chase were silent now, waiting.

"Alessandro, Gio's grandfather and my father-in-law," Francesca continued, "died behind the house where we live."

Gavin considered a moment, then asked, "Like a heart attack or something?"

"Sì," Gio said. "He was building Nonna a small stone, how do you say it, Mamma?"

Francesca replied, "Sanctuary. That's the word you're looking for, Giovanni."

"Sì. Yes," Gio continued. "He was building Nonna a sanctuary in a secret garden, with a water fountain and flowers."

Imagining the beauty of such a tiny little getaway from the busy streets of Rome, Chase said to Gio, "It sounds wonderful."

There was more silence now, as Gio explained, "He was down on his hands and knees putting in the paving stones when . . ."

The boy's voice drifted off. There was no need to finish the thought; Chase and Gavin understood.

Francesca then said, "It was beautiful, whatever he was building. The stones were different colors and shapes. I asked him once what he was creating, and he told me it was a surprise for Nonna."

Gavin then asked, "He didn't finish it?"

Gio shook his head and said, "No."

A sad expression overtook Francesca's face, picturing Alessandro, too old to be doing that kind of work, down on the ground toiling away in the summer heat.

She finally said, "He just ran out of time."

The four of them sat silently, sipping their cocoa, when Gavin shifted the mood again, asking, "So what is this Torta Borta the priest went on about?"

Gio spit out his cocoa and started choking and laughing at the same time.

"What? What did I say now?" Gavin asked seriously.

Francesca was trying not to laugh, but couldn't hide it, answering, "It's called Torta Barozzi."

Chase was laughing now, saying, "Oh, Gavin."

After a brief pause, Chase asked, "What is it, exactly?"

Francesca smiled at the two of them, saying, "It's a chocolate dessert with eggs, flour, butter, nuts, rum, and a bunch of other stuff I forget."

"Like a pie?" Gavin asked.

"No." Gio replied.

"A cake then?" Gavin followed up with.

"Nope," Gio came back, "Not a cake either. Or a cookie or a gelato or like anything you've ever had. And nobody makes it like Nonna."

Gio took the last sip of his cocoa and added for emphasis, "Nobody!"

Chase chimed in, "It sounds amazing, and it sounds like the priest at the church misses it and her."

Francesca and Gio were silent, thinking about their Nonna and Alessandro, and how happy they had made each other.

Finally, Francesca said, "He used to go with her to church, every day."

"Did he?" Chase answered, picturing the old couple walking hand in hand together.

"I suspect that's why Nonna has stayed away. At least for now. Too hard, you know?" Francesca added.

Chase answered, "I do."

Chase's wheels started turning in her mind, causing her to give Gavin a look he's seen before.

"What?" Gavin asked.

"Tell ya later," Chase replied, adding, "You know, we should probably get home if we're driving to Venice tomorrow for this Bridge of Sighs."

The four of them rose from the table and placed their empty cups on the counter with the other dirty dishes.

Gio turned to Chase, asking, "You'll tell him what later? We have no secrets in this family."

Gavin, being playful said, "But we're not family, are we?"

After a long pause he asked more sincerely, *"Are* we?"

Francesca put her arm around her son, looked at Gavin and Chase, and said, "You're getting to be, the both of you."

Gio, not letting go of his question, asked it again, "So?"

Chase smiled and said, "No secrets, Gio. I was going to tell Gavin later that I've always wanted to learn how to make an authentic Italian dessert."

Gavin looked at Francesca and said, "Do you think Nonna would teach her?"

Francesca just smiled and said, "Hmm . . ."

Gio took his mom by the hand, and they started their walk home.

Chase looked at the two of them and yelled after them, "What does *hmm* mean?"

The boy replied, "*Vedrai.*"

Gavin looked at Francesca for help with the translation, and without taking her eyes off the busy sidewalk, she said, "You'll see."

CHAPTER 13

Hurry or You'll Miss It

A t the oceanfront home of Rico and Rosa Lombardi, in Genoa, Italy, sat an ornate hourglass. Rico spotted it in a shop in Cairo when they celebrated their twenty-fifth wedding anniversary with a trip to Egypt. Being romantic, he liked to buy something on every trip, so they could look at it later and reignite a wonderful memory.

Rico had purchased this expensive home on the water ten years prior, with the inheritance from his father's furniture business. He told Rosa it would be a wonderful place to retire when they reached old age.

Old age? Just saying those two words reminded Rico of the famous expression, "Announcing your plans is a good way to hear God laugh."

But nobody was laughing now as Rico sat motionless in a wheelchair, staring at the ocean, knowing that was about all he could do with the time he had left.

His health troubles started when he tripped at work, repeatedly. The first time, co-workers chuckled. On the second occurrence, there was less laughter. The third time he fell, while leaving someone's office, Rico went down hard, cutting his forehead on a file cabinet. Lying in bed later that night, he whispered in Rosa's ear three words no spouse wants to hear: *something is wrong.*

Doctors called it *drop foot*, Rico's habit of not lifting his right foot the way he used to, catching it on doorways.

Something *was* wrong, so Rosa took him to the first of a half-dozen doctors to find out what. The last one, a neurologist, was the man who shared the horrible news. He hooked Rico up to a machine called an EMG and sent tiny electric currents into Rico's muscles. They budget a half-hour to conduct this test, but Rosa could see the truth on the doctor's face five minutes in.

He shut off the machine and said to Rico, "You have ALS."

The prognosis was two to four years to live, and just as promised, Rico's muscles were slowly shutting down, one by one, as if his brain was a large breaker system and someone was methodically flipping the switches from green to red.

Two to four years, that would be it, so get it all in, young man, before the sand runs out of the hourglass.

"When the end is near, I don't want you hooking me up to machines to make this go longer," Rico begged Rosa. "I know you love me, but you can't keep me around that way."

The words felt like acid on his tongue because he adored his wife and hated disappointing her, but this was different. This was personal, and Rico wasn't worried about himself. What bothered him most, was knowing how sad Rosa would be when he was gone and knowing he would not be there to catch her tears and kiss them away.

Once Rico was confined to a wheelchair and his speech began to slur, he lost his appetite for crowds. His ocean view on that veranda in Genoa was his entire world now, a place to sip brandy and wait for the inevitable.

Today, December 15, was Rosa's birthday, and Rico didn't have a present. At least that's what he thought.

As the sun rose over the ocean, Rosa hugged him and said, "I do want a gift from you today. It won't be easy, but you can do it."

Rico reached up to push the strands of gray hair off her loving face and said slowly, "If it's within my power, my love, I'll do it."

It was then Rosa told Rico they were taking a drive to a special bridge. A bridge where love was eternal. She'd hired a driver with a van that had a lift for the wheelchair, and both van and driver would be downstairs to pick them up in an hour. Rico was afraid and excited at the same time.

At the same moment, across Italy in Rome, Chase and Gavin shared breakfast with Nonna and the others, excited about their plans. The man at the Colosseum gave Gavin four clues that he said would lead to romance, and today they would pursue the second on that list: *a kiss.*

"How far is this Bridge of Sighs in Venice?" Gavin asked.

Francesca looked at her son, and Gio shot up from his chair, raised a piece of paper and cleared his throat, as if about to make a speech.

"From our house to the Bridge of Sighs is almost six hours by car," Gio began.

"Wow, that's a drive," Chase replied.

Francesca explained, "It's in the northeast of Italy."

"Excuse me," Gio said sharply, "I'm not done with my presentation."

Gavin smiled and said, "Apologies, young man, continue unabated."

"Un-what?" Gio asked, confused.

"Just keep going, he means," Francesca assured him.

Gio looked down to the paper in his hands and continued. "As I said, the drive is almost six hours, and the sun sets today at exactly 4:27 p.m."

Francesca looked to Gavin and Chase and said, "That's important. Remember you have to kiss under the bridge at exactly sunset to achieve eternal love."

There was a light knock on the door, then it opened to reveal Gio's uncle Jules.

When he saw everyone looking at him, he asked, "What? Am I late?"

"No, no," Francesca replied, "Right on time. Gio was just mapping out the day for us."

"Us?" Chase asked, "Are you coming?"

Francesca smiled, "If that's okay, I thought Gio and I might tag along."

Gavin smiled back, "Of course, the more the merrier."

Gio then said, "Just to finish what I was saying. If it's a six-hour drive and the sun sets at 4:27, we need to be on the road by ten."

Gavin got up to grab orange juice from the fridge and responded, "Sounds good, Gio, thanks for figuring all that out."

He noticed an Italian word separate from the other letters on the refrigerator door, that read B O L L E T T A.

When Gavin silently pointed at the word, Nonna said, "*Bolletta* is a utility bill. I left myself that note to remind me to pay the electric bill."

Gavin nodded, then said, "Smart."

Chase then raised her hand as if in a classroom.

"What are you doing?" Francesca asked with a smirk.

"I had a question," Chase replied sheepishly.

Nonna chimed in, saying, "We Italian in this house, just speak you mind."

Gavin trying to be funny, echoed Nonna's words, "Yeah, Chase, speak you mind."

"Right," Chase replied with a smile, "I just wanted to ask a dumb question. Are they even doing gondola rides in mid-December when it's chilly outside?

Gavin's jaw dropped, as he said, "Oh man, I didn't think of that. Yeah, they might be closed."

Francesca looked at Jules and said, "Do you want to handle this?"

Jules was stuffing a piece of blueberry muffin in his mouth and said, "Sure. Just let me swallow."

After an exaggerated gulp, Jules burped and said, "Excuse me. Sorry."

"Really, Uncle Jules," Gio said while laughing.

"I said sorry," Jules replied, giving Gio a gentle push on the shoulder.

Jules then continued. "Your question is not a dumb one, Chase, because it is cold in Venice this time of year."

"Oh no," Chase responded.

"But they still do gondola rides, just not nearly as many as in the busy season," Jules replied.

Gavin then said to Chase, "I hope we can get one, then. That's a long way to drive, only to get shut out."

"You're not kidding," Chase said sadly.

"Hello?" Jules said with a smile. "Do you think I'd let you drive all day and not get your kiss under the bridge?"

With hopeful eyes on him now, Jules said, "I have a friend who works for one of the companies that run the gondolas and arranged one just for you two, ten minutes before sunset, right near the Bridge of Sighs."

Chase clapped, then Jules said, "Go ahead, you can say it."

"Say what?" Gavin asked.

"That I'm the best," Jules replied.

"You *are* the best, Jules," Chase exclaimed.

With that, the man who had become their driver and friend took a bow, causing Francesca to say, "Oh stop that nonsense, you made a phone call, that's all."

Nonna pointed to the clock on the wall and said, "You better stop this talking and get moving, if you going to make it."

Gavin darted toward the bathroom and said, "Dibs on the first shower."

Chase ran after, calling out, "You'd better save me some hot water, Gavin Bennett."

The ride from the coast of Genoa to the canals of Venice was not an easy one for Rico and Rosa. The bouncing along those roads for four hours was difficult on him.

Every time Rosa insisted they stop, Rico waved her off and through labored speech, said, "I'm fine, keep going."

The ALS weakened his muscles, making everything a chore, including speaking. A simple conversation took so much out of Rico, he'd sit silent for hours, building up his strength to converse with his perfect bride. And that's what Rosa was to Rico, decades later, still his perfect bride in his eyes and heart.

He hated that this was how their love story would end, with him shutting down like lights in a stadium after a big game. One by one the bulbs would go out until there was only the darkness. He wished sometimes she would run away and let him face it alone, but he knew better than to ask such a thing. He knew, however his fairytale ended, she'd be at his side.

When they arrived in St. Mark's square in Venice the clock had just struck four p.m. Rosa knew this because she could hear the clock tower on the corner count out the time with four loud gongs. The driver they hired for the day, wearing a black suit and matching driver's cap, activated the lift, which lowered Rico to the cobblestone sidewalk. He then gently pushed the chair off to a spot away from foot traffic, where Rico would be safe.

"Do you need me to help you with the chair or should I stay with the vehicle?" the driver asked Rosa.

She reached out to take the driver's hand and placed a hundred-euro note in his palm, saying, "I've got him from here. We'll be back after the sun goes down."

The driver looked at the folded hundred, then his eyes met Rosa's, asking, "*Signora?*"

"That's extra, for getting us here," Rosa said with a grin.

She then pointed at the money and said, "That hundred has a twin brother you'll be meeting when we return home."

The driver, a younger man in good shape, had kindness in his eyes and sympathy he was hiding from the man in the wheelchair. He didn't know what was wrong with the gentleman, but it was clear he was in rough condition.

Two blocks away, another vehicle pulled up to the curb, and Chase, Gavin, Francesca, and Gio all hopped out delighted to stretch their legs.

Gio looked up at the harsh gray sky and said, "Sun is getting low, we probably shouldn't wait too long."

Francesca turned to her brother and asked, "Where do we go, Jules?"

"It's called Verano Family Tours. I pre-paid it, so they'll meet us down at the canal on a dock about fifty meters from the Bridge of Sighs," he replied.

"Thank you for that," Gavin said to Jules. "We'll reimburse you afterward."

Jules nodded, and the five of them started down the busy sidewalk.

"Lots of Christmas shoppers today," Chase observed, watching a throng of people carrying bags in and out of the colorful stores that lined both sides of the street.

"Always," Francesca replied. "Especially in Venice."

As the group continued their walk, they could see the dock with a single gondola waiting ahead of them.

Because Rosa knew this would likely be her final birthday with Rico, she wanted to do something to make it memorable. After talking to friends and scouring the internet for a romantic gesture, the Bridge of Sighs was the one that captured her attention.

"I know I'm going to lose him," Rosa told friends, "But our love is eternal, just as the legend says about that bridge."

Most thought Rico was too sick with ALS to make Rosa's birthday wish happen, but she knew her husband, and if he thought this was something she wanted, he'd find the strength to do it.

She timed his medication and gave him extra rest in the days leading up to this moment. She booked the van and driver and pre-packed snacks and drinks. Rosa planned everything perfectly, except unfortunately, the most important part.

She assumed there would be scores of gondolas waiting along the canal for tourists eager to spend money. It was Christmastime after all, a bit chilly for sure, but still a perfect time to make a love wish under a bridge at sunset.

When she wheeled Rico down to the dock, she was shocked to see just one gondola tied to the post. Standing in the boat was an older gentleman leaning on the pole he'd use to guide the vessel through the water. Everything was fine though, because she only needed one gondola and there it was, waiting.

"Are you warm enough, my sweet," Rosa asked Rico.

He was bundled up under three layers, with a heavy coat on top. His blue wool cap was pulled down over his ears, and a matching scarf was wrapped tightly around his neck.

"Yes, I am. You go ahead and talk to him, Rosa," he struggled to say.

As Rosa slowly approached the gondola driver, he raised his hand to stop her and said, "*Mi dispiace, ma non sono libero.*"

He was saying, *Excuse me, but I'm not available.*

Rosa asked the gentleman why, and he explained he was already hired for the sunset ride under the famed bridge.

"*Chi lo ha ingaggiato?*" Rosa asked, wondering who hired the man.

With that the driver pointed at five people walking toward the dock, and said, "*Loro.*"

It meant *them*.

As Gavin, Chase, Francesca, Gio, and Jules slowly approached, all eyes instantly went to the frail man in the wheelchair.

"Hello," Chase called out, "Merry-almost-Christmas."

Rosa and Rico both spoke English, and Chase's chipper demeanor caused both to smile instantly.

Rosa replied, in her Italian accent, "Hello to all of you."

Gio, misunderstanding the situation, asked, "Did you just finish your gondola ride? How was it?"

Rosa's eyes went from the gondola driver, down to her ailing husband and then back to the teenage boy, "No, son, we did not. We, um . . ."

She didn't finish the thought. She just fell silent, her eyes seeming to search for something to say.

Finally, Rico reached up to touch her hand, sensing she was upset.

"Is everything alright, ma'am," Gavin asked, with tenderness in his voice.

"Yes," Rosa replied, "I just messed up a bit."

Francesca, staring at the couple asked, "Messed up how?"

Rosa pointed toward the Bridge of Sighs, which was well within sight, then pointed to the empty gondola and explained, "I thought there would be dozens of gondolas lined up. Every time I see this place on TV, they show so many gondolas going up and down the canal."

Gio, a smart young man who had spent time researching this place, replied respectfully, "They do, *signora*, just not in December. It's quieter now."

Rosa looked at the calm, chilly water, void of any boats, and said, "I see that."

The sun, which was almost down to the horizon, began peeking out between two buildings, causing a flash of light to appear on Rosa's jacket.

Chase saw it right away, squinted her eyes, then asked, "What is that on your lapel?"

Having no clue what the stranger was talking about, Rosa looked down at her own jacket and said, "This? Just a pin."

Not much larger than a quarter, the pin had bright silver tinsel in a circle and a tiny green and red bow attached.

"Is that a Christmas wreath?" Chase asked, leaning in closer to see it.

"Yes," Rosa answered.

Gavin changed the subject to the reason everyone was there, asking, "You thought there would be more gondolas? So, you didn't get a ride?"

Rosa looked down at her husband, tucked neatly under a thick red blanket to stave off the chill, and answered, "No, we didn't, and we came a long way."

"As did we," Jules said.

Gio looked at the clock on his phone, then observed, "The sun sets in four minutes."

Gavin nodded, acknowledging the time crunch, but Chase was still fixated on the woman's pin on her jacket, asking, "Is that homemade, ma'am?"

Rosa touched the pin now, smiled and said, "Yes, it is, how did you know?"

Chase inched closer and reached out to touch the pin, saying, "I had one just like it once. A long time ago."

Gavin then said to his fiancée, "Chase, we should probably get moving."

She broke her gaze and looked into Gavin's eyes, answering, "Right. I'm sorry."

Francesca then asked the gondola driver in Italian if he should take all of them at once, or just Gavin and Chase.

He answered in Italian, and Francesca turned to Chase and said, "If you want the legend to come true—eternal love—he says it should just be the two of you on the boat."

Gavin reached to take Chase's hand and help her on the boat, when she said, "I'm sorry, hold up. Ma'am, can I ask who made that for you? The pin."

Rosa smiled again at the memory of it and replied, "My son at school, I think he was in primary school, six years old. A Christmas gift."

"Me too, first grade," Chase answered back. "I made one for my mom just like it, with tinsel, wire, and some glue. Elmer's."

Rosa could see the joy in Chase's face now and said, "I'm sure your mom loved it."

Chase met the woman's eyes and said, "Oh she did, she was heartbroken when she lost it."

Rosa replied, "Lost it how?"

Chase brushed the auburn hair off her face, revealing that her cheeks were starting to get red from the cold, then said, "She used to wear it to church every Christmas, and one year she dropped the jacket at the drycleaners and forgot to take the pin off."

Gio, now curious, asked, "And the machine ruined it?"

"No, Gio," Chase replied. "They just lost it."

There was an awkward silence for a moment, when Chase said to Rosa, "I'm sorry, going on like that about an old pin. And I'm sorry you didn't get your ride."

Rosa liked this young woman she had just met. There was a graciousness to her that was undeniable.

Rosa then said, "You two should go, if you plan to kiss under the bridge at sunset."

Chase reached for Gavin's hand, but he was staring at the man in the wheelchair, sitting under the mountain of blankets, and said, "Do you mind if I ask, sir . . . Why are you in the chair?"

"GAVIN," Chase said sharply, "That's private."

"She's right," Gavin said, feeling a bit foolish. "She's always right."

The man, who was only in his mid-fifties, yet looked so much older and weaker from the illness, motioned for Gavin to come closer.

Once Gavin's face was only a foot away from Rico's, he said slowly, "A L S."

A friend of Gavin's father back in Vermont had died of ALS a few years prior, so Gavin was aware of how horrible and unfair a disease it could be.

Gavin reached down and gently touched the man's arm, then said, "I'm so sorry, sir."

Gavin stood up straight and looked back at Chase, seeing the sadness in her face.

Gio broke their gaze when he announced, "Two minutes, guys."

Gavin looked from Chase's eyes back to Rosa's and said, "You two came here to kiss under the Bridge of Sighs at sunset?"

Rosa looked at Rico, then back to Gavin and said, "It's alright, there will be other days."

In that instant Gavin thought *when?* When will you find the time and energy to ever do this again with your husband slowly withering away in that wheelchair? When?

Gavin looked at Francesca and Gio, who were watching and waiting. He looked at the gondolier, who was standing with one foot in the boat, the other on the dock holding it steady. Then Gavin looked at Chase and found the answer to a question he didn't even need to ask.

She simply smiled and said, "Gavin, can you lift him onto the boat?"

Rosa brought her trembling fingers up to her lips and said, "No, we couldn't."

Gavin, nodded silently to Chase, then turned toward Rico in the chair, saying, "I grew up on a farm tossing hay bales all day, so if you trust me, sir, I'd like to carefully get you into that gondola."

"One minute till sunset," Gio called out, "You're gonna miss it."

Chase shot back, "No they're not. Hurry, Gavin."

"And up you go," Gavin said, lifting the frail man up and then down into a seat on the boat.

"Are you sure?" Rosa asked, tears now filling her eyes.

Chase replied, "Yes. Hurry, or you'll miss it."

As the gondolier was about to push off from the dock, Rosa called out, "WAIT."

Rosa quickly fumbled with the lapel on her jacket, then reached out to Chase on the dock. She placed something in Chase's hand, closing her fingers around it.

"A gift from me," Rosa said.

With that the boat pushed away and quickly made its way toward the bridge. Chase looked down, opened her fingers, and saw she was holding the woman's homemade Christmas pin.

As the sun slipped into the horizon, Gio, Francesca, Jules, Gavin and Chase all felt their hearts swell, as they saw the silhouette of the couple they just met, Rosa and Rico, embrace under the Bridge of Sighs for one eternal kiss. Just as their lips touched, the bells from the nearby church rang out in adulation.

Gavin, not taking his eyes off them, said to Chase, "That old man at the Colosseum told me these four clues would show us true romance."

"Right," Chase answered.

"First the young lovers with the lock, and now this," Gavin said.

Chase, watching the couple embrace with the red glow of the sunset on the water, replied, "Makes you wonder what might happen next?"

Gavin put his arm around Chase and answered, "Yes, it does."

CHAPTER 14

Know It When I See It

Chase forgot to set her cellphone ringer to "silent" before turning in for the night, which was a mistake.

After helping the couple at the Bridge of Sighs, the five of them walked to St. Mark's square in Venice, famished. Gavin spotted a Hard Rock Café, which reminded him of home.

"No, absolutely not," Francesca insisted.

"Why?" Gavin asked.

Francesca explained, "You two are in a country with the best food on the planet; I am not letting you get a cheeseburger."

Chase agreed, so dinner took them to Ristorante San Gallo for pasta, cheese, bread, and wine. Jules, feeling bad that Chase and Gavin had given away their romantic gondola ride, picked up the check.

By the time they got back to Rome it was just shy of midnight, so when Chase's friend Riley called at seven-thirty the next morning, that ringer on the phone hit like a bucket of ice water.

"What? Who is this?" Chase barked into the device, waking Scooter, who was sleeping at her feet.

"Geez, sorry, love, I thought you'd be up and about your day," Riley answered.

Chase saw the sunlight coming through her bedroom window, rubbed her sleepy eyes and said, "It's alright, I should be getting up anyway."

Riley, already dressed and on her second espresso, replied, "How about this. You shower, drink some coffee, and I'll pop over to hear all about your romantic kiss under the bridge."

Chase thought, *yeah, about that kiss,* but decided to save the story for when Riley arrived.

"Give me an hour," Chase replied.

Chase emerged from her room to find Gavin was already up and sharing tales from the previous day with Nonna.

"You gave away eternal love to that nice woman and her husband?" Nonna asked.

Gavin smiled and replied, "I think our love will be eternal either way, Nonna, like yours with your husband. I'm sorry, I forgot his name?"

"Alessandro," she replied, taking another sip of her tea.

Gio darted into the kitchen just long enough to grab a pastry and said, "I have to get to school. Yesterday was fun."

Gavin looked at Gio and replied, "Next time we eat at the Hard Rock, and I teach you about American rock and roll."

Gio gave Gavin a *high five* and out the door he went.

"He likes you," Chase said.

Gavin, who never had a little brother growing up, looked down with a smile and said, "I like him too."

There was a thoughtful pause when Gavin added, "Must be tough losing his dad. I mean, not having him around to do things."

Chase looked Gavin and said, "You're here, maybe you can do something about that."

Gavin nodded and gave Chase a look that told her he'd make time for the sweet boy.

The three of them then heard a loud voice coming up the stairs and lingering just outside the door. Chase thought it might be Riley arriving early, but it was Francesca on the phone.

"Yes, thank you for calling me back. I do appreciate it," Francesca said, as she stepped inside, the phone still to her ear.

After a pause, Francesca responded, "I have no idea what it means either, but I appreciate the information."

Francesca hung up the phone, placed it on the kitchen counter and let out a loud grumble.

"What now?" Nonna asked.

Francesca gave Nonna a quick hug hello and replied, "Nothing."

Gavin then said what everyone in the room was thinking: "It didn't sound like nothing."

Francesca poured herself a cup of coffee and took a seat opposite Chase at the kitchen table and began. "Do you remember the painting your dog barked at in my gallery?"

"Of course," Chase answered. "The one you donated for the church auction."

Francesca replied, "And do you remember I had my assistant contact the dealer who supplied it to the gallery?"

Gavin answered this time. "Yes, he wasn't sure where it came from, but you guys looked up artists with the last name Alexander and figured out it was painted by a nobody."

Chase asked then, "What about it?"

Francesca pointed toward her cell phone resting on the counter, and said, "That man on the phone is the art buyer who supplied the painting to my dealer. He just got the message that I was curious about the work and finally got back to me."

Gavin spoke up: "So? Were you right on which Alexander it was?"

"No," Francesca said firmly. "We weren't even close."

Chase, looking confused, asked, "Why not?"

Francesca stood up and said, "Because the guy who painted the one that your dog went nuts over doesn't have the last name of Alexander."

Chase responded, "But that's how he signed it."

Francesca smirked. "This artist, who painted it some three hundred years ago, was Alexander Francis Lido Johnson."

Gavin chuckled, "Wow, put that guy's name on *Wheel of Fortune*."

Chase, ignoring the joke, said to Francesca, "So, this Alexander Francis whatever, he signed his paintings with his first name?"

"Yes," Francesca answered. "According to the art buyer, he signed them all that way."

Chase then asked, "Was he local? Italy? Europe?"

"Nope," Francesca replied. "Someplace in the West Indies."

Gavin, taking the last bite of raspberry scone, said, "While that's all interesting, it doesn't answer our real question."

Chase replied, "Why is Scooter barking at that man's painting?"

There was silence, then Nonna made them laugh, saying, "Maybe your dog, he is ah, *pazzo*."

Francesca wagged her finger. "Nonna, Scooter is not crazy."

Francesca then turned to Chase and asked, "Is he?"

Chase didn't respond, instead getting up and looking out the window. She glanced down and saw Riley was outside talking to someone.

Chase realized who it was, turned back to the room, and said, "Riley and Jules are here."

Chase then looked thoughtfully at Francesca and Nonna, and said, "My pup isn't crazy or pazzo. This is something else."

She looked at Gavin now, searching for a way to explain it, so he helped.

"What she's trying to say is, he's done this kind of thing before," Gavin began. "Barking at something and directing Chase toward information."

"What kind of information?" Francesca asked.

Chase replied, "The kind that helps people."

Gavin, to emphasize her point, added, "Save people sometimes."

Francesca then: "Save them? From what?"

"That's a story for another time," Gavin replied. "The point is, when Scooter acts strange or barks at something, we pay attention."

Just then the front door opened, and Riley and Jules walked in. "Pay attention to what?" Jules asked.

Francesca went to the fridge to take out another plate of pastries, answering Jules, "We just learned the real name of the artist who painted the picture Chase's dog was barking at. They were saying he's done this kind of thing before, and it usually means something."

Riley smiled and said, "You're not saying your dog is psychic, are you? 'Cause that would be something to see. We could make money on that."

Riley spotted Scooter in the corner and called out, "Who's going to win the next Super Bowl, Scooter? Oh, the Dallas Cowboys? Great, let me put a thousand euros on them!"

Riley laughed, cracking herself and Jules up, but could see Chase and Gavin were not smiling.

Gavin, taking a deep breath, finally said, "I know it sounds silly, but we're not *fooling about*, as you'd say."

Jules then said, "You two are serious?"

Chase nodded her head, adding, "We are."

Riley then turned to Francesca. "Do you have a piece of paper we can write on?"

Nonna rose slowly from her chair and opened a drawer next to the stove, pulling out a piece of white scrap paper and a black pen.

"Here," she said, handing it to Riley.

"Where's your girlfriend, Tessa?" Chase asked.

Without looking up from her seat at the kitchen table Riley answered, "Work, all day, unfortunately. Okay, I'm ready."

"For what?" Gavin asked.

Riley answered back in a serious tone, "If when your dog barks it means something, tell me the name of the artist he was in a twist about."

"What was it again? Gavin asked Francesca, "Francis Johnson?"

Francesca answered, "Not even close."

Francesca then looked up at the ceiling as if trying to retrieve a memory, and said slowly, "The dealer said his name is Alexander Francis Lido Johnson."

Riley wrote the name out in big block letters, separating each word so they stood out on their own.

She scratched her head and said, "Scooter's bark means something, and this is the artist's name?"

"Yes," Chase answered quickly.

She pondered a moment, then Riley asked, "And this was the only thing he barked at? The only painting?"

"Yes," Chase answered.

"Hmm," Riley said, "So, the obvious question is, do you have a connection to any of these names?"

Chase looked again at them. "I don't."

Francesca then added, "The dealer said this artist's work dates back to early 1700s, if that helps."

Chase answered, "It doesn't. I'm telling you, none of these names mean anything to me. How about you, Gavin?"

"Not at all," Gavin answered right back.

Francesca sat next to Riley at the table, just noticing her thick, flowing red mane.

"God, you've got great hair," Francesca observed.

"Thanks, love," Riley answered with a smile.

"Do you use special shampoo to get it that way?" Francesca asked.

"No," Riley replied, "Just the regular brand."

Gavin cleared his throat loudly on purpose, and said, "Ladies, hello, trying to solve a mystery here."

"Oh, well excuse us, mister. I'm in a hurry," Riley shot back playfully.

Chase got up and walked toward Scooter, who was still sitting in the corner, then stopped and spun quickly around, getting everyone's attention.

"What?" Gavin asked, knowing his fiancée was on to something.

Chase said, "You asked if this was the only thing Scooter barked at, the painting by Alexander What's His Pants."

"Johnson," Francesca corrected her.

"Right, Johnson," Chase replied.

"So?" asked Riley.

Chase looked at Gavin, smiled and said, "It wasn't."

Gavin caught Chase's eyes and said, "She's right."

Nonna chimed in, saying, "He went pazzo with the refrigerator too, a few days ago."

Riley was confused, then Francesca said, "I forgot about that. He was barking at some random letters on the fridge. What were they again?"

Nonna remembered, responding, "Ostia."

"Ostia?" Riley asked, "What does that mean?"

Francesca answered her, "It has a couple of definitions, but one of them is host, like the bread the priest gives you at the Mass."

There was silence for a solid minute before Riley took up her pen and paper again, writing the word OSTIA, and saying, "So we have Scooter barking at the word *Ostia* and the painting done by Alexander Francis Lido Johnson."

"Right," Chase said,

"Right," Francesca echoed.

Gavin, staring at both women said, "Right."

There was another pause when Chase said out loud, "I've got nothing. These words mean nothing to me. Any of you?"

Blank faces stared back at her, and it felt like this journey down the rabbit hole was leading absolutely nowhere. That's when Jules saw it.

"Lido," he said. Repeating it even slower the second time, "Leeeeee-Doh."

Gavin then asked, "Are you having a stroke?"

Jules smiled, "No, my friend, watch this."

Jules grabbed up the pen and a fresh piece of white paper. He then wrote out in big block letters LIDO di OSTIA.

Francesca looked closer and said, "There it is."

"There what is?" Chase asked.

Gavin then inquired, "Who is Lido di Ostia?"

"Not a who," Nonna said. "A what."

Jules held up the paper with the words printed out and added, "Thirty minutes from here. It's one of the most popular beaches in Italy."

"What is?" Gavin asked.

Francesca answered, "Lido di Ostia is a place."

"A beach?" Chase asked.

"More than that," Jules answered. "There are shops, restaurants, houses."

"Boats," Riley said. "They have boats too."

"*Hai ragione*," Nonna agreed. "You are correct. Lido di Ostia used to be Rome's port. There are still ships there."

No one noticed Chase was standing at the window now, staring out at nothing. Gavin approached her slowly, placed his hands gently on her shoulders, and said, "What are you thinking?"

Chase turned and said, "I think I love you, and . . ."

She drifted off, her eyes fixed on nothing, deep in thought.

Finally, she added, "And I think if Scooter led me to this Lee Doh dee Oh-stee-ah—am I pronouncing that right, Jules?"

He nodded *yes,* without speaking.

"Then I should go there," she finished.

"The beach will be closed," Jules observed.

Gavin answered back, "Well I'm sure we'll find something open."

Francesca then asked what the rest of the room was already thinking, "And what will you be looking for, Chase?"

Chase turned and took in their faces, knowing they all thought she was a tad *pazza* right about now, answering, "I'll know it when I see it."

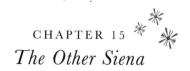

CHAPTER 15

The Other Siena

A light snow drifted over the streets of Rome that morning, giving everything it landed on a gentle kiss before melting. Chase's eyes, big as saucers, peered out of the backseat of Jules's car on the short ride from the apartment to the neighborhood known as Lido di Ostia. Gavin tagged along of course, holding Chase's hand the entire way, the two of them lost in their own thoughts.

Breaking the silence, Gavin asked, "Do we have a game plan, or do you just want to wander around?"

As Chase pondered the question, Jules said, "It's too big to just wander."

Realizing they were waiting for him to offer a strategy, Jules added, "I would split up. Gavin, you take the old port and the beach. Chase, you look around the business district for, um . . ."

There was an awkward pause, then Jules finished the thought, "Whatever it is you think you'll find."

Chase smiled, responding, "That's the fun part, Jules, I have no idea what we'll find."

Jules caught her eyes in the rearview mirror, "So you've done this before, run off having no idea what you're doing."

Gavin smiled and patted the top of the backseat, answering, "You have no idea."

Jules nodded his head even though he didn't understand, then put his eyes back on the road and got them there safely.

He dropped Gavin near the docks and continued on a few blocks away to the commercial district. The locals skipped the formality and called this area *Ostia* for short.

Chase, wearing a bright blue trench coat with the sash pulled tight around her waist, hopped over a slush puddle near the curb, calling back to Jules, "Give me two hours and I'll meet you back here."

Jules waved and drove off in search of a café to kill the time, while Chase played Nancy Drew.

The business district of Ostia was pleasant but unimpressive; a series of offices and shops occupied the ground floor of buildings, with apartments housed above. Chase wandered into a butcher shop and a bakery, causing her to think, *I've seen the butcher and baker, I just need the candlestick maker to complete the nursery rhyme.*

She was smiling at the thought, when her eyes fell on a quaint candy shop hugging the corner where two streets merged like a large V. A black wooden sign hung above the door with faded red lettering that read *RAVENOUS*. With a name like that, Chase had to go in.

Gavin was about a mile away and quickly realized his part of this investigation was a waste of time. Since it was mid-December with temperatures in the 40s, Jules was right: the beach was empty, save for a few seagulls sharing brunch on the broken shells that washed in with the morning tide.

The next stop for Gavin was the port, which a hundred years ago would have been bustling with activity. Today, however, it housed just a pair of shipping companies. The largest was Lilly shipping, which had locations all over Europe. Lilly's setup here at Lido di Ostia looked impressive but was the company's smallest operation by far. Lilly transported goods from high-end Italian merchants and exported them to cities splashed across the Mediterranean.

The second shipping outfit was far less impressive: a dirty brown building with a pair of long wooden docks, where a half-dozen smaller boats were tied. A rusty sign with the words CRANE SHIPPING was attached to a tall fence with razor wire on top. A piece of dirty bloodied clothing was tangled in the razor, indicating someone once tried to scale the imposing fence and did not come away unscathed.

Crane was a bottom-feeder, handling the jobs that no one else wanted, primarily delivering small items like refrigerators and furniture to the dozens of islands just offshore. People in town joked that Crane was like their own personal UPS, minus the brown uniforms, fancy trucks, or soap.

Gavin took one look and said, "That place should come with a tetanus shot."

The people at Lilly were open and friendly to Gavin when he wandered onto the property. He looked around but everything seemed exactly as you would expect. He had a much different experience at Crane.

"What business have you here?" were the first words out of the mouth of a surly security guard.

The man was eating lunch and had a mustard stain the size of Rhode Island blotted across his dingy white shirt.

"Just poking around," Gavin responded. "How are you today?"

Gavin wondered why the guard didn't speak to him in Italian, given where he was, then realized he was wearing his New England Patriots sweatshirt. The man must have assumed he was an American.

The guard wearing the mustard stepped out from the small booth he was in, giving Gavin an opportunity to see the size of him and the shiny black club that hung from his leather belt. It was the kind cops carried in old crime movies, used to thump people on the head.

He looked at Gavin like he was the next item on the menu.

"How I am is impatient with people who *poke around* where they don't belong," the guard said curtly.

Gavin raised his hands up high, as if he were the victim of an armed robbery, and replied, "Sorry, got it. Didn't mean to offend."

Gavin backed up slowly, like a man trying to extricate himself from a conversation with a rattlesnake. As his heels hit the public sidewalk, taking him off the private property, Gavin saw a worker in Crane's main building open a door, look at him, then shut the door quickly.

Why does he look familiar? Gavin thought. It mattered little; Gavin was not welcome, and it was time to go find Chase.

The front door to the candy shop tended to stick, so it took Chase a good tug to pop it open, causing an electric sensor to *ding*, letting the owner know they had a customer.

Before she was one step in, the sweet smells of sugar engulfed her nose and instantly made Chase feel like she was four again and her mother was taking her to her favorite candy shop back in Seattle. Eagle's Treats, it was called, run by a gentle soul named Abner Eagle. The man appeared so old you imagined him selling licorice whips to Benjamin Franklin.

Chase's eyes scanned the small shop, which had a long glass case, housing dozens of types of chocolate and a variety of penny candy.

Suddenly, she heard a woman's voice spilling out from a back room. It was a normal volume at first but then rose louder and sounded more urgent with each new word. The woman didn't appear angry as much as frustrated with whomever she was speaking to. Because Chase couldn't hear anyone speaking back, she knew it must have been a phone call. As the woman's voice intensified, she switched between Italian and English, sometimes in the same sentence.

The woman pushed through a door, entering the shop, lowering her voice immediately when she saw she had a customer. She was older than Chase, perhaps late forties, her hair a mixture of black and gray, pulled back into a ponytail. Her face was absent any makeup, but Chase could see why: the woman was so pretty she didn't need it. When her green eyes engaged Chase's, she ended the call abruptly in Italian and did her best to hide her embarrassment.

"*Salve*," she greeted Chase.

"I'm sorry," Chase answered, "I don't know that word."

The woman smiled and said in perfect English, "It means hello."

"Oh," Chase replied, "I thought *ciao* meant hello."

As the shopkeeper plugged her cell phone onto a charger behind the counter, she answered back, "It does. Both words mean hello, but *salve* is more formal. Can I help you?"

Chase put her hands on her hips and looked around the small shop, marveling at how much candy one could fit in such a confined space.

"Miss?" the shopkeeper asked again, "Do you need something?"

"I don't know," Chase finally answered. "I mean I can always go for chocolate."

The woman quickly put disposable plastic gloves on her hands and then approached the counter to take Chase's order.

"Although," Chase added, "I don't think I'm here for candy."

With that Chase walked around the store, looking as if she had lost something.

"Miss?" the woman inquired. "We're a candy store, so perhaps another shop on this street might suit you."

"Miss?" Chase shot back. "Wow, I haven't been called *MISS* in a while."

The woman behind the counter smiled and said, "Trust me, it beats being called ma'am."

Chase smirked, and, as she continued looking around the store, she replied, "Good point."

Chase then asked, "Is everything okay?"

The woman, forcing a grin, answered right back, "Yes, of course. Why?"

Chase replied, "I couldn't help but hear you raising your voice on the phone. Not my business, but you sounded upset. It sounded like it was about money."

The woman paused, as if she was deciding in that instant whether to trust this stranger, then said, "Everything is fine, just business stuff."

Chase then observed, "For an Italian you speak wicked good English."

The lady replied, "Wicked good, eh? That's probably because my mom is American."

Chase was intrigued now, and asked, "Whereabouts?"

"New York State, a tiny town called Fort Covington," she answered.

Chase thought a moment, then said, "I lived in Manhattan and a place called Briarcliff Manor, but I've got no idea where Fort Covington is."

The woman pointed toward the ceiling, then said, "It's way north. In fact, if you get to the Canadian border, stop, and turn around—"

Chase completed the sentence, "Fort Covington?"

"Bingo," the lady replied with enthusiasm.

The shopkeeper then said, "So if you don't want candy, why are you here?"

Chase took a few paces, looked around some more, let out a deep breath and said, "That's a great question. Something sent me to this neighborhood, and I'm kind of just looking around."

"Looking for what?" the woman asked.

Chase threw her hands in the air, "No clue."

The candy store clerk thought Chase seemed nice, but her actions were a bit odd, so it might be time to move the stranger along.

"Anyway, if you don't want candy, I have some work to get back to," she said firmly.

Chase spied into the glass case and said, "Tell you what, give me a few pieces of that peanut butter fudge. Gavin will like it."

As the woman took up a small white paper bag to put the fudge in, she asked, "Husband? Gavin?"

Chase looked up from the yummy candy, then replied, "Fiancé. For about two more weeks."

The woman put the bag of fudge on a small scale, turned back to Chase and said, "How does two bucks sound?"

Chase smiled, "Sounds like I'm back in America, since everything here is euros."

Chase fished some money from her pocket, placed it on top of the glass counter, and happily took possession of the bag of treats.

As Chase inched toward the door, to continue her investigation of the neighborhood, she stopped and said, "Have a good day, um?"

The woman with the gray in her hair smiled again and answered, "Siena."

"Beautiful name," Chase replied. "I'm Chase."

"It was nice to meet you, Chase," Siena answered back.

Chase put her hand on the doorknob, then turned to ask, "So you're named after the place in Italy?"

Siena smiled and replied, "Everyone assumes that but no, my parents named me after the other Siena. The college in upstate New York."

Chase tilted her head and grinned, causing Siena to explain further, "That's where they met, at Siena College. So . . ."

Chase took a piece of fudge from the bag, gave it a taste, and said, "They named you after a college? Good thing they didn't meet at Gonzaga."

The thought made both women laugh and pause. It was clear they liked each other already.

Siena then briefly explained, "Mom is from Fort Covington, New York; Dad is from a small town here in Italy. He got a scholarship to study business at Siena, and when he was a junior, he met my mom, who was a freshman."

Chase could picture it in her mind, saying, "And it was love at first sight between Italy and America?"

Siena nodded, "Pretty much. After graduation, mom came here to live and two years later I was born."

There was a pause when Siena looked off as if she was thinking, then asked, "Did you say your name was Chase? Like if you are chasing someone?"

"Yes," Chase replied, taking a second bite of fudge, adding, "This is delicious, by the way."

"Thanks," Siena said. "We make it in the back. That's so strange, your name."

"'Cause it's a boy's name?" Chase asked.

Siena leaned on the clean glass countertop and said, "No. My little sister, who lives in France, is an avid reader and is always telling me about her latest book."

"Okay?" Chase inquired.

"At Christmastime she likes to read a Christmas book," Siena continued.

"Makes sense," Chase replied.

Siena then said, "She told me she just got done reading one that was supposed to be a true story about these crazy events that happened to an American woman, a writer, in Vermont."

Chase, already knowing where this was going, didn't let on, instead asking, "Crazy how?"

Siena answered, "Like she could see things before they happened."

"So, she was psychic?" Chase asked.

"No, not really, my sister could explain it better," Siena added. "Anyway, the main character's name was Chase, just like yours."

Chase just stood and smiled, finally saying, "What are the odds, huh? Especially with me being an American."

"Exactly," Siena replied.

Chase then said, "Did I mention I did live in Vermont once and that I'm a writer?"

Siena considered her words, then narrowed her gaze and focused on Chase's face. Chase then smiled, raising one eyebrow mischievously.

Siena said, "No way."

Chase crossed the candy store, extended her hand, and said, "Chase Harrington, pleasure to meet you."

"You're kidding," Siena said more insistently.

"I'm not." Chase replied.

Then much louder from Siena, "YOU'RE KIDDING ME."

Chase raised up the white bag the candy was in and said, "Swear on this bag of fudge."

Siena seemed stunned, still not believing this odd coincidence.

Chase finally said, "If you don't believe me, Google the novel *Manchester Christmas*. My photo should be right there with the book."

Siena grabbed her phone off the charger, answering with glee, "I'm doing it right now, because I think you're full of fudge."

Chase looked in the half-empty candy bag, and replied, "I will be if I don't stop munching this."

She watched Siena's eyes fly open and then turn the phone around showing Chase her photograph from the inside of the book jacket.

"Wow, you weren't kidding," Siena said.

After a slight pause, Siena then asked, "Why are you here, again?"

"What do you mean?" Chase asked.

"Europe, Italy, Ostia, my shop?" Siena insisted. "Why?"

Chase replied, "Well, I'm in Italy to be married. I'm in your shop to obviously do damage to my waistline and sort out a mystery."

Siena came from behind the counter and took off the apron that was tied around her waist, asking, "What mystery?"

Chase saw a small table with two chairs and asked, "Do you mind if we sit?"

Both women did, then Chase explained. "I'm not psychic, I'm just someone who occasionally gets nudged one way or the other in life and tries to follow along."

Siena, who was quite bright, took a beat to think, then said, "And something nudged you to come to my store?"

"No," Chase answered, "more like it nudged me to come to Lido di Ostia. I just saw your cool sign and wanted to stop in."

Chase's phone then buzzed in her pocket, so she raised it to her ear and said, "Yes, I'm almost done too."

Siena could hear a man's voice on the other end. Then Chase said, "I'm in a candy store called Ravenous. It's on the corner not far from where Jules dropped us."

Chase hung up, prompting Siena to ask, "Fiancé?"

"Sì," Chase said, using Italian for the first time that day, adding, "he's meeting me out front in five minutes."

Neither woman seemed to know what to say, so Chase dealt with the elephant in the room, saying, "Now that you know who I am and that something nudged me to come down here, I have to ask—"

"What?" answered Siena.

Chase made an awkward face. "Are you sure something isn't wrong?"

Siena started fiddling with a napkin holder on the table, not answering the question.

Chase then said, "I'm not prying, but you were pretty heated on the phone when I walked in."

Siena looked a bit embarrassed now, her face turning a light shade of red, and answered, "Bill collectors, that's all."

Chase didn't say a word, she just waited for more.

"I'm fine. Really, I'm fine," Siena insisted.

Chase could sense it would be wrong to push, so she raised her bag of fudge and said, "Well. Thank you again for the treat. It was really nice to meet you, Siena."

Siena smiled and nodded, and just as Chase opened the door to go, Siena said, "Merry Christmas."

Chase turned back from the busy sidewalk, found Siena's eyes, and in the softest voice answered, "You too."

A moment after making her way to Jules's waiting car, Chase spotted Gavin and gave him a hug, squeezing him extra tight.

"Wow, that was nice," Gavin said.

Chase looked Gavin in the eyes and said, "Say it for me."

Gavin knew what she wanted, so he said, "I love you now."

On cue, Chase replied, "I love you always."

Gavin stepped back, looking at Chase, asking sincerely, "You okay?"

Chase nodded, "Yes, I most certainly am, and I got you a treat."

She handed Gavin the half-eaten fudge and asked if he had any luck in his adventures.

"Not really," Gavin answered. "I did meet the rudest person in all of Italy, but that's about it. How about you?"

"No," Chase said. "I met a nice lady in the candy shop."

Gavin took another bite of fudge, then said, "There was one odd thing."

"What?" Chase inquired.

"I thought I saw someone familiar, but it was probably just my imagination," Gavin answered.

"Who?" Chase asked.

Gavin hesitated, then answered, "At Crane Shipping, where the guard was rude. I saw this kid and he looked like the teen at church who grabbed Scooter's leash that day. It was far away though, so . . ."

After finishing the candy and putting the empty bag in the trash, Gavin asked, "So, was coming down to Lido di Ostia a waste of time?"

Chase looked back toward the candy shop in the distance, focusing on the fun sign that hung out front.

"Chase?" Gavin asked a second time.

Chase starèd at the word RAVENOUS, then said, "I guess so."

As Jules drove the two of them back to the Monti neighborhood of Rome, Chase felt like something was coming, some invisible thing hiding just beyond the margin of view. What she didn't know was, sometimes to truly see, you need to close your eyes.

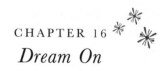

CHAPTER 16

Dream On

Chase didn't dream. I don't mean in the sense of making plans and dreaming of achieving things in life. I mean when she closed her eyes to sleep, dreams did not come. It wasn't until she was ten years old that someone told her how odd that was. When her mom grew concerned and asked a doctor about it, she assured her that Chase was mistaken. *We all dream,* she said, we just don't remember our dreams unless they happen right before we wake up. This quirk of Chase's nature is important because of what happened the night after she walked into a candy shop and met a young woman named after a college in America.

The clock had just struck four a.m. when Chase felt her feet getting wet. She opened her eyes and found herself standing on a beach, her toes in the sand a few inches from where the ocean was breaking. Back and forth the water went, inching high enough to cover Chase's bare feet.

It was daytime, and after looking around, Chase realized she didn't recognize where she was. The only thing she was certain of was, this must be a dream.

Off in the distance was a hill covered in mist. Chase could sense someone was watching her, but the mist concealed them. She didn't feel threatened by the presence, just curious as to who it might be.

Another swoosh of the water, a bit colder this time, caused Chase to look down, her feet completely submerged now. When the wave retreated to the sea. Chase saw letters written in the sand, as if a child had scribbled them with a finger.

They looked Italian, and Chase tried to memorize them before the next wave arrived: AIUTANTE.

The next wave then hit, the salty water rising up to Chase's waist. When the ocean took the water back, her eyes immediately went down to the sand nearby and the letters were gone, taken away with the tide. She instinctively looked back toward the hill, only to find the mist was gone and the hill was empty.

A loud bark filled her head, causing Chase to sit up in bed and find Scooter standing next to her in the darkness, barking to wake her.

"Shh," she said, placing her hand on Scooter's head, "Mommy is fine, it was just a dream."

She could only imagine she had been thrashing or talking in her sleep, alarming the poor pup.

Chase turned on a light, looked at the dog, and said, "We need a glass of water, and pen and paper."

Two hours later, Nonna found Chase sitting alone at the kitchen table, Scooter and the other dog of the house, Giuseppe, both asleep on a blanket on the floor.

"I heard Giuseppe growling earlier and then he was quiet," Nonna said. "I knew one of you couldn't sleep."

Chase smiled through tired eyes, and said, "Strange night."

The two sat quietly drinking coffee for an hour before Francesca awoke and joined them at the kitchen table, asking why Chase was up so early and holding a note pad.

"I had an odd dream," she explained. "Saw some letters in the sand, Italian, and looked them up."

Francesca smiled, then joked, "And the letters said get up and go make everyone coffee?"

Chase chuckled at the thought, answering, "No, the word was *HELPER*."

Nonna, looking down at the notepad repeated, "Helper?"

Chase nodded, answering, "Yes. Whatever that means."

Francesca paused a moment, then smiled and said, "I've got it. I was planning to do laundry today; I think the message in your dream is telling you to be my helper."

Chase giggled at the thought and answered, "Who knows, you might be right."

Gavin was next to rise and join the breakfast club, each of them taking turns teasing Chase about the word in her dream.

Finally, when Gavin saw Chase had had enough, he asked seriously, "Was there anything else in the dream to help make sense of this?"

"No," Chase answered quickly. "Well, there was one other thing. I felt like someone was watching from the fog on this hill."

"What did they look like?" Francesca asked.

"I couldn't see them," Chase replied. "It was more a feeling."

As the clock struck 8 a.m., Chase's phone starting ringing, and Gavin held it up to reveal it was Riley calling.

"Hey, luv," Riley began. "Want to go with me to the big Christmas Market? Tessa's store has a booth set up and I promised her I'd pop by and say hello."

Chase looked at Gavin, and he said, "You go. I'll hang back here and see if Gio wants to do something fun."

Gio held up a copy of *Harry Potter and the Goblet of Fire* and said, "I have to return this to the library. Wanna come?"

Gavin smiled at Chase and said, "Sounds like we both have plans."

Chase turned her attention back to the phone and said, "Riley, you still there? I'll have Jules pick me up in an hour and then we'll come get you."

With that, Chase ate a quick breakfast and pushed the dream out of her mind.

Rome is home to several large outdoor markets at Christmastime. Riley hopped in Jules's car and told him what he already suspected: she wanted to show Chase the Christmas Market at Piazza Navona. It was by far the largest and most beautiful outdoor market, stretching the length of several football fields.

Piazza Navona was home to three ornate fountains: Fontana di Nettuno, Fontana dei Fiumi, and Fontana del Moro. And in the center of it all, the breathtaking Sant'Agnese church. All of the architecture dated to the 1700s, which meant any direction Chase turned her camera, she'd capture something amazing.

A large merry-go-round that lit up at night was slowly spinning, with children waiting for their turn. Police on horseback slowly made their way through the thick crowd, the clip-clop of their hooves like music on the cobblestone street.

"This is crazy," Chase said to Riley. "Where do we even begin?"

Riley pulled her by the hand and said, "You just start walking and shopping, my dear."

More than a hundred tents lined both sides of the plaza, some with food, others with jewelry, trinkets, and clothing. Chase noticed several of the tents had red and black placards on them with two words written in Italian: CERCASI AIUTANTE. Chase recognized the second word on the sign from her dream.

"What do those signs say?" she asked Riley.

Riley replied, "Oh, that just means they have jobs available."

"The second word is *HELPER*, correct?" Chase asked Riley.

Riley looked at the sign a second time and answered, "Yes. And the first word is *SEEKING*."

Chase nodded, saying back to her, "So *seeking helper*. Ah, I got it now, in America it would say HELP WANTED but here they say SEEKING HELPER."

Riley smiled a bit and said, "Why are you obsessed with that sign? Are you looking for a job?"

"No," Chase answered, "Just curious."

There was an awkward silence, when Riley said, "Don't take this the wrong way, but you can sure act strange sometimes."

Chase looked her Irish friend in the eyes and answered, "Guilty as charged."

A dozen blocks away, Gavin stood with his mouth agape looking up at a beautiful stone building with four large pillars out front. In Gavin's mind the columns looked like the kind they'd chain Hercules to.

"Are we going in or are you just going to stare at it?" Gio teased.

Gavin looked down at the teenager and said, "Sorry, I just can't get over these buildings in Rome. It's so cool you get to see them every day."

Gio paused, then asked, "Are the mountains beautiful in Vermont?"

Gavin replied, "Sure."

"Do you stare at them all day?" Gio asked.

Gavin slapped the boy on the back playfully and answered, "I see your point."

Once inside the library, Gio dropped the Harry Potter book into the return bin and asked Gavin, "Want to look around?"

Gavin was mesmerized by the wrought iron railings, the circular staircases, and the clear glass floors that allowed patrons to see floors below and above as they explored.

When they reached the second floor, Gio said, "My father used to take me here all the time."

Gavin felt for the boy, knowing he had just recently lost his father, then replied, "He must have known you liked books."

Gio grinned and said, "It wasn't just for me—my dad loved to read too."

Gavin could see Gio light up at the mere mention of his father, so he asked, "What kind of stories did he like?"

Gio was smiling broadly now, as he said, "He loved adventures. His favorite author was—"

With that Gio stopped talking.

Gavin nudged him, asking, "His favorite author was?"

Gio turned on his heels and said, "Follow me."

Off the teen dashed around one corner, then another, and finally a third, with Gavin right behind.

Finally, Gio stopped in front of a rack of books.

"His favorite author was Alexandre Dumas," Gio said, while pointing.

Gavin looked at a shelf full of books, each with the last name DUMAS in bold print on the spine.

He examined the titles, then called out, "*The Three Musketeers*, I know this one."

Gio was focused on a different novel. He took it down from the shelf and said to Gavin, "This was my father's favorite."

Gio showed Gavin the cover, causing him to read it out loud: "*The Count of Monte Cristo.*"

Gio turned the book over, and asked, "Wanna see something?"

Gavin smiled at the boy, answering, "Sure."

Gio opened the back of the book, exposing a small pouch with an index card tucked inside. Gio slid the card out, revealing his father's name, *Matteo,* written over and over again.

"Every time he borrowed it, they had him sign this card," Gio said.

He took one finger and slowly traced his father's name, as if just touching it brought him closer somehow.

"You must miss him terribly," Gavin said.

Gio didn't answer, he just stood holding the open book, a single tear falling to the card with his father's writing on it.

Gio then said, "You know what's strange?"

Gavin met the boy's eyes and waited for him to continue.

"We were so close, my dad and I," Gio continued. "I always assumed when I lost him some day, I'd feel it. I'd feel him gone."

"And you don't?" Gavin asked.

Gio shook his head.

Gavin put his hand on the boy's shoulder and said, "It's only been a few months. I'm sure you and your mom and grandma are still in shock."

Gio wiped the tear away, trying to be brave and answered, "Yeah."

"Can I ask how he died?" Gavin asked.

Gio, still staring at the novel, answered, "He was on his way to a job when there was an accident. Three men died that day."

"A car accident?" Gavin asked.

"No," the boy replied. "He was on a boat, getting a ride to work. I don't like to think about it."

Gavin could sense the boy's pain.

The teen slowly leafed through the pages of the book, causing Gavin to change the subject. "It looks like someone underlined some of the passages."

Gio smiled and said, "Yeah, my dad. You're not supposed to, but he was the only one who ever took it out, so—"

With that, Gio closed the book quickly and placed it back on the shelf.

"Maybe you should take it out and read it," Gavin suggested.

Gio, more composed now, looked up at Gavin and said, "I have."

Gavin asked, "Does it have a happy ending?"

Gio smiled, answering, "Yes, the hero who loses his way, in the end, finds true love."

Gavin replied, "My kind of ending."

"Me too," the teen said.

The two smiled as they made their way toward the large staircase that would return them to the street.

Back at the Christmas Market, Riley and Chase found Tessa's booth where she was selling expensive clothing.

"A hundred euros for a silk scarf, no way," Riley said, teasing her girlfriend.

As the three of them were laughing, a man's voice called out, "Young lady."

Chase turned around to find an older man in a long dark jacket and matching winter cap waving at her.

It took a second, then Chase recognized him, answering back, "Father Leo?"

The priest approached, then exclaimed, "How fortuitous, running into you here today."

"For-what?" Riley asked in her Irish accent.

"Fortuitous. It means lucky," the priest answered. "Do we have a bit of the Irish in that voice?"

"More than a little," Riley answered. "And why is Chase lucky?"

Father Leo touched his chest, answering, "No, I mean me, lucky for me, because I wanted to talk to Chase about Nonna."

"What about her?" Chase asked.

"I'm curious if Francesca talked to her about helping us with the auction, baking the Torta Barozzi?"

Chase answered, "I don't think so, father. I'm not sure anyone wants to push her."

The priest shook his head, looking frustrated, and answered, "Sometimes a push is what people need. I just wish someone could help her."

Chase paused, then asked, "What did you just say?"

Father Leo answered, "I said I wish someone would help her."

"Help her?" Chase repeated, then said to herself "Help her. Helper."

Chase thought of her dream, the words in the sand, then the signs she saw all over the Christmas Market. Now this random meeting with the priest and that word again—*helper.*

"Chase, are you okay?" the priest asked.

"Yes father, just have a lot on my mind," Chase answered.

It was then that Riley tugged at Chase's arm and said, "I think your phone is vibrating in your pocket."

Chase retrieved the device and, seeing it was Gavin, pushed the button immediately and put him on speaker.

"Chase?" he began. "I need you back home right now. It's happening again."

CHAPTER 17

A Sweet Plan

Chase took the stairs two at a time to reach the apartment as quickly as possible. The moment she opened the door Scooter stopped barking and sat in front of the refrigerator.

"What?" she asked out of breath. "What now?"

Gavin and Gio pointed, and Chase saw an alphabet soup of random letters on the fridge. They read: FAMELICO.

"What am I looking at? Is that a word?" she asked.

Gavin replied, "It's Italian."

Chase, asking right back, "Which means what?"

"You're not going to believe it," Gavin said.

Chase, clearly impatient now, demanded, "GAVIN!"

Her fiancé handed her his phone with the English translation spelled out in large letters: RAVENOUS.

Chase was at first perplexed, then it hit her, "Ravenous? The same name as the candy shop I went into yesterday in Ostia?"

Gavin took a seat and said, "We're trying to figure out how it might connect with your dream. First, *helper* and now this word."

Chase took a seat near Gavin and said, "I've been thinking about that. What if the word I saw in the dream didn't mean *helper* but *HELP HER.*"

Francesca then asked, "But wouldn't it be spelled differently if that was the case?"

Chase shot back, saying, "It's a dream! I don't think dreams have to follow any rules."

Gavin thought, then said, "So if you're right, Chase, we have two messages then: *help her* and *Ravenous.*"

Nonna was listening quietly, then said, "It's possible this is a coincidence. Those letters move around every time someone closes the refrigerator door."

Francesca added, "It's true, Chase, we find random words all the time. It doesn't mean anything."

Chase looked to Nonna, and said, "It's been my experience there are no coincidences."

"So? Gavin asked, "What now?"

Chase looked at her fiancé and replied, "It's obvious, someone or something is telling me to go help that nice lady at the candy store."

"Help her with what?" Nonna asked sincerely.

Chase stood up and grabbed her coat off the back of the chair and replied, "I have a hunch it has to do with money. Do you want to tag along, hon?"

Gavin took up his coat and said, "Of course."

Jules had just gotten home and was on his couch watching a soccer game when Chase's text arrived telling him she was sorry, but she needed another ride.

He put his bowl of gelato back in the freezer, slipped on his cap, and made quick work of getting over to Chase and Gavin for this latest adventure.

A stiff wind blew off the sea, causing the candy shop's sign to rock back and forth, that word RAVENOUS swaying in the unforgiving December air.

Gavin decided to wait in the warm car with Jules, allowing Chase to talk to the woman alone.

The buzzer on the door sounded as Chase entered the shop, and Siena sat up from behind the counter, taking off her glasses and setting down the book she was reading.

"Anything good?" Chase asked. "The book, I mean?"

Siena smiled and said, "Well, well. If it isn't the author from America."

Chase nodded warmly and said, "Chase."

"I remember," Siena replied. "After we met, I ran out and bought your book. You're just as pretty as the photo on the dust jacket."

Chase blushed and replied, "I wish, but thank you."

"So, let me guess, Gavin loved the fudge, and you came back for more?" Siena asked.

Chase looked toward the floor, uncertain how to get into this, simply replying, "No, not exactly."

Siena picked up Chase's novel *Manchester Christmas,* and said excitedly, "I love how you two met, by the way, in chapter one, you lost in Vermont and him looking like a hunky cowboy from a dime store novel."

Chase smiled at the memory, "Yes, that was a great day. How far are you in the book?"

Siena looked at where she had left the bookmark, and replied, "You just saw something in the second window at the church."

Chase nodded, "Ah, the crazy stuff is about to happen."

Siena held up the book in her hand and said, "And this really happened, not fiction?"

Chase walked around the store looking at all the candy and answered, "It did, although many don't believe it."

"Amazing," Siena answered. "So, you're not here for candy?"

Chase turned to engage Siena's eyes and said, "No Siena, I'm here for you."

"Me?" Siena responded.

Chase leaned on the glass countertop and said, "I don't want to get into everything, but something tells me you are in trouble and need help."

Siena, drew back from the comment, and said, "I told you yesterday, I'm fine, Chase."

Chase pouted and replied, "The phone call? The money stuff? I know something is going on."

Siena looked away, deep in thought.

Outside on the street Gavin and Jules were listening to the soccer game on the car radio. Since the broadcast was in Italian Gavin had no clue what was going on, so his gaze was fixed on the shoppers going up and down the sidewalk. It was less than two weeks until Christmas, so you could see the urgency in their steps.

Suddenly Gavin's eyes went wide when he saw that same teenager from the church, the one he thought he saw at the shipping yard, now coming out of a sandwich shop.

Gavin didn't know why but something compelled him to hop out of the car and call over to the young man.

"Hey, kid," he yelled, but the teen didn't seem to hear him.

Gavin ducked his head back in the car and yelled to Jules, "How do you say *excuse me* in Italian?"

"*Mi scusi*," he replied.

Gavin called out again to the teen, louder this time, "MI SCUSI, you, boy, MI SCUSI."

An older man on the street got the teen's attention and pointed toward Gavin, causing the teenager to look over. When he saw Gavin's face, the boy quickly bolted away.

"What the heck?" Gavin said. "This kid acts like he owes me money."

He was about to give pursuit, but the teen disappeared around a corner.

"What was that about?" Jules asked, as Gavin got back in the car.

"Nothing," Gavin replied. "I've just seen him a couple times and he keeps acting squirrely."

"Squirrely?" Jules asked, not understanding.

"Strange," Gavin replied.

Jules chuckled and said, "Maybe he thinks you're *pazzo*."

Gavin laughed, then replied, "He might be right."

Back in the candy shop, Chase was waiting silently for Siena to tell her what was troubling her.

Siena started fiddling with items behind the counter, then, looking away said, "It's just been tough, but I'll figure it out."

Chase stepped around the counter, standing next to Siena now, and said, "I know we just met, but I'm here as a friend. Please tell me what's going on."

Siena silently walked through the swinging door into the back office, then reappeared a moment later with a tax bill from the city.

She explained, "This shop was my mom's and she never told me how far in debt she was."

"Okay," Chase replied.

"I cleaned up most of the financial mess with the vendors, but the city won't budge, and if I don't come up with ten thousand euros in back taxes by January first, they plan to close me and take the property."

"Money? That's what you need?" Chase said almost happily.

"Yes, why are you smiling?" Siena asked.

Chase picked up her novel and answered, "Because this novel put a lot of money in my pocket, and I can loan you what you need."

"Loan me?" Siena shot back with a sharp tone. "You don't even know me."

Chase put the book back down and said, "True, but something sent me to you to help and I can help . . . so let me."

Siena looked at Chase and replied, "Something sent you? What does that mean?"

"Irrelevant to this conversation," Chase fired back. "Now, let me help you."

Siena was stone silent for a solid minute before responding, "No."

The short answer prompted Chase to reply, "No?"

Siena looked thoughtfully at this American who was trying to be kind and said, "All due respect, I've done everything on my own and I won't take charity now. I'm sorry, but your generosity is rejected, with thanks and respect."

Chase looked in Siena's eyes and could tell instantly the proud woman was not going to budge. She recognized the look because Chase saw it in the mirror every day as she was growing up poor.

Chase paced the candy store floor, thinking now. Twice she stopped and was about to speak but continued pacing in circles, mumbling to herself.

"If you're wearing a Fitbit your steps are certainly adding up today," Siena joked.

Chase wasn't listening. Instead, she was thinking about everything she'd encountered since she arrived in Rome: the young couple on the bridge; the older couple in the gondola; Francesca, Gio, and Nonna, who felt like Chase's own family at this point.

That's when it hit her. "Nonna," Chase said out loud.

"Who is Nonna?" Siena asked.

"Help her," Chase replied, out loud again.

Siena moved close to Chase and said, "Are you alright? Help who?"

Chase started laughing and said, "It was right there in front of me, I just didn't see it."

"See what?" Siena asked. "You're freaking me out, Chase."

Chase looked at Siena, then in a serious tone explained, "Nonna is a wonderful woman I'm staying with. She needs help starting her life again after losing her husband and son. You need help with money. This shop, Ravenous, is the connection."

Siena, looking confused, said, "Chase, you lost me completely."

Chase then said excitedly, pointing toward the back room, "You melt the chocolate on the premises, right? You told me that."

Chase ran into the candy store's kitchen before Siena could even answer.

Chase saw four stoves lined up like soldiers against a back wall, ready for battle, saying, "This is perfect."

"What is?" Siena asked, still confused.

Chase saw a coat hanging from a rack and handed it to Siena, saying, "I need you to trust me. We're closing for an hour and you're coming with me."

Siena was about to speak when Chase touched her arm, and said, "I know what I'm doing. Trust me."

Back at the turn of the last century, the early 1900s, there was a pastry chef named Eugenio Gollini. He wanted to create a chocolate dessert unlike anything anyone had ever tasted, something so decadent people would travel hundreds of miles for just one bite.

Chef Gollini was a huge admirer of an architect from the sixteenth century named Jacopo Barozzi, so when the dessert he created was finished, he named it *Torta Barozzi*.

The dessert was so popular in Italy, others tried to recreate it, but none could come close. Sure, they mixed nuts, butter, rum, chocolate, and the other ingredients, but something was missing; the taste wasn't the same.

Nonna learned to cook as a little girl, growing up in the Modena Province of Italy, outside Bologna, only a few miles from where Chef Gollini invented Torta Barozzi. She tasted it in the original pastry shop where it was sold and knew right away what was different about Gollini's creation, compared to the others. It was the balsamic vinegar.

You could walk into any store in Europe, then or now, and find a bottle of balsamic for less than ten dollars, but Gollini's balsamic was special. He was using what the locals called *balsamico di Modena,* which was mixed and aged in the attics of local homes in Modena, sometimes taking decades for the flavor to ripen. It tasted nothing like traditional balsamic, and Nonna knew several families who still made it the old-fashioned way.

One bottle of this special mixture cost two hundred euros, so only the elite bought it, and none knew it was the magic ingredient in Gollini's Torta Barozzi. None but Nonna, that is.

When Chase arrived at the apartment with Siena, Nonna was waiting.

Chase didn't beat around the bush, saying simply, "Nonna, this is Siena. Both she and the church you love are in financial trouble and I have a way to fix it. Will you help me?"

Nonna smiled, then asked, "In your dream you saw the words *helper* or *help her.* Is Siena the one who needs help? Or am I? Or are you, Chase?"

Chase gave Nonna a hug and said, "Maybe we all are."

Riley spoke to her girlfriend, Tessa, about the booth her store set up at the popular Christmas Market. When Tessa explained the situation, her boss was more than willing to allow Chase, Riley, and Nonna to sell their decadent dessert there.

Gio printed up fliers on hot pink paper and stapled them all over Rome, announcing that for one day only, the famous Torta Barozzi dessert that sold at auction at the Santa Maria church would be available to the general public. Gio's flyer made it clear this had never happened before and would never happen again.

Jules drove to Modena to secure two large bottles of the special balsamic, aged twenty years, while Nonna took Francesca, Gio, Chase, Gavin, Riley, Tessa, and Siena to the store to buy the rest of the ingredients.

The plan was to sell the dessert at 20 euros a slice, with each cake supplying ten slices. If they could bake 100 of Nonna's special Torta Barozzi desserts and sell them all in one day, that would raise 20,000 euros, more than enough to pay Siena's tax bill, help the church's poor, and cover their expenses.

Four ovens, seven helpers, and one old woman with a gift in the kitchen.

"Nonna?" Chase asked. "We need a Christmas miracle. Can we really do this?"

Nonna looked at her grandson, Father Leo, and the candy shop owner, all with such hope in their eyes, and answered, "Christmas is the time for miracles."

With the stoves working nonstop in the back of the Ravenous candy store, it took from sunup until sunset the following day to produce 100 of Nonna's Torta Barozzi creations. They even managed to make five extras, so they could offer free samples to the customers passing by.

As luck would have it, the sun was shining, and the temperature rose into the low fifties, bringing out a massive crowd of Christmas shoppers and tourists. Gio's flyers did their job, driving customers to Tessa's tent, and in that one twelve-hour day, every slice of Nonna's Torta Barozzi was gone.

The candy shop was saved, the church finances were put back in the black, and Nonna seemed more like her old self, with pride and purpose.

As Chase cleaned up the mess behind the counter at the Christmas Market, Gavin took his thumb and smudged a dab of chocolate on her nose, looking at her fondly.

"What's up, silly?" Chase asked him lovingly.

"I'm just so proud of you," Gavin replied.

He then let out a deep sigh, causing Chase to ask, "What's wrong?"

Gavin wrapped his strong arms around her and said, "I know this romance stuff I'm in charge of hasn't gone as planned, but I think, in some ways, what has happened is better."

Chase looked over at Siena, who was laughing with Francesca and Nonna, and replied, "Me too."

What neither could know, at that moment, was the surprises and adventures they'd encounter chasing around Rome had only just begun.

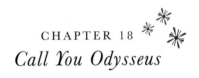

CHAPTER 18

Call You Odysseus

That night, as everyone slept soundly after such a busy day, the thermometer dipped sharply in Italy and on the islands off her shores. On one of them, Brother Levi woke to the sensation of cold air rushing into his room. He rose from his bed at five in the morning, hoping to find the source of the chill. It was the front door, wide open, in the home he shared with a dozen other monks. Footprints were visible on top of the fresh snow, so Levi threw on a coat and scarf and set out to make sure everything was okay.

There was a small work shed that stood between the main house and five wooden docks that poked out like fingers into the Tyrrhenian Sea. There, in that shed, Levi found a lantern turned on and a man with his back to the door, fiddling with something.

"Strange time to be working on a project," Levi called out, startling him.

The man, without turning, answered back, "It's just me, Tommaso."

"What are you doing up?" Levi asked.

Tommaso turned to meet his eyes, saying, "I could ask you the same question."

Levi replied, "Do you remember when you first came to live with us, I told you that front door needed to be pulled hard or the lock wouldn't click?"

Tommaso gave him a bewildered look, then replied. "Not really."

"Well," Levi pressed on, "you didn't shut it tight, so the door blew open."

"Sorry about that," Tommaso said remorsefully.

Levi walked into the shed to get closer to Tommaso, answering, "No big deal, you just gave the house a chill."

Levi noticed a small brass item in Tommaso's hands, asking, "What's that there?"

Tommaso held it up in the light, answering, "An old compass. It didn't work, so I popped the glass off and cleaned the pin."

"How did it get dirty?" Levi asked with curiosity.

"Moisture got in and caused it to rust," Tommaso answered. "But now it works, pointing north again."

"You should keep that," Levi said.

"Me? Why?" Tommaso answered.

Levi replied, "You never know when you might get lost."

Tommaso rubbed his thumb along the tarnished brass and carefully placed the compass in his pocket.

Levi paused a moment to consider his next words, then said, "I've avoided asking you this, trying to respect your privacy, but where are you from, Tommaso?"

The good-looking man in his early forties answered, "Someplace nicer than this, I think."

Levi then asked, "Are you happy with us here?"

"I suppose," Tommaso replied.

"Not exactly a rousing endorsement," Levi answered back.

Tommaso, trying not to offend, responded in a friendly tone, "I suppose not."

With the door to the small shed still open, Levi could hear the ocean crashing on the shore, prompting him to ask, "More boats are coming and going today from the island. Would you like to go ashore with me?"

"No," was Tommaso's answer, at little more than a whisper.

Levi then asked, "Tomorrow?"

Again, Tommaso gave him a quiet, "No."

Levi then asked, "Is it the ocean you don't like, or the boats?"

Tommaso took a deep breath and replied, "Both."

Levi motioned with his hand for Tommaso to follow him out of the shed. Outside, even though it was still dark, the ocean was having a conversation only the rocks and sand could understand.

"So, you're not entirely happy here and you don't want to go out there," Levi said, pointing toward the ocean. "Maybe I should call you Odysseus."

Tommaso turned to Levi, asking, "Who?"

"Odysseus," Levi answered. "From Homer's *Odyssey*."

Tommaso dropped his hands to his side, then said, "I don't understand."

"It was a poem written long ago," Levi continued. "My father made my brother and me read it each summer when school was on break. I told you about my brother, didn't I?"

"The priest?" Tommaso inquired.

"That's right," Levi confirmed.

"A priest and a monk. I bet if you had a sister, she'd be a Sister," Tommaso said lightheartedly.

Levi paused and said, "I'll bet you're right."

"Anyway, I remind you of someone in the poem your dad made you read?" Tommaso asked.

"Honestly, I'm just teasing you. I get silly when I wake up early and wander in the dark," Levi answered.

Tommaso was now curious, asking, "No, tell me. Please."

As the two men slowly made their way up the snow-covered path toward the house, Levi shared the story.

"Odysseus was a man sent on a long journey where he faced many hardships, and by the end of it, much like you, he was sick of the sea," Levi explained.

"Okay," Tommaso replied.

"Anyway," Levi continued, "He's visited by a ghost, and the ghost tells him to pick up an winnowing oar, find land, and then walk with his back to the ocean for as long as it takes until someone sees the oar in his hand and mistakes it for a winnowing fan."

Tommaso considered what he had just said and then asked, "Why a winnowing fan?"

Levi concluded the story, saying, "Because that would mean Odysseus had reached a place where no one has ever been troubled by the sea."

"Because they didn't know what an oar was," Tommaso answered, understanding the parable.

"Exactly," Levi replied. "Perhaps that's you."

Tommaso smiled at the notion, as Levi said, "Let's get back inside before we catch a chill out here."

As Levi reached the door, he felt Tommaso take hold of his elbow to stop him.

"Tell me one last thing," Tommaso asked. "Does Odysseus find happiness at the end of the poem?"

Levi gave him a smile that answered the question without words.

Back in Rome, Chase and Gavin saw Nonna, Francesca, and Gio dressed in fine clothes.

"Something special happening today?" Chase asked.

Gio said to Chase, "We have to make a visit to Verano."

"Is that a village?" Gavin asked.

Gio looked at his mother, that back at Gavin, answering, "It's a cemetery."

Before Chase or Gavin could ask why, they heard footsteps on the staircase, followed by a quick knock, and Jules walked in holding a small Christmas wreath. It was nothing elaborate, just simple evergreens with a red bow.

"Is this good?" Jules asked Nonna, who was dressed in a modest black dress.

"Sì. Good, Jules," she answered.

Suddenly it hit Chase that everyone was up early and dressed this way because they were going to the cemetery to pay their respects to Nonna's late husband, Alessandro, and son, Matteo.

Chase touched the wreath and said, "Is this for the grave?"

"Yes," Francesca replied, her face a bit pale, absent of any makeup.

Gavin, trying to be thoughtful asked, "Do you need a second wreath, for both graves? Chase and I could run out and get one."

Francesca looked at Gio, and the boy was visibly upset now, excusing himself from the room.

"I'm sorry," Gavin offered, "if I said something wrong."

Francesca touched Gavin's arm and said, "There is only one grave."

Chase and Gavin were quiet now, trying to understand why, when Nonna said, "One body, one grave."

Chase looked at Nonna, then asked, "One body?"

She then turned to Francesca and Chase asked, "You said he died in an accident, but there was no body?"

"Sì," Francesca replied, adding, "they never found any of them."

Gavin took a seat at the table and said, "Can you tell us what happened?"

Francesca sat across from Gavin and tried her best to explain. "Matteo was a mechanic who could fix anything. Sometimes that meant traveling out to the islands for work."

Chase joined Gavin at the table now, then said, "Go on."

"To reach the island, he took a ride on a boat," Francesca continued.

She paused to collect her thoughts, then said, "There was a storm, and the boat lost its way and got caught in it."

Francesca took a deep breath and finished. "The boat capsized. There were no survivors."

The room was dead quiet, then Gavin asked, "How many?"

"Three," a boy's voice said from behind.

It was Gio, returning to the kitchen to join the others.

Jules, who was standing silently by the door, then said, "Tell them the rest, about the insurance."

"Jules," Francesca snapped. "What's done is done."

"What about the insurance?" Chase asked.

Francesca shook her head angrily and responded, "Because a storm is considered an *act of God* the insurance company wouldn't pay for the funerals or survivor benefits."

"So, they gave the three families nothing?" Gavin asked, his tone disgusted.

"Sì," Nonna answered. "Not that money would change anything."

The room fell quiet now, as the others prepared to make their somber trip to the cemetery.

"If you don't mind," Chase said. "We'd like to come."

Gavin put on a blue sport coat, Chase a lovely dress, and the couple joined the others on the trip to Verano. Just as they were told, they found one grave for Nonna's husband, Alessandro, but no marking of any kind for Matteo. The grave felt sad and incomplete.

Driving home, Gio tried to put everyone's minds on something else, when he asked, "So the four clues you got from the man at the Colosseum?"

Gavin looked across the backseat of the car, asking, "What about them?"

"You only did two, the bridge with the locks and the gondola with the kiss," Gio observed.

"True," Gavin said. "Your point is?"

Chase took Gavin's hand in hers and said, "You know what his point is: there are still two left."

Gavin looked out the car window at the beautiful passing homes and asked, "Do you really want to finish them?"

Francesca, who was in the front seat, smiled for the first time today and turned and said, "I think I know what the third one was about."

Gavin had to think a moment, then said, "The third clue was a letter."

"Correct," Francesca replied.

Chase was smiling now because she could tell Francesca was excited about something, saying, "So, don't leave us hanging here."

Francesca grinned wider and asked one question, "Have you ever heard of Casa di Giulietta?"

Gavin replied, "*Casa* means house, but the rest, I'm lost."

Gio laughed and said, "It stands for House of Juliet."

Gavin looked at Chase and said, "Juliet who?"

Chase burst out laughing, saying, "I think she's talking about Romeo and Juliet, honey."

"WAIT," Gavin exclaimed. "They were real?"

Francesca answered, "Sort of. Legend says that Shakespeare based the story on a real couple."

She turned her whole body around, facing the back seat, and added, "The house with the balcony where Juliet lived is certainly real, and I know where it is."

Chase pondered a moment, then asked, "What does this have to do with a letter."

"Not *a* letter," Francesca said, "Letters, plural. Thousands of them. It's really something to see."

Chase looked at Gavin, prompting him to say, "Two down, two to go. I guess we're finishing the list."

Chase gave him a kiss, making the rest of the drive go as fast as his heart.

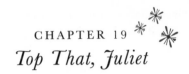

CHAPTER 19

Top That, Juliet

It was more than 300 miles to Juliet's balcony in the city of Verona in northern Italy, so Chase wanted to be certain of what they'd find should they make the long journey. There were only twelve days until Christmas Eve, the day Gavin and Chase were to wed, and there was still much planning to do. Where would they marry? Who would perform the ceremony? If family wasn't flying in from America, how could they take part?

As Chase sat on her bed with her laptop, learning everything she could about Casa di Giulietta, Gavin was outside getting expert instruction on how to kick a soccer ball from Gio. Francesca was at the gallery and Riley was on the way with fresh pastries from the corner café, planning to help Chase with what she called her *Romeo research.*

Traffic was busy in front of the building where Gavin was kicking the ball, so Gio showed him a small hidden garden tucked behind the house. It was invisible to the world unless you knew about the entrance from the back alley. Gio called it his *secret passage.*

"This is pretty neat back here," Gavin said, looking at the rows of rose bushes that were asleep for the winter but lining each side of the garden.

A large brown fountain was flush against the back of their home, the water continuously flowing from a statue of a lion's mouth, even during these cold winter months.

"Nonno always kept it running so the birds had someplace to drink," Gio said.

"I'm sorry, who?" Gavin asked sincerely.

"Nonno," Gio answered. "It means grandfather in Italian."

Gavin smiled, then said, "Wait, so grandparents in Italy are No-Na and No-No?"

Gio kicked the ball his way and said, "You got it."

Gavin stopped the ball with his foot and replied, "We just called mine Nanny and Pops."

Upstairs in the apartment, Nonna was making a racket in the dining room, opening and slamming drawers. Whatever she was looking for, the more she couldn't find it, the louder the banging got.

"Are you okay out there?" Chase called from her bedroom.

Nonna didn't answer, just more slamming.

Riley arrived, and when no one answered her knock on the door, she let herself in with a loud, "HELLO? Chase?"

Chase ducked her head out of the bedroom, saying, "I'm in the back. Bring the pastries—I'm starving."

Gavin played basketball growing up in Vermont and summers were spent chasing baseballs around the sandlot, but soccer was foreign to him.

"This is our number one sport," Gio explained. "And we call it *calcio* or football."

As Gavin tried to return a pass, the ball sailed over Gio's head and into a small pile of bricks in the corner.

"I'll get it," Gavin said.

After retrieving the ball, he walked past the fountain and noticed the unfinished work of Gio's grandfather on the ground in front of it. Bricks had been carefully laid into a large square area, but the middle was incomplete, exposing the bare dirt that was partially covered by December's slush.

Looking down at the unfinished business, Gavin remembered the story about how Gio's grandfather died, on his hands and knees, laying these very bricks to create a sanctuary for Nonna.

"You okay?" Gio asked, as Gavin just stood with the soccer ball in his hand, staring silently.

"I'm sorry," Gavin answered, "I just realized where we're standing."

Gio walked over and took the ball from Gavin, saying, "Yeah, I haven't been back here since it happened."

There was a pause, then Gio asked, "Wanna see something?"

Gavin followed the boy over to a tiny shed in the corner of the yard, which had a wooden door being held shut by a tiny hook. Gio popped the hook loose, and the door creaked open on its own, revealing two shelves filled with paint cans, tools, bags of sand, and mortar mix. Next to the mix, Gavin saw long thin sticks that looked like rulers, sticking out of an empty coffee can.

Gio touched a metal tool and said, "He'd use this to tamp down the sand and get it level. The mortar went around the stones to keep them in place."

Gavin just listened, enjoying the young man talking about his grandfather.

Gio continued, "The rubber mallet gets the stones tighter if they won't go down."

He picked up the mallet and looked at Gavin, adding, "It has to be rubber because a regular hammer would crack the stones."

Gavin smiled, answering, "That makes perfect sense."

Gio picked up one of the thin sticks from the paint can and said, "I'm not sure what he used these for."

Gavin replied, "I do."

Gio looked back, surprised, then waited for Gavin to explain.

Gavin took the stick from Gio's hands and said, "Your Nonno used these sticks to mix the paint or mortar."

Gio could imagine it now, his grandfather standing in the garden, mixing, hammering, and finishing the patio as a surprise for Nonna.

Gavin said to Gio, "You are very lucky, Giovanni."

Gio looked up to Gavin, answering, "I am?"

Gavin put his hand on the boy's shoulder and said, "Despite what you've all been through, you have your family. That's so important."

Gavin then handed Gio a single stick from the coffee can, and said, "Do me a favor and break that."

"Break it?" Gio asked surprised.

"Yes. Snap it in half," Gavin said with glee.

Gio shrugged his shoulders, gripped the long stick tightly on each end, and with one quick movement over his knee snapped in two.

It made a loud *pop*, like a tree branch breaking, causing a sparrow that was getting a drink at the fountain to be startled and fly away.

Gavin then picked up a half dozen of the sticks and put them together as one, stacked on top of each other like a thick board.

He handed it to Gio and said, "Now, try to break this."

Gio took the six sticks, merged as one, into his small hands and could feel the strength and weight of them.

He tried to bend them but there was no give, unlike when he was holding the single stick.

"Go ahead," Gavin encouraged him.

Gio hesitated and then raised the sticks up and brought them down on his knee again, only this time they didn't break. Gio looked up at Gavin, a bit embarrassed by the effort.

Gavin took the unbroken sticks from Gio and said, "My father taught me this long ago, when I was younger than you."

Gavin held up the six sticks in his right hand and a single stick in his left.

Raising the left hand first, he said, "Alone."

Then he raised the right hand with the half-dozen sticks, and said, "Together."

Gio was pondering the lesson when Gavin handed him the stack of sticks and said, "That's the power of family."

Back upstairs, Chase and Riley finished their pastries and walked out of the bedroom, disappointed. Their food wasn't the problem, it was what Chase had read about the home in Verona, Italy, with the balcony of Juliet.

"Oh Romeo, my Romeo, what's your problem with Juliet?" Riley asked sarcastically.

Chase plopped on the couch, her laptop still in her hands, and said, "It's a silly tourist trap."

"How so?" Riley asked.

"Where do I begin?" Chase replied, "The house isn't the one where the real Juliet lived, the girl Shakespeare based the play on. And the balcony she supposedly called Romeo from was added years later to make the tourists happy."

Riley made a troubled face, and said, "Ewww, that's not good."

"No, it's not," Chase replied, adding, "and while it's neat people write love letters and pin them to the wall there, the so-called *Letters to Juliet*, they're letters from people looking for love."

"What's wrong with that?" Riley asked.

"Nothing," Chase answered, "Except, I'm not looking, I have my *happy ever after*."

Riley thought a moment then said, "So, you're saying the third clue from the guy at the Colosseum may be about a letter, but not one to a fake Juliet?"

"Exactly," Chase replied.

"And we're not wasting an entire day driving up there for nothing?" Riley concluded.

"No, we're not," Chase answered firmly.

Chase closed the laptop and said, "If the word *letter* leads to romance, it's got to be something else."

"Sorry," Riley said, "I'm lost on this one."

Chase let out a sigh and said, "Maybe I'm not supposed to complete this little adventure and I should be focusing on my wedding."

Riley then asked, "Who is marrying you by the way? Doing the service, I mean?"

"Good question," Chase replied. "Gavin is Catholic, but I never really went to church that much. At least not enough to belong to a con-gregation."

Riley considered the dilemma, then suggested, "You know, that priest from Nonna's church seems nice. I know he can't marry you, but he might know of someone who can."

Chase saw Gavin and Gio walking through the front door and replied to Riley, "Good idea."

Gio grabbed a bottle of water from the fridge and disappeared into his bedroom, leaving Gavin with Chase and Riley in the small living room off the kitchen.

"How was soccer?" Chase asked her fiancé.

"Fun," Gavin answered, "although they call it something else here."

"Football?" Riley asked.

"Yes," Gavin answered. "They have another name for it too. It begins with a C."

Nonna was on her way to the kitchen when Chase called out to her, "Is everything okay, Nonna?"

The old woman stopped, looked in, and replied, "Sì. Just *frustrata.*"

Gavin asked, "What does that mean?"

Nonna answered, "Frustrated. I am *frustrata!*"

"What's wrong?" Chase asked. "We heard you slamming drawers."

Nonna answered, "I was looking for my Alessandro's old watch, for Gio."

Gavin replied, "For a gift?"

"Sì," she answered. "For him to wear Christmas Eve, at your wedding."

Nonna looked at Chase and Gavin, then asked, "You still getting married, yes?"

"Absolutely," Gavin said, "I'm just working on the details."

Nonna paced around a room a moment, then said, "I can't find the watch and I can't find the box."

Chase asked, "What box?"

Nonna sat on a chair for a moment to explain. "My husband, he have a small box he keep important things in. Since his death, I cannot find."

Chase looked around the room and said, "We can help you look if you want."

Nonna threw her hands in the air, replying, "I looked everywhere, it's not here."

Gavin thought a moment, then asked, "Did you say box?"

"Sì," Nonna answered.

"Was it about the size of a pillow, brown, wooden?" he asked, using his hands to help describe the size and shape.

Nonna got excited now, "Sì, yes, do you see it somewhere?"

Gavin answered, "I think I tripped on it when I was up in the attic. Remember you sent me up there for decorations after we moved in?"

Nonna clapped her hands and said, "Sì, Gavin, can you go back up and find it?"

It took Gavin less than a minute to pull the ladder down, climb up and return with Alessandro's memory box, covered in dust. They placed it on the kitchen table, used a wet cloth to remove the grime, and then tried to open it.

Unfortunately, the lock was engaged and the box, which had to be a hundred years old, was shut tighter than a submarine door.

Gavin shook it gently and could hear several things rattling around inside.

Riley, seeing Nonna's frustration, took out her phone, and a moment later was speaking Italian with someone on the other end. When she hung up, Riley immediately made a growling sound, like she was frustrated.

"What's wrong?" Chase asked.

"That was a locksmith," Riley explained, "He said with locks this old, you can force them open, but he'd have to punch the lock to do it."

"What does this mean?" Nonna asked. "Punching the lock?"

Riley touched her hand gently and said, "It means he'd have to break it to get inside. If you don't care about the box—"

Nonna shook her head sharply left to right, "No," she said. "I don't want to break Alessandro's box."

Everyone was perplexed now on how to move forward.

Just then, Gavin snapped his fingers and said, "Wait a sec."

"What?" Chase asked.

"Do you remember when we bought the old lock from the antique store?" he asked.

Everyone nodded yes, so Gavin continued. "Behind the counter he had a ring with what had to be a hundred keys to old locks. He might have one that fits."

Riley gave Gavin a friendly shove and said in that Irish accent, "You're as smart as you are handsome. Not that you're my type."

With that, Riley gave Chase an exaggerated wink.

Chase smiled and said, "Yes, we've already covered that ground, thank you very much."

Gavin grabbed the box from the table, tucked it under his arm, and said, "Give me an hour and let me see what I can do."

In five seconds flat, Gavin was out the door.

Nonna had a machine in her kitchen to make fresh pasta. It had worked effortlessly for decades, yet for some reason, today, she couldn't get her mind and hands on the same page, and her pasta was stringy.

"It's just nerves," Chase said to her. "Waiting like this stinks."

Nearly an hour had passed when they heard the doorknob finally turn and Riley called out, "Did he get it open?"

To their surprise, it was Francesca peeking over the grocery bag she was holding, answering, "Get what open?"

Nonna took the bag from Francesca's hands and said, "Gavin went someplace, we waiting for him."

Francesca smiled and said, "He's right behind me on the stairs, or at least he was."

All eyes went to the front door just as Gavin walked through with a grin stretching ear to ear.

"I didn't look inside, but Mr. Carlucci at the antique store got it open on the thirty-seventh key," Gavin said, laying the box on the kitchen table.

Nonna sat down in front of it, lifted the lid and immediately smiled.

"There is the watch," she said.

As she started going through the other items in the box, her eyes suddenly went wide with surprise. First, she saw a small dried red rose with a pin sticking out of the short stem.

Nonna held it up and looked at Francesca, saying, "He wore this on his jacket when you married Matteo."

Francesca instantly started filling up with tears, thinking of that wonderful day and how much she missed her husband.

Nonna's wrinkled fingers delicately picked up a small photograph of a baby.

"This is you," she said to Gio. "The day you were born."

Francesca wrapped her arm around her son, giving him a squeeze.

"Oh my," the old woman said, as she raised up a pair of half-torn concert tickets.

She raised her eyes to meet the others and said, "Luciano Pavarotti, 1975."

She found birth certificates and some old insurance forms neatly tucked away as well.

Then she discovered something that really surprised her: letters she had written to her husband years earlier when he was away at war. They were carefully preserved, with a pink ribbon tied around them, keeping them safe.

Nonna ran her hands over the letters, the concert tickets, and the rose, as if touching them took her back to such wonderful memories.

"Did you know he kept all these things?" Francesca asked.

Nonna could only shake her head no.

Then Gio pointed, "What's that, there?"

The teen had spotted the white corner of an envelope sticking out from what looked like a hidden compartment inside the top of the memory box.

Nonna couldn't get it with her trembling fingers, so Gavin pulled hard, and out came the envelope with a single piece of white paper, folded into three, tucked inside.

It was clear from Nonna's expression that it was Alessandro's handwriting.

"Is that—" Francesca began to ask.

When Chase answered, "A letter."

Chase looked at Gavin, remembering the third clue from the old man at the Colosseum, as he nodded back in agreement.

"Open it, Nonna," Gio urged.

"What does it say, *mia madre?*" Francesca asked.

Nonna looked into Francesca's eyes, realizing in all their years together, it was the first time she ever referred to Nonna as *mother.*

Nonna raised the letter in her hands, slowly opened the fold and read these words silently to herself.

Mia bella Ava,
Come dire addio a qualcuno che è stato tutto il tuo mondo? La risposta è che non si fa.

Se stai leggendo questo, ora sono con Dio, ma questo non è un addio.

Ti farò un posto e ti aspetterò con cuore aperto e paziente.

Nel frattempo, nei giorni in cui ti manco, vai a metterti al centro del mio cuore e cerca un segno.

Finché non ti stringerò di nuovo, sono tuo sempre,
Alessandro

Nonna, her eyes now filled with tears, brought the letter up to her face and held her husband's words against her quivering lips, as if giving Alessandro a kiss wherever he may be.

Francesca, without prompting or permission, gently took the letter from Nonna, and started reading it out loud in English, as the others looked on.

My beautiful Ava,
How do you say goodbye to someone who has been your entire world? The answer is that you don't.

If you are reading this I am now with God, but this is not goodbye.

I will make a place for you and will wait for you with an open and patient heart.

In the meantime, on the days when you miss me, go stand at the center of my heart and look for a sign.
Until I hold you again, I am yours always,
Alessandro

Nonna took the letter back, carefully folded it, and placed it back in the memory box.

She stood up to leave, but she paused at the doorway and turned back to Chase and Gavin, saying, "That letter is the best Christmas gift I've ever received. *Grazie.*"

As Chase wiped a tear from her eye, Riley made her burst out laughing when she said in her Irish accent, "Top that, Juliet."

CHAPTER 20

He Saved Everyone

The next two days in Rome passed uneventfully, with Gavin coming and going from the apartment like a secret agent on a mission. Chase asked Gavin to pick the romantic place where they'd be married, and if he had settled on one, he was certainly keeping it quiet. Until today.

Chase woke to a small note on the pillow next to her, with six words written in Gavin's hand: *Meet me at Baccano at noon.*

When Chase joined the others for breakfast, Francesca looked at the note and said, "I know this place. It's in the heart of the Trevi district of Rome, not so far."

"What is it?" Chase asked.

Gio poured himself some orange juice, and answered, "A restaurant."

Chase took the fresh pastry that was in her hand and placed it back on the large plate in the center of the table, saying, "If I'm eating lunch that early, better save room."

Nonna came around with a pot of coffee to freshen everyone's cups, asking Chase, "Have you decided where you'll be married? And who will be there?"

"I think Gavin is working on the *where*," Chase answered. "As for *who*? We plan a simple ceremony here and then a big party with our families this spring in America."

Nonna sat next to Chase, pressing further, "And who will marry you? A priest?"

Chase was taken aback, not expecting the question, then answered, "We're still figuring that out too. I'm not Catholic, but I was going to get some advice from Father Leo, at your church. He seems very nice."

Gio then said, "He's a good guy, Father Leo—a little heavy on the wine, though."

Chase was alarmed by the statement, asking, "Are you saying he has a drinking problem?"

Francesca laughed and covered her mouth, causing Gio to do the same.

"What? What did I say?" Chase asked.

Gio explained, "I was an altar boy and Father Leo doesn't like to drink more wine than he has to, so when he'd fill the chalice for Mass, he'd guess how much he'd need, based on how many people were in the pews."

Francesca continued the explanation, saying, "You don't want to run short, so the priest puts in a little extra. Except in Father Leo's case, he'd go heavy on the wine and have too much."

Chase, thinking she understood, asked, "So what happens then, you dump it down the drain?"

This brought another laugh, when Francesca said, "I keep forgetting you're not Catholic. No, you can't because at that point of the Mass it's considered the blood of Christ. So, someone must drink it."

Chase marveled at the scenario, then asked, "Who?"

Gio raised his hand and said, "Me."

"You?" Chase asked surprised.

"Yeah," Gio continued, "Father Leo would drink as much as he could and then wave me over. Once he handed me half a glass and I had to go to school right after that."

Chase looked at the boy and said, "Oh my."

Francesca chimed in: "'Oh my' is right. He fell asleep in his math class—the teacher didn't know what to make of it."

"I just told my teacher, blame Father Leo," Gio said with a chuckle.

Nonna, listening to all of this, tapped Chase on the arm and said, "He'll help you, the father."

Chase looked at her watch and said, "I should have enough time to shower, stop by Santa Maria church, and get over to Gavin at, whatever that place was called."

Francesca said the name slowly so Chase wouldn't forget it, "Bah-ca-no."

Jules was kind enough to give Chase a ride over to church, even though it was only a few blocks away. For the first time since she'd arrived in Rome, Chase noticed how many nativity scenes were set up around the city. Back home in America, you might see one outside a church or on the lawn of a random home, but here? The three wise men and the rest of the gang were plentiful.

When she opened the church door, Chase noticed the same young man who helped her catch Scooter when he broke free, kneeling quietly alone. Gavin told Chase he thought he had seen the teen near the shipping yard, and definitely, a third time, when she was visiting the candy shop, but the boy ran off. Chase was curious why this boy was so aloof, but he was in church praying, so she thought it best to leave the matter alone.

"Father?" she called out, getting the priest's attention.

Leo was dressed in jeans and a gray T-shirt, his work gloves filthy from the morning's labor.

"I almost didn't recognize you," Chase said.

"Yes," the priest responded, "moving some tables and chairs up from the basement, it's amazing how dirty things can get."

Father Leo took off the gloves and tossed them on a pew, saying, "You were cryptic when you called. How can I help you?"

Chase made a pained face and replied, speaking very quickly, "This is a bit awkward, 'cause I'm not what you'd call a regular churchgoer. I mean, I like church when I'm there but it's not something I normally do. And since I don't normally go, I hope you don't mind me asking for some advice. I'd understand if you thought it was strange, me coming here."

The priest raised both hands, stopping her, and said, "Noah could have built the ark in the time it takes you to ask a question. What do you need?"

Chase smiled and replied, "Gavin and I are to be married Christmas Eve and we can't do it in a church like this 'cause I'm not Catholic. I guess my question is, do you know of someone who does the kind of nondenominational, bingo bongo, sprinkle some fairy dust on it and go live happily ever after, ceremony?"

"Bingo bongo?" the priest asked with a grin. "Is that from the Old or New Testament?"

Chase shrugged and said, "Sorry. *Bingo bongo* does sound like something you'd see in an ad for the Gap."

Father Leo replied, "You could get married at the Gap. Believe it not, we have them here in Rome along with McDonald's and Burger King."

Chase smiled, paused, and then got serious, saying, "I don't want you thinking I'm taking my vows lightly. I adore Gavin and we *WILL* be together forever."

The priest looked into Chase's eyes and said, "I can see that. So, not a priest, but someone to help you with the vows, correct?"

Chase nodded silently, and Leo surprised her when he said, "Do you remember my brother, Levi? He was here playing chess with me the day your dog came crashing in."

Chase thought back and said, "Yes, kind of."

"Well," Father Leo replied. "He's what you might call a monk, who lives at a retreat on an island, BUT he's also licensed and can perform marriage ceremonies."

Chase lit up, "Do you think he'd do it? We'd need him Christmas Eve."

Father Leo rose from the pew and said, "I can give him a call for you. I'm sure if he's free he'd be happy to help."

Chase extended her hand to shake the priest's and said, "Thanks a lot, padre, I knew you'd help me."

Chase looked over and realized the teen she'd seen several times before was gone, always leaving as quietly as he came in.

As Chase looked down at her phone to see what time it was, Father Leo said, "Before you go, can I ask one question?"

Chase smiled and said, "Sure."

The priest leaned on the top of the pew and asked, "Is your *not going to church* because you were never taken as a child, or did something happen to sour you on the whole thing?"

Chase, being a writer, loved asking questions, but had never been on the receiving end of one so pointed and complex at the same time.

"Hmm," she began. "I guess I never really thought about it."

Chase was silent a moment, then said, "The short answer is, my mom only took me a few times a year for the big ones—Christmas, Easter, you know?"

"I do," he replied. "Every priest on the planet is associated with that phenomenon." He then asked, "Now. What's the long answer?"

Chase took a deep breath, exhaled, and said, "Are we really having this conversation right now?"

The priest looked around at the now empty church and said with a welcoming smile, "I think we are, yes."

Chase looked off, as if thinking, then said, "The truth is, some of what the church sells is hard to buy or at least understand."

Father Leo, undaunted, asked, "Give me a *for example*."

Chase paused again, then said, "Okay, for example, God sends his only son, Jesus, down to help us, knowing it's going to end bad for him."

"Beyond bad," the priest added, pointing to a crucifix hanging behind the altar.

"If he loved his son, why would he do that?" Chase asked. "Why not fix things from above and not put the poor guy through all that?"

The priest walked in a small circle thinking, causing Chase to say, "I'm sorry if it's a stupid question. I've always just wondered."

The father raised his right hand up and said, "Heavens no, it's a great question, Chase, one that scholars have been debating for centuries."

Chase smiled and said, "Do they ever come up with a good answer?"

Father Leo stopped pacing, smiled back, and said, "Yes, they do."

He then asked, "What do you do for a living? You and your fiancé?"

"I'm a writer and he's a farmer," Chase answered.

"A farmer?" the priest said, "Perfect. You're a writer, so you must like stories."

"Sure," Chase answered.

Father Leo said, "Once there was a terrible snowstorm coming and a farmer did all he could do to secure his home and animals. He put extra hay in the barn, some heating lamps to stave off the cold, and secured all the latches and locks, until everyone was safe."

Chase could imagine Gavin and his father back on the farm in Vermont, doing that exact thing before a storm, so she said, "Go on."

"The storm hits," the priest continued. "And it's worse than anyone expected, with raging, blinding snow, and wind. A true blizzard."

Chase leaned back on the pew waiting for the rest.

The priest said, "Everyone was safe, but then the farmer saw a flock of beautiful birds outside caught in the storm. He knew they were doomed if he didn't do something to help them."

"What did he do?" Chase asked.

"Well, he ran out and opened the barn door, giving them a place to go," the priest replied.

Chase then asked, "Did they fly in?"

"No," Father Leo answered, "They couldn't see it through the snow, so the farmer put some large powerful lights just inside the open barn door."

"And then they flew in? Chase asked.

The priest grimaced, then answered, "No, the light seemed to scare them, so they flew in circles and eventually landed in a tree with no leaves or protection from the storm."

"Did they die? I don't think I like this story if they die," Chase said sincerely.

Father Leo leaned in and said, "No, Chase, they didn't die. The farmer found a way to turn himself into a bird and he flew out the window, leaving the safety of his home, into that terrible storm."

"What happened to him?" Chase asked.

The priest moved even closer to Chase now, so she wouldn't miss his words, saying, "Because he became one of them, he got the birds to follow him toward the light and safety and he saved everyone."

Chase was quiet a moment thinking about the story.

Then the priest said, "I know I'm not officiating your marriage, but I'll give you some free advice."

Chase looked over and listened.

"Act that way with Gavin and he with you, risking it all and putting each other first," the priest said, "and your love will last forever."

Chase looked up at the altar and the large cross with the suffering Christ, pointed and said, "Your story: when you put it that way, what he did, it's pretty amazing."

Father Leo started walking toward the door that led back to the rectory and said, "I've always thought so."

He turned then, raising both hands out to his sides, looked up toward the ceiling of the beautiful church, and added, "That's why I'm here."

With that the kind priest said, "Good luck," before vanishing behind the door.

Over at Baccano, Gavin was waiting with a rose in his hand and a violinist ready to play upon Chase's arrival. The moment she sat at an outdoor table under a heat lamp, the music started, and Gavin took her hand.

"I wanted to meet you here because," Gavin began.

Only to have Chase shout, "WHAT? I CAN'T HEAR YOU."

Gavin looked at the violinist, a stout man with a large mustache, who was only three feet away, then back at Chase, raising his voice, "I WANTED TO MEET HERE BECAUSE—"

Chase held her hand up to her ear, indicating she still wasn't catching a word of it.

Gavin stood abruptly, peeled a twenty-euro bill from his wallet, and shoved it at the violinist, saying, "That's fine, we're good. You can go now."

The violinist, confused, said in a heavy Italian accent, "But you pay for half-hour."

Gavin pointed to people sitting at other tables and said, "I'll bet they'd love to hear you."

The violinist huffed in protest, "AMERICANS," before storming away, causing Chase and Gavin to burst out laughing.

"Why is it every time I try to do something romantic in Italy it back-fires?" Gavin asked.

Chase took his hand and said, "I thought it was sweet. So, what's up?"

The waiter came and Gavin ordered them both a glass of champagne, prompting Chase to ask, "Are we celebrating something?"

Gavin answered, "We were going to, but I changed my mind."

Chase then asked, "I'm lost, what's wrong?"

Gavin pointed off to their right, across the plaza and said, "Did you catch the view?"

Chase looked over and said, "Oh, WOW, the famous Trevi fountain. How did I not see that when I walked in?"

Chase looked back to Gavin and asked, "What about it?"

Gavin answered, "I've looked at about a dozen places to get married in Italy: on the beach, on top of cliff, under a famous bridge, and of course, the Trevi fountain."

"And what did you decide?" Chase replied, placing her chin on both hands, batting her eyes at him romantically.

"Keep that up and I'll marry you right here before we get appetizers," Gavin answered.

Chase leaned back and looked again at the fountain and saw swarms of people taking photographs and said, "It's pretty, but busy."

Gavin responded, "That's the problem. I got here twenty minutes early and I swear, Chase, three hundred people walked up and took photos in front of it."

Chase looked back at the fountain and said, "So, if we did get married in front of it, we'd have strangers photo-bombing our private moment, right?"

Gavin nodded, "Exactly. My plan was to show it to you over lunch and announce that's where we'd get hitched, but now—"

"Now, you want something more intimate?" Chase said, finishing his thought.

Gavin sighed and said, "Yeah, this isn't it."

The waiter brought the two glasses of champagne, causing Chase to raise her flute and announce, "Here's to you getting one perfect romantic idea then."

They clanged the glasses, took a sip, and Gavin replied, "Cupid, don't fail me now."

What Gavin didn't realize was, it wasn't Cupid, but a large bag of bird seed that would answer his prayers.

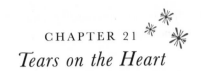

CHAPTER 21

Tears on the Heart

After lunch, Chase and Gavin returned home to relax.

Gavin took a glass down from the kitchen cabinet and started filling it with water, when Nonna said, "What are you doing?"

Gavin, answered, "Getting a drink."

"No, no," she said, taking the glass from Gavin's hand, dumping it in the sink.

She pointed toward the refrigerator and said, "Bottled water is better."

Gavin didn't understand the difference, but did as he was told, going to the fridge. As he reached for the handle, he noticed the previous letters stuck to the door were gone, replaced by new gibberish: CIBO PER UCCELLI.

After taking a bottle out and enjoying a healthy swig, Gavin pointed to the fridge door and said to Nonna, "This isn't a word, is it?"

Nonna looked over, answering, "Sì. *Cibo per uccelli* is bird food. I put it there to remind Francesca to buy some."

Gavin thought a moment, then asked, "Oh, for the garden, with the fountain, right?"

"Sì," Nonna answered. "We like to feed the birds, especially in winter."

"Do you have a favorite bird?" Gavin asked.

Nonna smiled, answering, "I always loved robins, but Alessandro's favorite was a bright red cardinal. He never got to see one in person though."

Gavin shrugged, asking, "Why not?"

Nonna replied, "We don't have cardinals in Rome, unless you count the ones who wear robes and live at the Vatican."

"None?" Gavin replied, surprised. "Not even one?"

Nonna smiled again, answering, "Not in all of Italy. So, if you see one let me know, because that would be something special."

Chase entered the room now and said, "Guess what, Nonna? Father Leo helped find a person to marry us!"

Nonna smiled, answering, "I knew he would. You have a place to be married?"

Chase looked at Gavin and he replied, "No. We thought we did but changed our mind."

Gio came into the kitchen, took a bright red apple out of a bowl, gave it a hearty chomp, and asked, "Changed your mind about what?"

Chase answered, "Where to be married. We were thinking the Trevi fountain, but it's too crowded."

Nonna joked to the couple then, saying, "So no church, no fountain, maybe you go to the Colosseum and have gladiators as ushers."

Chase smiled, answering, "If we don't figure something out soon it may come to that, Nonna."

Gio, still working on the apple and with mouth half full, asked, "What ever happened to your list? The four things the guy told you to do?"

Gavin looked at Gio, bewildered, then said, "Oh, at the Colosseum, the old man who was painting."

Gio pointed at Gavin and said, "Yes, that guy. You did three of them, right?

Chase said to Gio, "That's right. We gave our lock away at the bridge, our ride away in Venice, and we opened your grandfather's memory box and found the letter for Nonna."

Nonna reached into a pocket of her blouse and produced the letter, clutched tight in her hand.

"I keep it with me," Nonna said, rubbing the letter against her cheek.

Chase stood up and was staring at nothing, when Gavin asked, "What? What are you thinking?"

Chase turned and responded, "If we dial this thing back. You talk to that man in the Colosseum, and he says he'll give you four clues to finding true romance."

"Right," Gavin agreed.

Chase then replied, "They may not have worked out exactly as we had planned, but you can't deny that all three—the young couple, the man with ALS, the letter Nonna is holding now—are all really romantic."

Gavin nodded in agreement, "You're right, they were. They are."

"So?" Gio asked Gavin.

Gavin looked at the boy, waiting, then said, "What?"

Gio answered, "Finish the clues. What's number four?"

Gavin looked at Chase and she counted them out loud on her fingers, "Lock, kiss, letter, and puzzle."

Gio then asked, "Haven't they all been puzzles?"

"I guess you're right," Gavin answered. "But this last clue feels more literal."

"I don't know what that means," Gio replied.

Chase explained, "I think what Gavin means is, we should be looking for some kind of puzzle. Does anyone have suggestions?"

Chase looked at Nonna and Gio, and both seemed clueless on this one.

She then picked up her phone and said, "Hang on," punching in a name they couldn't see.

When Riley saw Chase's name appear on her cell phone, she answered on the first ring. "Hey, sweetie, how's my favorite American girl?"

"I'm good, thanks," Chase replied cheerfully. "I have you on speaker, and we have a question. Do you remember how the guy gave Gavin four clues to find romance?"

"Of course," she responded.

Chase continued, "Well, the fourth clue is the word *puzzle*. Does that mean anything to you? Is there some big puzzle that needs solving in Italy?"

Riley put her hand through her thick red hair, thinking, then said, "I can't think of anything, hon, but let me ask Tessa. She's here keeping me company."

Chase could hear Riley talking in Italian on the other end to Tessa, then she returned to the call saying, "The only thing she can think of is Villa Pisani in the town of Stra."

"Straw?" Chase asked, "Like you find in a barn?"

"No, Chase," Riley answered. "Stra, S-T-R-A. It's a town way up north, not far from Venice."

Gavin moved close to the phone now, saying, "Riley, it's Gavin. What is Villa Pisani?"

Tessa took the phone from Riley, answering, "It's a lot of things, Gavin, because it's a town, but I know it has a very cool outdoor maze made of hedges. This is Tessa, by the way."

"Oh, hi, Tessa," Gavin answered, and then asked, "A maze? Like the kind you get lost in?"

"Exactly," she answered. "But very beautiful and romantic."

Gavin looked at Chase and said, "It sounds nice, but is a maze really a puzzle? The word the guy used was *puzzle*."

Chase called back into the phone, "What do you ladies think?"

"Honestly, I don't know, guys," Riley said.

Chase thought a long moment in silence, prompting Riley to ask, "Chase, are you still there?"

"Yes, sorry," Chase replied. "Just thinking. Something tells me this Pisani place is not it, but thank you both for trying to help."

Riley replied, "If we think of something else, we'll let you know. Sounds like you and Gavin want to finish this romantic adventure."

Chase looked at Gavin again and said, "Maybe, but with just a little over a week to get married, we're not going to go *Chasing Rome* for the answer."

Tessa yelled into the phone again, "I hope we're invited, to the wedding I mean. I have a killer dress."

"Really?" Gio said. "What color?"

Nonna smacked the teen on the arm with a folded newspaper from the table, causing him to blush.

"What?" he replied. "I'm into fashion."

Gavin looked at him and said, "Especially if it's a beautiful woman wearing it?"

"Alright, alright, leave the boy alone," Chase said.

Then Chase called back into the phone, "Of course you're both invited. We'll let you know when and where. Bye, ladies."

Just as Chase hung up the phone, Francesca walked in with a grocery bag.

"Did you get everything?" Nonna asked.

"I did," Francesca replied, as she emptied a brown paper sack. "Fish, milk, chocolate, and a large bag of bird food."

As Nonna put the items away in the fridge, Gio picked up the bird seed and started curling it with one arm as if he was lifting weights at the gym.

"A hundred of these a day and I'll be as strong as you, Gavin," he said.

"No doubt," Gavin replied.

Gio then asked his mother, "Do you want me to take this out back and fill the feeder?"

Francesca smiled proudly at her son, and said, "That would be nice. Thank you, Giovanni."

Chase looked at Gavin and motioned with her eyes toward Gio.

This prompted Gavin to ask, "Do you want some help with the birds?"

The teen instantly smiled and said, "Sure, let's go."

Chase mouthed words *thank you* to Gavin as he and Gio headed for the door. Francesca saw this, and when Chase realized it, she wasn't sure if Francesca would be annoyed with her meddling.

On the contrary, once the boys were gone, Francesca said out loud, "No, thank you. It's helping him, spending time with Gavin."

Chase didn't answer, she just looked back with kind eyes, happy for the boy.

Downstairs and around the back of the building, Gavin opened the gate to the secret passageway and the two of them snaked their way to the secret garden and fountain. A small pear tree was growing opposite the fountain, about thirty feet away, and hanging precariously from one of the branches was a wooden bird feeder.

As Gio stood beneath it and struggled to get the plastic tie off the end of the bird seed bag, two sparrows made expert landings on the fence to his right. They looked like restaurant patrons waiting for the *all you can eat* buffet to open.

He filled the feeder as best he could, with a fair amount of seed spilling out and bouncing off the hard ground at Gio's feet.

"That's the good thing about bird seed," Gio said to Gavin. "It's okay to spill it 'cause the birds will eat it anyway."

"Good point," Gavin answered.

As Gio closed the bag and did his best to refasten the tie, Gavin found himself looking from the pretty water fountain, over to the shed and the pile of bricks that lay haphazardly in the corner of the yard.

"You ready?" Gio asked.

There was no response. Gavin was standing still as that pear tree, his gaze fixed on the unfinished patio that Gio's grandfather died trying to complete.

"Earth to Gavin? Come in, Gavin?" Gio said jokingly.

Gio was starting to feel uncomfortable with the silence and lack of response, so he dropped the bag of seed to the ground and walked over to Gavin with haste.

"HEY," he said much louder.

Gavin seemed to snap out of whatever world he was in for those twenty seconds and turned to see the worry in Gio's face.

"Hey right back," he answered. "Were you calling me? I'm sorry."

Gio took his first breath in a minute and replied, "It's fine, you just scared me for a second."

Gavin put his hand on the boy's shoulder and looked at him a moment. He'd been in Rome nearly three weeks now, but this was the first time Gavin really looked at the boy. He didn't know his exact age, likely fifteen or sixteen by Gavin's estimate. A tough age because you are caught between the devil and the deep blue sea of childhood and what comes next.

There was more to this kid, though, and Gavin could see it. He'd had to grow up fast these last few months, losing his father and grandfather only weeks apart.

At sixteen, Gavin had only had to worry about milking the cows, basketball practice, and chasing girls around Manchester, Vermont. This kid had it all squarely on his narrow shoulders. Gavin felt such admiration for the boy at this moment, causing him to grin proudly.

"What?" Gio asked.

Gavin shook his head and replied, "Nothing. You're a good kid is all."

Gio didn't respond, uncertain what to say.

Gavin then pointed to the unfinished stonework and asked, "What does that look like?"

Gio looked down and said, "A patio."

Gavin shook his head no, then said, "Look again."

Gio did and kept staring, not sure what he was supposed to be seeing that wasn't there.

Gavin then asked, "Did you ever put a jigsaw puzzle together?"

Gio's eyes then traveled from the incomplete patio over to the pile of bricks his grandfather never got to finish.

He smiled and looked back at Gavin, saying, "Your fourth clue."

Gavin nodded in agreement. "My fourth clue. It was right in front of us the whole time."

Gio took another deep breath and asked, "So? Do we try to finish it?"

Gavin walked over to the pile of loose bricks, one on top of the other, gave them a gentle kick with his foot, and said, "I think we do."

Gavin poured the mortar mix into the large white bucket Gio's grandfather used, as the boy slowly added water from a hose.

"Not too much," Gavin cautioned. "You can always add more but you can't take water out."

Using the paint sticks Gavin had showed Gio earlier, demonstrating the power of family, the two of them mixed the mortar until they had just the right thickness.

Sand was placed on the bare ground; Gavin used a level to be certain things lined up correctly, and then the difficult process of choosing the right stones began. Alessandro, Gio's grandfather, did things the old way, meaning there were no blueprints or plans on how this project should proceed. They'd have to do it using instinct and common sense.

"Why don't we lay all the pieces out on the side so we can see what we have to work with," Gio suggested.

"Brilliant plan," Gavin replied, high-fiving the boy as he went by.

Ten minutes later the stones were lined up and the pair of new best friends started carefully laying them into place. The outside edges came easily but the corners and turns took a bit more thinking before they put them down. The mortar was used to hold them in place, and very quickly Gavin and Gio realized they were capable of doing this.

"Wait, some of these are a light shade of red," Gio observed.

Gavin saw it too, answering, "You're right.".

Gavin kept backing up from what they were working on but couldn't get the right perspective.

Finally, he looked up at the building behind them and said, "Who lives there?"

Gio answered, "Lots of people. Why?"

Gavin smiled mischievously, then said, "Come with me."

They walked around to the front of the building, went up the front steps, and saw a dozen doorbells with names they didn't recognize next to them.

"What are you doing?" Gio asked.

Gavin answered, "I want to look at the patio from above, so we need to get into this building."

Gio asked the obvious question, "What's wrong with our building?"

Gavin shot back, "Wrong angle, can't see the garden, has to be this one."

Gio then asked, "And how do you think we're getting into this building?"

Gavin smiled devilishly and said, "By ringing all the buzzers at once, not answering the call box and hoping someone gets so annoyed they buzz us in."

Gio considered the plan and asked, "And if they call the police?"

Gavin waved him off saying, "Ah, that never happens, but if they do, we run."

Gio looked around, already feeling guilty, then said to Gavin, "Worst plan ever in the history of plans."

Without hesitation, Gavin started hitting the buzzers all at once. They heard a few voices squawk out of the speaker above the buttons, all calling out in Italian, but Gavin didn't respond.

Finally, just as he predicted, someone hit the buzzer, followed by a loud click, and Gavin opened the front door.

Gio smiled and said, "I can't believe that worked."

"Let's go," Gavin said to his fellow miscreant.

Once inside, the pair went up the long staircase as high as it could go, and Gavin looked around for another door. Sure enough, he found it unlocked, and using the flashlight on his phone, the two went up to the roof.

"Do NOT walk to the edge," Gavin said to Gio. "Get down on your hands and knees and crawl over to look down."

Once they did, the pair peered over the side of the roof, directly down to the secret garden. They had to be six stories up but could easily make out the pattern in the unfinished patio below.

"Look on the left and right sides," Gio observed. "It looks like a vine in the stones."

Gavin saw it, then said to Gio, "Your grandfather was an artist. It's beautiful."

Then Gavin looked to the center of the patio, the part not finished, and said, "I know what he was planning to do. I've got it now."

"What?" Gio asked.

Gavin slid back, making certain to hold Gio by the arm as he did the same.

"What did you see?" Gio asked again.

Gavin winked and said, "I'd rather show you."

Once they got back downstairs, they quickly looped back around to the passageway and Alessandro's secret garden. Gavin went to work with the red stones, placing them in a pattern at the center of the patio.

In a matter of minutes, Gio saw it too.

"It's a heart," the teen exclaimed.

Gavin nodded and said, "We'll need more mortar."

For the next hour, they worked feverishly on the patio. So diligent was their labor that both took off their jackets because they were sweating in the cold December air.

Soon there was one round red stone left and Gavin made certain to hand it to Gio.

"For your grandfather," Gavin said.

Gio's eyes were filled with tears, realizing what they had done, finishing the dream that they thought had ended with Alessandro's life. He placed the final stone in the center of the heart and, just as with an elaborate puzzle, his vision was complete.

Both stepped back to see the fruits of their labor. A large stone patio with vines running up each side, and at the center, a beautiful red heart. It was so perfect you could almost hear it beating.

Both stood speechless, looking at Alessandro's dream, now complete, when a voice called from behind, "How long does it take to feed birds?"

It was Francesca with Nonna and Chase, the three coming down, worried because the boys had been gone so long.

Chase saw it first, the completed patio, and said, "What did you two do?"

Francesca raised her hand to her face, touching her trembling lips, trying to stifle tears, but it was Nonna who was the most stunned. She gently moved the other ladies aside and walked to the center of the patio, the heart resting beneath her feet.

No one spoke as she looked down, her silent tears falling and wetting the dry red stone. The moisture from her tears on the heart made it glow even brighter.

Francesca looked over at Gavin and Gio and said, "You boys are something."

After putting the tools away and locking the shed, the five of them made their way toward the passageway that would guide them home.

Gio then asked, "Hey Gavin, can we look at it from the roof of the other building? It must look so cool from up there."

Francesca stopped and said, "Absolutely not, young man. Do you think I'm going to let you on a rooftop?"

Gio replied, "But mom, we already—"

Gavin grabbed the boy firmly for a hug and said, "Listen to your mother, Giovanni."

Francesca, suspicious, looked at Chase, who in turn squinted her eyes and said, "Gavin Michael Bennett, is there something you want to tell us?"

Gavin looked from Chase, to Francesca, to Nonna, then to Gio, and said, "Nope."

As they started toward the stairs Gavin gave Gio a gentle kick on his backside, hoping no one saw it.

Chase did, asking, "What was that for?"

Gavin flashed that country boy smile and answered, "He had a bug on him."

CHAPTER 22

Not a Police Matter

With the four clues complete, Chase and Gavin felt a sense of accomplishment and liberation. The artist who set the couple on this path may well have vanished, but his four suggestions on where they would find true romance were unmistakably perfect. Seeing Nonna so happy, standing in her late husband's secret garden, made the entire trip worth it.

When morning came the two decided to take that long overdue walk to see Rome's biggest attraction.

"Give me your hand and don't let go," Chase said, as the two walked side by side in St. Peter's Square in Vatican City.

It was exactly three miles from the apartment in the Monti neighborhood to St. Peter's, and the sunshine was kind as the lovers made the slow walk over. Both agreed the trip home would be by taxi, but for now they were enjoying the view at one of the most iconic places on earth.

The square is embraced, like two large arms, by two oval-shaped colonnades with nearly three hundred columns each. Piercing the cobalt blue sky above, Chase saw dozens of white statues keeping watch on everything below.

"Who are they again?" Chase asked Gavin, knowing he had spent hours poring over tourism books.

"Let's see," he said pointing up. "That one is a monument to Derek Jeter and over there is Magic Johnson."

Chase gave him a gentle shove and said, "Ha, ha. Tell me for real?"

Gavin stopped and squinted as he looked up at several statues, saying, "They're saints and martyrs, I think. Some with names you'd know, most you wouldn't."

They thought about taking a Vatican tour, but Gavin wanted to get back and make an important phone call to the monk Levi about their wedding.

Chase hugged him tight and said, "It's all becoming so real, I can't wait. Let's grab a cab."

A half-hour later, when Chase and Gavin returned, an argument was underway at the apartment between Francesca, Nonna, and a police detective named Stefano Bianco.

Chase could hear the raised voices as she came up the stairs and decided to knock loudly before opening the door.

"Come in," Francesca called, her eyes staying fixed on the detective.

When Gavin saw the older man standing in the kitchen in a neatly tailored blue uniform, he instantly felt protective of his new Italian family and puffed out his chest, before asking, "Is everything alright?"

The officer launched into a barrage of Italian words, when Francesca waved her hand in front of his face and said, "They only speak English— say it in English, *per favore.*"

Officer Bianco nodded out of respect for the American couple and said in a strong Italian accent, "I'm sorry. I was explaining to them that there is nothing I can do, the weather is the weather."

Francesca turned to Chase and said, "This is about my husband's death. He investigated the boating accident and says a boat getting caught in a storm is not a matter for police."

The officer, listening to Francesca's explanation, took on a very apologetic tone, saying, "Ladies, I am heartbroken over your loss, but this is not a police matter."

Gavin then asked, "If it's not a police matter, why are you here? And who are you with, anyway?"

Officer Bianco produced a small business card from his shirt pocket, handed it to Gavin, and said, "I'm with La Polizia di Stato, the National Police, stationed in Rome."

Gavin took the card, saw it looked legit, then said, "Go on, you were saying."

Officer Bianco explained, "Whenever there is a death of an Italian citizen we investigate, and, in this case, we had three people die. But a storm felled the ship, and there is no evidence of, how you say in English, foul play."

Gavin nodded and asked, "And you're here to tell them that?"

"Sì," Bianco replied in a hushed tone. "It felt like news, best told in person. I'm sorry, but the case is closed."

With that the officer bowed his head and excused himself from the room, closing the door gently behind him as he left. Chase and Gavin saw Nonna fall back into a kitchen chair, emotionally exhausted over the death of her son.

The front door opened again, and it was Gio this time, with a look of hope in his eyes, asking his mother, "The police again? Is there something new in Papà's case?"

His mother's look gave Gio his answer, without the need for words.

"I see," the teen said, before hanging his head and heading toward his room, a black backpack bursting with schoolbooks hanging from his shoulder.

Nonna got up from her chair then and went to the left side of the kitchen, opening a drawer that was filled with papers, bills, and letters.

She pulled one specific envelope out, tore it in half, and said, "*Finito,*" before tossing it into the garbage can in the corner.

Francesca hugged her mother-in-law and said, "I'm done too."

Chase looked at Gavin, still not certain what was happening at this moment.

Gavin, reading her face, asked Francesca, "Are you two okay?"

Francesca, looking exhausted herself, replied, "Yes, we just wish Matteo's death mattered to these people."

Gavin replied, "You mean the police?"

"The *polizia,* the boat company, all of them," Francesca answered.

Chase looked away, uncertain how to help, and saw the half-torn envelope sticking up from the trash. She saw the return address in the upper left-hand side and was able to make out four letters: C R A N.

She crossed the room then and picked up the two pieces of the envelope and put them back together, allowing her to read the entire name: CRANE SHIPPING.

Her mouth dropped open as she turned to Gavin. "Wait. Gavin? Crane Shipping? Isn't that the place you went to the day we were in Lido di Ostia?"

Gavin looked at the envelope in her hands and said, "Yes, there were two shipping places there. The large one where they were nice to me and—"

"Crane," Chase answered for him.

"Yes," Gavin said, taking the envelope from Chase's hand.

Gavin stared at the name, then held it up and asked Francesca, "Why do you have a letter from Crane?"

Nonna answered, "It tells us what we tell you already, the accident wasn't their fault and they sorry, but they owe us nothing."

"Wait a second," Chase called out with surprise. "Are you saying the boating company your husband died on, the one that was giving him a ride to work, that was Crane?"

"Yes," Nonna answered. "Matteo took rides with them sometimes if he had work on one of the islands."

Francesca looked seriously at Chase now, asking, "Why are you asking about Crane Shipping? What did you mean Gavin went there?"

Chase quickly took a seat at the kitchen table and explained. "When we saw the letters Scooter barked at on the fridge for Ostia and then learned that the artist who painted the picture at your gallery had Lido in his name—you remember that's why we went to that town?"

"Right, but how does that involve Crane?" Francesca responded.

Chase went on, "I walked around the town, which led me to Siena and the candy shop, while Gavin went to the beach and docks."

Gavin joined in now, saying, "The beach was empty, but at the docks, I walked onto Crane's property, and they were rude and chased me right out of there."

"Chasing you? Why?" Nonna asked.

"I don't know, Nonna," Gavin replied. "But they didn't want anyone snooping around."

Chase snapped her fingers and pointed at Gavin, saying, "That's also the place you saw that kid from church!"

Gavin moved closer to Chase now. "That's right, twice in Ostia, once at Crane, and the other time a few blocks away."

"He must work there," Chase guessed out loud.

"Who? What kid?" Francesca asked. "You two are confusing me."

Gavin answered, "There's a kid, late teens or early twenties, who is always at Nonna's church praying. I saw him at Crane Shipping, and he looked at me like he had seen a ghost."

Nonna got up and went to the window, looking out to see some gentle flurries drifting by the glass, then asked, "What does this have to do with anything?"

Chase looked at Gavin and answered, "Maybe nothing, Nonna."

Everyone was silent a moment when Gavin said, "Do you want to go to the church and see if we can find that kid?"

Chase nodded, "I do."

"Why?" Francesca asked.

Chase paused and said, "Something is spooking him. It might be why we keep seeing him at Santa Maria church."

Francesca again, asking, "What will you ask him?"

Chase looked Francesca in the eyes and said, "Two words: What's wrong?"

Nonna then said, "Church is closed right now, but there is a five o'clock Mass later today."

Chase wanted to go this instant, to find that kid and ask him why he was so reluctant to speak to anyone. Maybe he was just shy. Sure, that could be it—teenagers are strange by nature. Chase assured herself of that fact, again and again in her head. Yet something about that explanation didn't ring true. There was more to this; she felt it, as sure as she felt Gavin put his loving hand on her shoulder to get her attention.

"Chase?" Gavin asked. "Hon, are you listening?"

Chase broke her stare away from the kitchen wall and said, "What? No, I'm not. Sorry."

"I said," Gavin answered, "why don't we have some lunch? I'll call the monk, Brother Levi, to ask about the wedding, and you can rest a bit before we head to Santa Maria church."

Chase smiled and said, "Sounds like a plan."

Chase turned to Francesca and said, "Do you have the menu for that place down the block? We can order a sandwich or something."

Nonna rose immediately and said, "*Sedetevi, sedetevi, sedetevi.*"

Chase looked at Gavin, confused, when Francesca said, "She's saying *sit, sit, sit.* Both of you."

Nonna took out a large white bowl and announced, "*Zuppa di verze e patate.* With bread."

The old woman poured it into a large pot on the stove, causing Gavin to ask, "Is that soup?"

Francesca answered, "Best you've ever had."

Gavin saw Nonna fire up the gas stove and asked, "Wouldn't it be quicker to heat it in the microwave?"

Nonna spun around with a long wooden spoon in her hand and shook it, yelling, "*ESCI DA QUI!*"

"She's telling you to get out of the kitchen," Francesca explained.

Francesca then said, "Don't ever tell Nonna to cook with a microwave unless you want to get thumped in the head with a spoon."

Gavin respected the older woman's ways and replied, in his best fake Italian accent, "*Mi scusi.*"

He and Chase quickly retreated from the kitchen and waited to be summoned for lunch ten minutes later.

The soup, a cabbage, potato, and bean mixture, was just as advertised, absolutely delicious. Served with crusty bread, it was filling enough for two meals.

The full tummy made Chase want to step away for a short afternoon nap.

"Sounds tempting," Gavin said. "But I'm going to go to the café across the street for an espresso and call this monk."

Chase smiled at the thought asking, "Do monks have cell phones?"

Gavin replied, "I sure hope so."

With that the couple gave each other a peck on the lips and parted ways for the next two hours.

When Chase awoke from her slumber and came out of the bedroom, soft music filled the apartment.

"This is pretty," Chase said, as she entered the living room. "Who is it?"

Nonna replied, "Andrea Bocelli, 'Time to say Goodbye.'"

Chase listened to the lyrics, some of them in English, and suddenly got very sad.

Nonna saw it in her eyes and asked, "What's wrong, *mia dolce?*"

Chase realized she had a tear in her eye and wiped it, answering, "God, I'm such a pile of mush sometimes. Sorry."

"Is alright, Chase," Nonna said, taking her hand for the first time since they met.

Chase then pointed to the sky, and said, "These lyrics, 'time to say goodbye.' I just realized Gavin and I will be married soon, and I don't think I ever want to say goodbye to you and your beautiful family."

Nonna squeezed Chase's hand and said, "We always your family, Chase."

Chase smiled warmly at this woman who was truly starting to feel like her real grandmother, and asked, "What does *mia dolce* mean? You called me *mia dolce.*"

Nonna replied, "*Sweetie*—it means *sweetie*, which you are."

In the other room, Gavin was waiting for Chase to wake, and he had an expression on his face that Chase had seen before.

"What?" Chase asked, "I know that look."

Gavin picked up his phone and said, "So, to answer your earlier question, yes, monks have phones, and they pick up on the first ring."

"You spoke to him then, Brother Levi?" Chase asked.

"Yes," Gavin answered, "and he's ninety-nine percent sure he'll officiate and marry us on Christmas Eve."

"Ninety-nine percent. Not a hundred?" Chase replied.

Gavin let out a deep breath and said, "He wants to meet me in person first."

"Okay," Chase answered, "like here in Rome?"

"No," Gavin said, "on his island. Elba."

Chase then asked, "Well, how far is that?"

Gavin scrunched his face and answered, "By car and then ferry, five hours."

"FIVE?" Chase replied.

"Each way," Gavin finished.

"Ouch," Chase said. "Well, that kills a whole day."

"Yes, it does," Gavin agreed. "But I like the guy and I think he's the one to marry us."

Chase then responded, "Well, saddle up, cowboy, and get going."

Gavin then asked, "And what will you be up to while I'm meeting the monk with the cell phone?"

"One of us has to go to church and find that young man from Crane Shipping, remember?" Chase replied.

"Wait a second," Gavin replied sharply. "I don't want you talking to that kid alone."

"I won't be alone," Chase shot back. "Father Leo will be there."

"And I too," Nonna said, adding, "I wanted to go to Mass anyway."

Gavin thought a moment and said, "So, that's the plan. You go to church, me to the island of Elba."

Francesca heard voices and the music and entered the room now, saying, "Nonna, again with the Andrea Bocelli?"

The old woman smiled and joked, "He's my singing boyfriend."

Francesca then asked, "Did you say you were going to the island of Elba?"

"Yes," Gavin replied, "to lasso us a preacher for our service."

"Ah, very good," Francesca answered back. "Long trip, have fun."

Chase was lost in thought and asked Francesca, "I'm curious, Francesca. You said your husband, Matteo, was on that boat going to fix something on an island."

"That's right," she answered.

Francesca could already see where Chase's mind was going, so she added, "But it wasn't Elba, it was the island of Capraia, a bit farther north."

"Gotcha," Chase replied. "Hey, Nonna, you want to get to church early? I'm going to be on a stakeout."

Nonna, clearly confused, asked, "Steak, like you eat?"

Chase smiled and answered, "I'll explain on the way."

Gavin raised up his cell phone and said, "Jules says he'll drive me to a place called Piombino, to catch the ferry to Elba. He's on the way to get me."

"Good," Chase answered. "Now give me a kiss before you go."

As Gavin shared a gentle kiss, he asked, "How was your nap?"

Chase thought a moment and said, "Now that you mention it, kind of weird."

"Oh boy," Francesca said, "Don't tell me you saw more writing in the sand."

"No, nothing like that," Chase answered. "Something else. Nothing really."

Gavin sighed and asked, "And what does *nothing really* look like?"

Chase got herself a glass of fresh orange juice and after taking a sip said, "I dreamt I was back on a beach and there was lots of mist like before."

"Okay," Gavin said, "And?"

"I looked at my feet but there was no writing in the sand this time," Chase explained.

"But?" Gavin asked again.

"I could hear this weird noise but couldn't see what it was," Chase explained.

She could see them all looking at her, waiting for more. "The only way I could describe it is—have you ever put a sheet out on a clothesline to dry and the wind whips it around?"

Nonna said, "We used to dry all our clothes that way when I was a little girl."

"Right," Chase said, pointing at Nonna. "Then you know, when the wind blows hard it makes a sound, the sheet flapping in the breeze."

Gavin looked at her and asked, "And you could hear that sound but not see it?"

Chase took another sip from the glass and said, "Yep. Too much mist. Like I said, just a weird dream."

Gavin had been with Chase long enough to know that moments like this, what most would write off as silly or strange, often carried great weight and meaning. But right now, he had to get downstairs and into a car for a long journey off the coast. He'd have plenty of time to decipher Chase's dream along the way.

"Will you be back tonight?" Chase asked.

"Yes, I should get there by six, meet Levi quick, then catch the last ferry at eight," Gavin replied.

Francesca then, doing the math, said, "That doesn't get you back home here until after midnight."

"All the more reason to get moving. Love you," Gavin said. "All of you."

As he closed the door behind him, Nonna pointed at it and said to Chase, "All the fish in the sea, that's the one you keep."

Chase smiled and said, "Don't I know it!"

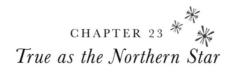
Chase and Nonna got to church a half-hour before Mass was to begin at five. They were greeted by large red candles to their left, a marble bowl with holy water to the right, and three people already taking up residence in the empty pews.

Chase looked around, then said, "Shoot," acknowledging the teen from the shipping yard was not here.

Father Leo saw Nonna and Chase standing in the back of the church and gave them a friendly wave. The pair approached, taking a seat in the front row as their stakeout began.

It was one-hundred and sixty miles from the apartment in Rome to the ferry at Piombino, and Gavin spent half of it thinking about Chase's odd dream and strange sounds in the mist.

"If there's something to it, I'm lost," Gavin announced from the front seat, as he looked out the window.

"Lost?" Jules replied. "We're not lost."

"No," Gavin said, "I'm, just talking to myself."

The ferries back and forth to the Island of Elba ran every two hours, and Gavin got there right on time to catch one. There were chairs on the open top deck, but the late December air carried a bite, so Gavin sat inside where it was warm.

As the ferry pulled into the long dock on Elba, Gavin noticed a man, by himself, holding a long bamboo fishing pole.

When Gavin stepped off the boat, the fisherman made eye contact with him, prompting Gavin to ask, "Anything biting?"

The man smiled and said, "No, they never do this late in the season."

Gavin, curious now, commented, "Maybe it's your bait."

The fisherman pulled the line from the water and said, "Hot dogs, you mean?"

Gavin laughed, "Hot dogs? I've never heard of someone using those."

"Oh, they work," the man replied. "Just not when it's this chilly."

As Gavin attempted to leave the dock, the fisherman said, "Besides, I already caught what I came here for. Gavin, right?"

Gavin quickly put two and two together, asking, "Brother Levi?"

"In the flesh," the monk answered.

The two shook hands, the monk retrieved his fishing line, and together they started up a stone path toward a hill and the hermitage where Levi lived with the others.

The sun was low in the sky, but just before they reached the house, Gavin saw spotlights hitting a long stone wall that bordered the yard. Gavin heard tapping and clicking sounds that grew louder with each step.

Then he saw it, three men dressed in brown robes, working on a rock wall.

"Building it or taking it down?" Gavin asked Levi.

"Fixing it," Levi answered. "Come help us."

Gavin looked at his watch, but before he could speak, Levi said, "Don't worry, we have lots of time."

Back at the church in Rome, the five o'clock Mass came to an end. Father Leo would hear confessions right after the service, and the church regulars were all jockeying to be first in line to spill their sins.

Unfortunately for them, a teenaged boy who had quietly slipped in was already standing by the confessional.

Chase saw him, nudging Nonna with her elbow, saying, "That's him. That's the kid from the shipping company."

Nonna wasn't sure what Chase thought she could learn from the boy, but she nodded and said, "You go, I wait."

Chase started across the church to approach the teen, just as he disappeared into the confessional. Two minutes felt like an hour as

Chase waited for the young man to emerge. She positioned herself perfectly between the confessional and the only door out, so the kid had to run into her.

When he finally appeared, Chase approached and said, "Don't run off, I just want to meet you."

The teen stopped, and as Chase examined his face, she could sense he was harmless and scared.

"I don't want to hurt you," Chase began. "Just talk for a moment, please."

The boy nodded yes and pointed to the back of the church where it was empty and quiet.

"What's your name?" she asked.

He looked thoughtfully at Chase and answered, "Flavio."

Chase paused and said, "Flavio, my fiancé saw you at Crane Shipping. Do you work there?"

He nodded, without speaking.

"He said when he tried to talk to you, you ran off," Chase said. "Can I ask you why?"

Flavio swallowed hard and said, "We're not supposed to talk to strangers."

Chase then asked, "When you say *we,* do you mean the employees at Crane?"

"Sì," Flavio answered anxiously. "Can I go now?"

"One more minute, Flavio, please," Chase replied.

Chase decided to just take a chance and explain why she was here, saying, "Do you see that old woman sitting in the pew up front?"

Flavio looked toward Nonna, nodding again.

"Her son died on one of Crane's boats, with two other men," Chase said. "They got caught in a storm. Do you know what I'm talking about?"

The teen's eyes seemed to dart away from Chase's now. He looked nervous, and finally he answered, "I can't talk about that."

Chase, feeling a bit aggravated now, shot back, "Why not? It was an accident, right? An act of God is what everyone called it."

Flavio looked like he wanted to jump out of his skin, pacing in a small circle just inside the church's front door.

"Flavio?" Chase said.

The boy suddenly got close to Chase, making her wonder if he was about to put his hands on her.

Instead, he put his face next to hers and whispered, "God had nothing to do with it. Now please, I must go."

With that the elusive teen pushed through the church doors and was gone into the night.

Chase returned to Nonna and as they were about to leave, she saw Father Leo wrapping up his last confession.

As the priest approached the altar, Chase moved quickly to him and asked, "What did that boy tell you?"

Father Leo grimaced and said firmly to Chase, "You may not be Catholic, but you know I cannot repeat what anyone tells me in confession."

Chase, clearly frustrated, said, "That's great, father. Thanks for all the help."

She returned to the pew and said, "Let's go, Nonna."

As the two women started down the church's main aisle, Father Leo called out, "Did you ask him why he's here at church so much?"

Chase stopped and answered, "No. I asked him about the place where he works."

Father Leo looked around, making certain others weren't listening, and called out, "You should ask him why he's here."

Chase stood motionless, not sure how to respond to that when the priest said, "That's all the help I can give you."

Chase took Nonna by the hand and the pair started home.

Back on the Island of Elba, Gavin was helping Levi and the others repair a stone wall.

"Where's the mortar?" Gavin asked. "Don't you need mortar to secure the stones?"

"No," Levi answered, "We do it the old way, look."

The priest was pointing to a large pile of rocks of all shapes and sizes.

"I don't understand," Gavin replied.

Levi said, "Watch what the others do. You find a gap in the wall, choose the exact stone to fit in that gap, and then use a hammer to tap it into place."

Gavin watched a moment, and that's exactly what the three monks were doing, sorting through hundreds of stones to find the perfect size, then tapping it in place.

Gavin spotted part of the wall that needed support, fished through the pile of stones, and returned with one that was just right.

As he tapped it, Gavin said, "This is kind of fun."

"Relaxing, isn't it?" Levi said. "Just ask Brother Marco."

Gavin saw a man in his sixties smile and wave hello without speaking.

Levi pointed at the men now, saying, "That's Marco, David, and the youngest of the bunch, Tommaso."

All three men continued working in the shadows of nightfall.

Then Levi said to Gavin, "Those discarded stones make a nice metaphor for life, don't you think?"

Gavin looked at rocks asking, "How so?"

"Big, small, long, wide, jagged," Levi said, "We're all just stones looking for a place to fit."

Gavin looked up at the monk's beautiful house, with the lights coming on inside, and asked, "And you fit here?"

Levi nodded, "I do."

Gavin then asked, "But no girls? Ever?"

The monk smiled and said, "That is the discipline."

As Gavin searched for another rock to work on the wall, Levi said jokingly, "But we do have plenty of time to fish."

"With hot dogs," Gavin answered, flashing his smile.

"As for your wedding," Levi said, changing the subject. "You adore this woman?"

Gavin stopped hammering, looking up, answered, "With all my heart."

"And you'll stay true to her?" Levi asked.

Gavin pointed his hammer up to the sky and replied, "As true as the northern star." \

Levi extended his hand to shake Gavin's and said, "Then I'd be happy to marry you both on Christmas Eve."

Just as Gavin was thinking about getting back to the dock and that ferry ride to the mainland, Levi snapped his fingers and said, "Speaking of northern stars, Tommaso, how is the compass?"

The younger monk, a man in his early forties, with a nasty scar above his left eye, reached into his pocket and produced a small bronze compass.

Tommaso held it up for Levi to see and said, "Works perfectly."

After returning the compass to his pocket, the monk said, "I'm going to head up."

As Tommaso and the others put down their tools and went into the house, Gavin said, "I should be heading home as well. Long drive ahead."

"Oh, I know it well," Levi replied. "I make it at least once a month for my epic chess match with my brother."

Gavin thought a moment and replied, "Yeah, I remember seeing you both at the chessboard in the church the day our dog got loose."

"I remember that day," Levi replied. "When Chase gave chase."

Gavin laughed, "She sure did."

As they reached the dock and Gavin stepped back on the boat to go, Levi called out, "Where are you getting married?"

Gavin smiled and said, "Up until this moment I would have told you I wasn't sure, but now I have the perfect place in mind. Let me talk to Chase first, then I'll call you."

"Sounds good," Levi answered with a wave. "Safe travels."

Just as expected, Gavin and Jules didn't get back to Rome until just shy of 1 a.m. He was shocked when he climbed the stairs to the apartment and found Chase awake and sitting at the kitchen table.

As he came through the door, both said at the same time, "I have to tell you something important."

Gavin laughed at the coincidence, then said, "By the look on your face, I think you should go first,"

Chase began, "I talked to that teen from the shipping yard."

"YOU DID?" Gavin exclaimed. "What did he say?"

Chase, obviously frustrated, answered, "It's what he didn't or wouldn't say."

"What wouldn't he say?" Gavin asked.

Chase got up and paced the kitchen floor, then lowered her voice to a whisper, answering, "I don't want to upset any of them," gesturing toward the bedrooms where Nonna, Francesca, and Giovanni were asleep.

She continued, "But that kid knows something about what happened to Matteo and the others on that boat."

"The cop called it an accident, a storm," Gavin replied.

Chase just shook her head defiantly, "I'm telling you there's more to this."

Gavin paced the floor along with her, thinking, then asked, "So what now? I mean if the police closed the case, and the kid won't talk?"

"Flavio, that's his name," Chase said.

"Okay, Flavio. If Flavio won't talk to you, what then?" Gavin asked again.

Chase looked at Gavin and said, "Father Leo told me there's a reason Flavio is at church so much. I'm going to find out why."

Gavin yawned and said, "Now? Or can we play Nancy Drew tomorrow?"

Chase yawned herself and replied, "Sleep now, sleuth in the morning."

As Gavin took Chase's hand and was leading her back to her room for some much-needed sleep, she stopped and said, "Wait, what was it you had to tell me?"

Gavin hugged her and said, "Brother Levi is going to marry us, and I know where I want to say our vows."

Chase lit up with anticipation, asking, "Where?"

Gavin grinned and said, "It sort of affects everyone in the house, so I'll share that news in the morning."

Chase put her hands on her hips, "You're really going to make me wait?"

Gavin gave her a gentle kiss on the lips, "I really am."

With that, Gavin flipped the light switch on the wall and the house, so full of love and light, suddenly fell dark.

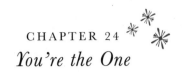
You're the One

Two blocks from their home in Rome sat Gio's favorite breakfast spot, a small café called La Licata that was known for its simple yet hearty meals. Gio had mentioned the place to Gavin when they were walking to the library the week before, so when everyone rose the next morning, Gavin instructed them to grab their coats and scarves, because he was taking them out for breakfast.

During tourist season, it would be impossible to get a table at La Licata, but with the eatery only half-full a few days before Christmas, the young hostess pushed two tables together for everyone to sit.

"Juice, Italian coffee, and caffè americano for the entire table," Gavin instructed the waiter. "And we're waiting on three more."

"Three?" Chase asked, surprised.

Right on cue, the small bell on the door rang and Jules, Riley, and Tessa all came in together.

"Hey," Chase called out excitedly, before giving her best friends in Rome a hug.

"This is on me," Gavin announced to the table.

Gio picked up his menu and teasingly said, "So, steak and lobster then."

"Who are you kidding?" Francesca commented. "You'll get blueberry crepes just like every time before."

As Gio laughed and everyone else perused the menu, Gavin tapped his water glass with a silver spoon, stood up and said, "If I could have your attention. I have a request of your family and our new friends here in Italy."

Everyone looked up in anticipation.

Gavin continued, "Levi, Father Leo's brother, has agreed to marry us on Christmas Eve."

"Yay," Riley called out, clapping her hands in approval.

"As you know," Gavin continued. "Chase and I have lots of family and friends back in America and it's too much to ask all of them to come."

Everyone seemed to nod in unison, understanding the logic and expense in that.

"So," Gavin went on. "We want to have a small ceremony here in Rome and we'd like all of you to be involved."

"How?" Francesca asked.

Gavin then crouched down, putting his head at Nonna's level, asking the grandmother of the house, "For starters, I've looked at every romantic place in Italy, but I can't think of a more perfect place to pledge my love to Chase forever, than the beautiful garden Alessandro built for you."

Nonna took Gavin's hands in hers and said, "The one you and Giovanni finish?"

"Yes," Gavin answered. "Is it okay with you if we get married there?"

Nonna smiled, answering, "*Certo*, Gavin. Of course."

Gavin rose to his feet again, took Chase's hand and asked, "How would you feel about getting married right in front of that heart in stone?"

Chase answered, her voice now quivering with emotion, "I think that would be perfect."

Gavin gave her a kiss on the cheek and then said to the table, "And to pull this off in three days I'm going to need all your help."

"Tell us what you need," Tessa said, clasping Riley's hand tightly in hers.

Chase rose from her chair now, her cheeks flush with excitement, saying, "Well, we'll need fresh flowers to brighten up the garden."

Riley stood and in her Irish accent announced, "I'm on it, luv, I know just the florist to help. This wedding is going to be the craic."

Everyone looked at Riley grinning, clearly not understanding what she'd just said.

"Crack?" Chase asked, confused.

"Craic? You don't know the word?" she asked.

Tessa stood next to her, saying, "Baby, they're not from County Cork."

"My apologies," Riley said. "C-R-A-I-C. It means fun."

Gio stood up, raised a glass of juice, and in his best Irish accent said, "I agree, this wedding is going to be the crack!"

Everyone joined in the toast, laughing at the silly boy.

As the waiter brought food, Nonna asked, "What about the party after—the, um, what you call it?"

"Reception?" Chase asked, trying to help.

"Yes," Nonna replied. "You must have a party after."

Gavin looked around the table and said, "Our families plan to have a big party for us in the spring, but I think Nonna is right."

"Meaning?" Francesca asked.

"We should have a celebration after the ceremony in Rome," Gavin answered.

Gio, while putting a fork into his hot crepes, shocked his family when he said, "What about Verdile's?"

The table fell silent, prompting Chase to ask, "What's Verdile's?"

Jules, who had been quiet the entire breakfast, then spoke, "It's a restaurant that's special to Francesca and Matteo, her late husband."

Gio, now regretting the suggestion, said, "I'm sorry. It's just that you love the food and it's right down the block. I just thought—"

With that the boy went silent, realizing he may have upset his mother.

Francesca patted Gio's hand on the table and said, "I think Verdile's is a great choice, Gio."

Chase looked at Gavin, and he, sensing the tension, said, "There are a million great places we can eat after the wedding. I mean, come on, we're in Rome."

Francesca smiled at Chase and said, "No, I think Verdile's would be perfect, and perhaps my Matteo will be there in spirit."

When the check came, Gavin peeled off a hundred euros, along with a generous tip.

As they started for the door Gio said to Gavin, "Best breakfast ever?"

Gavin gave Gio a high-five and said, "You know it."

Walking back to the apartment, Chase took hold of Gavin's hand and whispered in his ear, "I checked the Mass schedule, and Santa Maria church has a service at noon today."

Gavin looked at her and said, "You wanna?"

He didn't need to finish the question; Chase nodded. The two would make an excuse to break away from the others and find their way over to the church. If this teenager Flavio kept on schedule, he'd show up and Chase would have her chance to talk to him again.

"Actually," Chase said. "Can we stop home first? I want to grab my hat and gloves."

Gavin wrapped his arm around Chase, trying to keep her warm, as they finished the short walk back.

Gavin waited down on the front steps, while Chase dashed upstairs for her things.

When she emerged, Gavin looked at her in a matching lavender scarf and hat and said, "Snug as a bug in a rug."

"A bug?" Chase teased.

Gavin made a silly face, then said, "The prettiest bug in all of Italy is what I meant to say."

Chase then looked Gavin up and down and said, "And can we talk about Mr. G.Q. here?"

Gavin struck quite the pose in his jet-black navy peacoat and jeans, the collar turned up on the jacket giving the striking farmer just the right panache.

Before they began the five-minute walk to the church, Gavin noticed something on Chase's lapel, asking, "Is that the pin?"

Chase looked down and said, "Yes, the one the woman gave me at the Bridge of Sighs."

"That was so sweet of her," Gavin remarked.

"It was," Chase answered. "And it really does look a lot like the one I made for my mom when I was a kid."

"I'm surprised you're wearing it," Gavin said.

"Me too," Chase answered. "When I grabbed the hat, I saw it on the bedroom table and thought, it's almost Christmas, why not show it off?"

Gavin took her hand tight and the two started their short walk to church.

They arrived at Santa Maria shortly before noon. It was more crowded than on Chase's previous visit, and when she saw Father Leo, she threw him a quick wave.

Leo pointed to a row of pews to the right of the altar, the exact spot where Flavio had spent so many hours praying in recent months. He was already there.

Gavin looked at his watch and said to Chase, "You have nine minutes before the Mass starts. Do you want to talk to him now or—"

Before he could finish the thought, Chase was already moving in that direction, with Gavin soon to follow.

When she reached the pew, she saw Flavio's head pressed down on his folded hands, deep in prayer. Chase carefully entered the same pew and slid closer without the boy noticing.

"Flavio," she whispered, trying to sound as non-threatening as possible.

The teen raised his head, took one look at Chase and Gavin, did the sign of the cross on his forehead and chest, then stood up to go.

"Father Leo tells me there's a reason you are here so much, and I should ask you about it," Chase said quickly, before the boy could depart.

Flavio ignored her and started out of the pew, causing Chase to say firmly, "Before you run away, can you tell me why?"

The teen turned, looking defiant, then answered, "You only care about the place I work and those men who died. That's why you keep bothering me."

Gavin then spoke to the teen the way a father might to a son, "Flavio, look at me."

The boy looked up at Gavin, who was nearly twice his size, but didn't feel threatened. Instead, he stood still, waiting for Gavin to speak.

Gavin said, "We do care about the boating accident, that's true, but we also want to know if you're okay."

Flavio paused, clearly deciding in his mind whether he should trust these Americans.

It looked like he was about to share something, but instead answered, "I can't talk to you. Now leave me alone, please."

As Gavin went to move closer Chase stopped him with her hand and said, "It's alright, Gavin, he's right, we should stop."

She turned her full body toward Flavio now and said, "I'm sorry for whatever you are going through, and I promise we won't bother you again."

Father Leo moved closer to them and said, "Mass starts in five minutes. Are you three almost done?"

Chase looked at the priest and said, "We're done right now. We're leaving."

She then said to Flavio, "You should stay. Again, I'm sorry we bothered you."

As Chase took Gavin's hand to go, Flavio suddenly saw the pin attached to the lapel of Chase's jacket.

"STOP," he said, loud enough that other parishioners looked over.

"Where did you get that pin?" the boy asked.

Chase was a bit flustered, looked down at her lapel, and touched it gently and replied, "This? It was a gift."

"From whom?" Flavio asked, his voice calmer now.

Chase looked at Gavin, trying to remember their names, asking him, "The woman was Rosa, right? But the man . . . what was it?"

Gavin snapped his fingers, answering, "Rico. It was Rico and Rosa. I only remember because they both began with an R."

Chase smiled at that, saying, "That's right, I don't think they told us their last name, though."

"Lombardo," Flavio answered. "Rico and Rosa Lombardo."

Gavin smiled and said, "You know them?"

Flavio sat back down, took the hat off his head, and tossed it beside him in the pew. Chase and Gavin stood silent in curiosity. After shaking his head in disbelief, Flavio looked up at Gavin.

"You were the big man who lifted him into the boat?" Flavio said.

"That's right," Gavin replied, a bit confused at how this teen knew this.

"And you," Flavio said, pointing to Chase. "You're the one who gave up your romantic gondola ride so they could kiss under the bridge at sunset."

Chase just stared at Flavio now, only saying, "When the church bells rang."

"When the church bells rang," Flavio replied, repeating her words.

Chase's eyes filled with tears, as did Flavio's at precisely that moment.

Gavin moved closer now, putting his arm around Chase and said, "I don't understand what's happening."

Then she said out loud, what she knew already in her heart, "You're the little boy who made this pin. You're their son?"

Flavio wiped the tears and looked away, realizing Father Leo was standing off to the side, listening quietly.

The priest then called out to the thirty or so people waiting for the service to begin, "Noon Mass will begin at twelve-fifteen today."

An Italian woman in the front row asked, "*Perché?*", which meant *why?*

Father Leo shot back playfully, "*Perché Gesù lo ha detto*—because Jesus said so."

Gavin was trying to understand the connection between the teen and that older couple at the Bridge of Sighs, saying to Flavio, "But Rosa and Rico live on the other side of Italy and you're here."

Flavio replied, "That is their retirement home. They're from Rome. When they left, I stayed for work."

Chase sat next to Flavio in the pew and said, "I'm sorry for what is happening to your father."

Gavin added, "ALS, right? That's why you're here at church every day. You're praying for your dad."

Flavio looked over at Gavin, let out a deep breath and said, "That and other things."

Chase took the boy's hand in hers and said, "What else is wrong?" Does it have to do with the boating accident?"

Flavio looked down at the church floor, paused and thought carefully before answering, then raised his head and said, "Sì."

Gavin then said to the boy, "We don't want to get you in trouble, Flavio, but if there's something you know, something bothering you so much it has you hanging your head in church every day, maybe it would help to tell someone."

Flavio grimaced as if he was struggling to say the words.

Then, a calm fell over his face as he looked at Chase, answering, "For what you did to help my mamma and papà, yes, I will tell you what really happened."

As Gavin, Chase, and Father Leo all stood in stunned silence, the teen added, "And it wasn't an accident."

While church is a great place for confessions, Gavin and Chase thought it best to let Father Leo get on with his Mass and take Flavio somewhere safe to talk. Any of the restaurants or cafés would have customers who might eavesdrop, so Chase took Flavio back to the apartment.

Gavin still had the business card left by the Italian police detective Stefano Bianco, so he called him, and being as cryptic as possible, informed the officer they had a break in the case, and he should rush right over.

A half-hour later, with Nonna, Francesca, Jules, and Bianco present, Flavio unburdened his heart and his conscience.

"Crane Shipping has been in and out of bankruptcy several times over the last ten years," Flavio began.

"We're aware of the financial troubles," the detective said. "Go on."

"I was hired as a scheduler and tracker," the teen explained.

"What does that mean?" Gavin asked.

"Just what it sounds like," Flavio replied. "When items need to be delivered to one of the islands off Italy, my boss negotiates the price and then I schedule which boat will take it and when."

"Go on," Chase said.

"I mentioned the financial trouble because they couldn't afford to have boats out of service," Flavio explained.

Seeing they were all silently waiting, Flavio pressed on, "Crane has eleven boats in the fleet and the number seven vessel was the worst of the bunch."

"Worse how?" the detective asked.

"Chronic engine troubles, leaking oil, stalling for no reason," Flavio answered.

He continued, "It was so bad that when the port authority did their scheduled inspection, they pulled it out of service."

Francesca, listening carefully, then asked, "So they couldn't use it?"

"Sì," Flavio answered. "It was the number seven ship."

Nonna, silent up until now asked, "What does any of this have to do with my Matteo and the storm that killed him?"

"Summer is our busiest time and Crane didn't want any ships out of service," Flavio answered. "Including number seven."

Gavin, starting to see where this might be going, asked, "What did they do, Flavio?"

The boy swallowed hard and answered, "They took black paint and changed the number seven on the side of the ship into a nine, just in case anyone saw it coming or going from the harbor."

"So, you had two number nines on the water?" Chase asked.

"Yes, one that worked and one that didn't," Flavio replied.

Detective Bianco then pressed, "Get to the day of the storm."

Flavio glanced at the detective and a sick look came over his face, causing him not to speak.

Chase touched his arm and said, "It's okay, you can tell us."

Flavio continued, saying, "We had to make a last-minute run to the island of Capraia, but we knew there was a storm just south of there."

Francesca, remembering now, looked at Flavio, saying, "That's the island Matteo needed a ride to, to repair a motor for a business."

Flavio could see the hurt in her eyes, answering, "Yes, Matteo and others often took rides from us for a small fee. He was on the boat that day."

The detective asked the obvious question, "What number boat was he on?"

The teen answered, "It was the number seven, sir, the one they changed."

Chase then: "And what happened, Flavio?"

He wrenched his hands together and said, "The boat was supposed to go quickly and get ahead of the storm."

Detective Bianco interjected, "But it was too slow and got caught?"

"No," Flavio said. "That's not what happened."

The detective took the small recording device he was holding this whole time and inched it closer to Flavio now, "Go on."

"The boat was well ahead of the storm," Flavio continued. "But then the engine did what it had done so many times before: it stalled."

Gavin then: "So they were stopped in the middle of the sea, just floating?"

"Not just floating," Flavio answered. "Drifting, right into the path of the storm."

Chase then asked, "How do you know this?"

"They called in to Crane to report the problem," Flavio said, "and I could see their GPS signal on the screen."

Detective Bianco then raised his voice. "But there was no distress call. I talked to the maritime authorities—there was no call for help."

"They couldn't," Flavio said. "They knew they'd get caught with a boat on the water that was unsafe."

Francesca then, her voice shaking with anger: "So they let that crew, including my husband, just drift there with a storm approaching?"

Flavio could only muster one word, looking at the grieving widow, "Sì."

Gavin looked to the cop angrily, asking, "How does none of this come out in your investigation?"

Detective Bianco replied, "Because the few who would talk to me, all lied."

Flavio said, "They're afraid for their jobs. They were told if they spoke to the police we'd be shut down."

"Well, they got that part right," Bianco said. "I'll have the people running Crane brought up on charges."

Flavio, who was barely nineteen years old, looked to Nonna and Francesca and said, "I want you to know I had nothing to do with putting Matteo on that boat or changing the number. I didn't even realize the number seven was on the water until it was too late."

Chase looked from Francesca and Nonna over to the teen and said, "Nobody is blaming you, Flavio, and I know it took a great deal of courage to tell us this."

Francesca assured the boy, "She's right, Flavio. Hard as it is to hear, I appreciate knowing the truth."

Nonna was stone silent, in shock. Trying to find the right words.

Finally, she said, "So he didn't have to die."

The detective said to Nonna directly, "Signora, nothing will bring Matteo back, but I will hold the people responsible for this, and I'm sure you have grounds for a lawsuit."

Nonna thought a moment, then answered, "Money? You think money change anything?"

The old woman stood up and said to the detective, "You put them in jail, they can keep their money."

With that, Nonna slowly left the kitchen and retired to her bedroom, trying to process this harsh truth.

Francesca looked at the others and said, "It was easier thinking it was just a storm, an act of God as you put it, detective."

She continued, "Knowing it didn't need to happen."

Francesca could only shake her head in disgust, then got up from the table herself.

Chase looked at her friend and said, "I'm sorry."

Francesca smiled and gave Chase a loving hug, the first since the two met.

As they broke their embrace, Chase asked, "You wanna go grab a coffee? Maybe something stronger?"

Francesca took a deep breath and let it out as if she was exhaling the pain her heart was feeling at this moment.

She answered, "Coffee would be nice."

As the two women left, Gavin shook the detective's hand, thanking him for coming by on such short notice.

"Understand something, young man," Bianco said to Flavio. "What you did is brave, and as we move forward, I will protect you."

Flavio looked out the window down to the street below and replied, "Protection? When they find out I talked, I'll need a job, not protection."

Gavin then asked, "Can you move in with your folks? With what your dad is facing, the ALS, they might appreciate having you around."

Flavio started to fill up with tears, answering, "You call me brave for speaking the truth, but the truth is, I'm afraid all the time."

Detective Bianco asked, "Afraid of what, son?"

"Losing my dad, losing my job, losing myself in this mess," the teen answered.

Gavin put his hand on Flavio's shoulder and said, "Trust me, even the worst mess can be cleaned up."

Flavio looked at Gavin and said, "Not my father's. Not ALS."

Scooter the pup walked over and looked at the teen with kind eyes, almost as if he wanted to help in some way.

Flavio got down on one knee to pet the dog and said, "I pray and pray. Heaven seems to be fresh out of miracles."

Gavin looked at the detective, then back to Flavio and said, "I don't pretend to know everything, Flavio. But rather than spend every day at Santa Maria praying for a miracle, maybe go stay with your dad for his last months and pray together. Maybe being with his son on these final steps of the journey is the miracle he needs right now."

As the teen considered Gavin's sage advice, the detective noticed the logo on the yellow sweatshirt Flavio was always wearing, the red emblem with the word Torino and a bull kicking up his heels.

"You're Toro fan?" the detective asked.

"Sì," Flavio answered, happy to change the subject from his ailing father.

"Ever been to a game?" Bianco then asked.

Flavio managed a small smile, "Many—when my father was, you know, better."

The boy thought a moment and said, "Their retirement home on the water isn't that far from Torino, in northern Italy."

"What sport is that?" Gavin asked.

The detective shot back, "Football, or what you call soccer."

The detective, realizing everything this young man was dealing with, then said, "You know, Flavio, a good friend of mine runs the front office for the team. If you are moving back to be with your folks and need a new job, I could make a call."

Flavio seemed stunned at the prospect, answering, "Seriously?"

"Sure," Bianco answered. "Toros need men of good character."

Gavin, sensing some closure on the day's events, extended his hand to the detective and said, "Thank you for coming over, sir."

Bianco shook Gavin's hand firmly and said, "Thank you for getting Flavio to speak to me."

The detective offered to give Flavio a ride back to his home in Rome, and as the two opened the door to leave, Gio appeared with a smile.

"Ciao. What are you doing here, detective?" Gio asked innocently.

Bianco shot Gavin a look and replied, "We have some new information in your father's death. Gavin can explain."

After the detective and Flavio left, Gavin sat Giovanni down and shared the news about why the boat capsized in the storm, telling him it was negligence and greed, nothing more.

Rather than fly into a rage, Gio could only shake his head in disgust, saying, "I hope they put them all in prison."

"Knowing that detective," Gavin replied, "that fact seems certain."

Gio was anxious now, unable to sit still.

When Nonna returned from her bedroom, he gave his grandmother a hug and whispered, "I'm so angry I could scream, Nonna."

Nonna met his eyes and whispered back, "Sì, but we leave vengeance to God."

Gio nodded, then turned to Gavin and said, "I can't sit here. I think I need to walk, maybe go to the library."

Gavin asked, "You want company? I've been wanting to go back there myself to look for something."

"What?" Gio asked.

"Do they have books on artists from long ago? Painters, people like that?" Gavin asked.

Gio nodded, "I'm sure they do."

The pair grabbed their coats off the backs of some kitchen chairs and made their way out the door.

Something had been nagging at Gavin since they first arrived in Rome. It centered on that mystery man he met, standing at his easel inside the Colosseum. Gavin was hopeful that an old book buried in that library might quench his curiosity. At the pace he and Gio were walking down Monti's cracked sidewalks, he'd have his answer soon.

The pair were motoring along so quickly, they failed to notice that Chase and Francesca were sitting in the front window of a small café just two blocks away from the apartment.

How do you make someone feel better about the loss of their spouse, knowing it never had to happen? As the two women sat in silence, Chase realized it was an impossible task.

As for Francesca, she was done trying to make sense of so much loss. For the moment, she was content wrapping her hands around a cup of hot coffee on this cold December day, sitting quietly with her friend.

After ten minutes of silence, one of them had to be the first to speak.

It was Francesca, asking, "So, let's talk about your wedding."

"Nope," Chase replied. "You owe me a story first."

"A story?" Francesca responded.

"Yes," Chase answered. "A few weeks ago, you asked me when I knew Gavin was *the one* for me, remember?"

Francesca paused, smiled, and said, "The story about the lost sheep on his farm growing up."

"That's right," Chase answered. "That day you promised you'd share *your* love story about Matteo and when you knew he was the one?"

Francesca nodded in agreement. "I do owe you that story, don't I?"

"You do," Chase replied. "And after that I want to ask you about this restaurant called Verdile's. I could tell at breakfast there is something special about the place."

Francesca waved the waiter over to the table, saying to Chase at the same time, "I'm getting us more coffee, because we're going to be here for a while."

As Chase leaned closer, making certain not to miss a single word, Francesca added, "The truth is, my love for Matteo and Verdile's go together, as you Americans say, like peanut butter and jelly."

Chase got comfortable in her chair and a small smile rose in the corners of her mouth, knowing that whatever came next was going to be good.

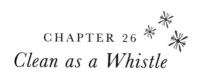
I'm not from Rome," Francesca began.

She sipped the hot coffee, adding, "I'm from Palermo, on the island of Sicily."

Chase looked confused, asking, "Is that not part of Italy?"

"It is and it isn't," Francesca answered. "I mean, technically it is one of the regions of Italy."

"Why do you say technically?" Chase asked.

"Because," she replied, "people from Sicily have their own variation on the language and customs."

Chase nodded, waiting for more.

"I mentioned I'm from Palermo, so you'll understand a traditional Roman family might be a little skittish about me," Francesca added.

Chase asked, "Like Nonna and her family, who grew up here?"

"Yes," Francesca replied. "Not that they were mean when they met me, just cautious."

"Go on," Chase said.

Francesca leaned back in her chair and continued, "I was a good student, and when it came time for college, I left Palermo to study art history at the American University of Rome."

Chase nodded, asking, "Is that how you met Matteo?"

"Sì," she replied. "But not at college, at Verdile's. I was a waitress there."

Chase smiled and said, "And he came in, got one look at the menu, and wanted you instead?"

Francesca laughed out loud, answering, "Not quite. He came in with his family to celebrate his twenty-first birthday, and I was their waitress."

Chase leaned in closer, "Did he ask for your phone number?"

"No," Francesca said. "He was too shy. We both just stared at each other that night."

"You didn't even speak?" Chase asked surprised.

"Once," Francesca answered. "When I asked if he wanted more bread."

Chase laughed and said, "So that was your Baby moment from *Dirty Dancing*."

"My what?" Francesca replied.

"You've seen the movie, right? With Patrick Swayze? *Dirty Dancing*?" Chase asked.

Francesca replied, "A long time ago. Remind me."

Chase stood up and said, "Remember Baby's first words to Johnny are *I carried a watermelon*."

Francesca burst out laughing, saying, "Oh my God, you're right. *Do you want more bread?* What a thing to say to a cute boy."

Chase took her seat again and the two laughed for what felt like a minute.

"Anyway, he came back another day and asked about me," Francesca continued. "That's when I gave him my number."

Chase thought a moment, then asked, "You mentioned Nonna being cautious with you. What does that mean?"

Francesca grimaced a bit and said, "If you Google pictures of Palermo, you'll see beautiful buildings and seascapes, but there is also poverty there, and my family didn't have much money."

"I've never gotten the impression Nonna and Alessandro were rich," Chase observed.

"No, not rich," Francesca replied. "But certainly middle-class. And a mom wants her son to do well with the girl he chooses."

Chase pondered that statement and answered, "I suppose so. Of course, love is what matters most."

"Yes, it is," Francesca answered.

Chase then asked, "So what happened to soften her? Did she see Matteo in love and just gave in to it?"

"No," Francesca replied. "It was a random trip to a, what would you call it in America, a low-income store."

Chase was confused, "You mean like Walmart, somewhere to save money?"

"No, I mean a place where people donate clothing and the store sells it very cheap to poor people," Francesca responded.

"Oh," Chase answered. "Thrift stores. Yes, we have those in America."

Francesca continued, "So Nonna was with her husband, Alessandro, dropping off a bag of clothes, probably stuff Matteo grew out of, and they saw me."

"Shopping?" Chase asked. "You mentioned you were poor."

Francesca smiled warmly, "No, my job waitressing was good to me, so I didn't need to shop in a store like that."

Chase replied, "I'm confused then."

"I was volunteering my time there," Francesca explained.

"Oh, got it," Chase replied.

Francesca continued, "My parents taught me it was important to give back if you are blessed. Between my studies and the restaurant, I didn't have much free time, but once a week I helped at that store."

"That's so good of you," Chase replied. "So, they saw you there, and—?"

"Well, they thought I was shopping and didn't want to embarrass me, so they didn't approach me," Francesca explained.

She continued, "They were about to leave when they saw me help a little girl find a jacket just her size. It was marked down to about ten euros, but I could tell the girl's mother didn't even have that."

Chase smiled at Francesca and said, "So you bought it for her."

Francesca nodded shyly. "It was no big deal, ten euros was part of one day's work at Verdile's. I could afford it."

"Let me guess," Chase replied. "Nonna and her husband saw you do it."

Francesca took another sip of her coffee and answered, "They did, but I didn't even know it. They left without saying a word."

"What happened then?" Chase asked.

"Like I said," Francesca continued. "Seeing that softened them toward me, and slowly I became part of that wonderful family."

Chase then realized something, asking, "What does any of this have to do with Verdile's or you knowing Matteo was the one for you?"

"I'm getting to that," Francesca said. "Verdile's is an old-fashioned Italian restaurant."

"Okay," Chase replied.

"They don't even hand you a menu. It changes so often that it is written in chalk on a big board up on the wall," Francesca explained.

She was smiling now as she continued. "And they had this old sea bell from a ship that dates back to the 1700s hanging near the bar."

"A bell? What for?" Chase asked.

"To ring of course," Francesca answered. "Every time something important happened at Verdile's, someone would ring the bell."

"Important?" Chase asked.

"You know, engagements, promotions, someone announcing they're having a baby," Francesca replied.

Chase could picture it, answering, "That's kind of sweet."

Francesca agreed, then explained the part that was not so sweet.

"Verdile's had a strict policy that they didn't want the workers eating there," Francesca explained.

"Ever? Even off duty?" Chase asked.

"Never ever," Francesca replied.

"Strange, but go on," Chase replied.

"And more than once I complained to Matteo that it wasn't fair. I got to hand out all this delicious food, but I couldn't sit and enjoy it," Francesca said.

"So, what happened?" Chase asked.

Francesca smiled as if she was reliving a wonderful memory now, saying, "Years later, after I graduated from the university and had quit that waitressing job, Matteo told me he had a special evening planned."

Chase was smiling now, "What did he do?"

"He put on a suit and tie, picked me up at my little apartment in Rome, and took me to Verdile's," she answered.

"Oh, that's nice," Chase said, her voice revealing she was expecting something more lavish.

Francesca read Chase's face and said, "No, you don't understand. When we got to the restaurant it was empty."

"Empty? Like closed?" Chase asked.

"No," she said shaking her head. "The entire staff was there, but no customers. Just one table with candlelight by the fireplace, with clean white linens and fine silverware."

"Where were the customers?" Chase asked.

"Matteo paid the owner to close for the night, to everyone but me," Francesca said.

Chase could just envision how romantic the table setting must have been.

She was lost in thought when Francesca said, "There's more."

Chase smiled and waited, as Francesca continued. "Instead of the dessert menu, the waiter brought a big silver tray, took off the top and revealed a black velvet ring box."

"You're kidding!" Chase said excitedly.

Francesca held out her left hand, which still had both her wedding band and her engagement ring on, then said, "This was my dessert."

Chase marveled at the beautiful diamond, then replied, "And you said yes!"

Francesca, her eyes getting moist looking down at the ring, answered, "I did, and then the owner, Mr. Verdile himself, rang the bell louder than I had ever heard it before."

The waiter returned and asked the women if they wanted another coffee, prompting Francesca to say, "I think we are good, thank you."

The bill was for ten euros, but Francesca handed the young man a twenty, causing Chase to say, "Big tipper."

"When you wait tables, you always tip more," Francesca said.

Chase then asked, "So earlier at breakfast, when Gio mentioned going to Verdile's for our little wedding reception—is it hard for you to go there now?"

Francesca pondered the question and answered, "I wouldn't say hard. It's just that I haven't been there since we lost Matteo."

Chase answered, "Like we said earlier, there are a million places to eat—"

Francesca stopped her, placing her hands on top of Chase's, saying, "I have lots of wonderful memories at Verdile's. I think it's the perfect place to go."

Chase sighed and asked, "Are you sure?"

"Positive," Francesca said, rising and giving Chase a hug.

"WAIT," Chase said loudly. "So that dinner, the fireplace, candlelight, the ring, that's when you knew he was the one?"

Francesca smiled and said, "No, that came moments after, when we went to leave."

Chase waited for the rest of it.

"This will sound silly to you," Francesca began.

Chase looked her in the eye and said, "No, it won't."

Francesca said, "I had a white blouse on and didn't realize I'd gotten a tiny bit of red sauce on the edge of my collar."

Francesca pointed to the blouse she had on now, saying, "Right here."

"Okay?" Chase answered.

"Matteo went behind the bar, grabbed a bottle of club soda, dabbed it on a napkin, and very gently cleaned my collar."

Chase stood silently, trying to imagine it.

"His face was only inches from mine, but he was so determined because he knew that was my favorite blouse," Francesca explained.

"You must have wanted to kiss him," Chase said with a smile.

"More than you could know, but he was like a little boy with a project," she answered.

"And did he get the stain out?" Chase asked.

She nodded. "He did. Then he took his index finger and traced it from my forehead, down my nose and eventually to my lips."

"And then he kissed you?" Chase said.

"No," Francesca laughed. "He pressed it on my lips and said, 'clean as a whistle.'"

Chase was silent, imagining it all when Francesca said, "I told you it was silly."

"I think it's sweet," Chase answered.

As the two women left the café, Francesca said, "I should tell you when we walked out of Verdile's that night it was snowing, so Matteo took his coat off and put it over both our heads."

Chase looked at the gleam in her eye and said, "And then you kissed him?"

"You bet I did," Francesca said laughing.

Chase looked at her friend and said, "Thank you for sharing your story with me."

Francesca didn't need to reply. One look told Chase they were friends for life, and these were the kind of secrets you shared.

As Chase and Francesca took the short walk back to the apartment, detective Bianco was across town sitting with a judge and prosecutors, plotting their next move against Crane Shipping to hold them accountable for what they'd done.

Flavio called work to quit his job, and at that very moment was already on a bus that would take him to Genoa and a long overdue visit with his mother and ailing father.

Brother Levi was going through books in his room at the monastery on the island of Elba, searching for the one with marriage vows, so he could brush up for the big day.

And Gavin and Gio were already inside the library searching for answers to two nagging questions the curious farmer could not let go of: Who was the artist who created the painting that Scooter obsessed over in the gallery? And, crazy as it might sound, did he have any connection to the artist Gavin met at the Colosseum?

One old and very dusty book was waiting patiently for Gavin in the library's west wing. What he found inside would seem impossible, but in all matters involving Chase, Gavin had learned long ago to strike that word from one's vocabulary.

I f Gavin Bennett had one flaw, it was his inability to let things go. Unfinished business felt like a sliver under the skin: he couldn't rest until it was dealt with.

A good example was back when he was a senior at Boston University, taking English composition. Students were graded on five short stories and several quizzes. Gavin worked hard and had a ninety-five average as the semester was ending.

The last week of classes, skipped by most seniors, Gavin had one final essay due to his English professor, David Kissick. Gavin spent the weekend in Vermont helping his father on the farm, planting peas by day and writing the essay by night.

When it was time to drive back to Boston on Monday morning, the alternator in Gavin's 1992 Chevy quit, leaving him without a ride. He spent several hours searching for wheels, and eventually his cousin Dominic offered his old Ford Fairlane.

The problem was, Gavin couldn't possibly make it back to Boston and Dr. Kissick' s office to meet the noon deadline. He called the professor and was told, in no uncertain terms, to stay in Vermont and not worry about the essay because it wouldn't affect his grade.

"You're getting an A, either way," Mr. Kissick assured him.

Gavin, being Gavin, couldn't let it go and made the 320-mile roundtrip journey to Beantown.

Knowing this about Gavin, you can now understand why, just two days shy of his wedding, he was wandering around one of Rome's oldest libraries, determined to tie off one last loose end.

"I thought it would be easy to find the art section," Gio said. "But maybe we should ask for help."

Gavin looked at the boy and replied, "This is one man who isn't too proud to ask for directions."

Gio found an older librarian with gray hair and a pair of reading glasses dangling from a gold chain.

After speaking quickly in Italian to the librarian, Gio turned to Gavin and said, "We weren't even close. It's way in the back on the second floor."

The two set off, determined to find a book that could satisfy Gavin's curiosity.

Back in the apartment, Francesca and Chase returned to find Nonna fussing with something on the kitchen table. Chase saw graham crackers, bags of hard candy, and little tubes of colored icing.

"What's this?" Francesca asked her mother-in-law.

Nonna motioned with her arm toward Chase and answered, "It's for her, so she feel at home."

Chase looked at the mess in front of Nonna and asked, "Me?"

Nonna continued stacking crackers and then let everything collapse, saying in Italian, "*Mi arrendo!*"

Francesca winced and said, "Maybe we can help you, if you tell us what you're trying to make?"

Nonna pointed and replied, as if it were obvious, "A gingerbread house, like they do in America."

Chase smiled and said, "That's so nice of you. Being a highly experienced gingerbread architect, I can definitely help Nonna."

Chase sat down and, using a generous amount of frosting, coated the edge of one of the crackers, connecting it to another. Once the crackers were standing on their own, she repeated this step repeatedly until the framework for a house appeared.

"You put the walls up first and then let it dry," Chase explained. "The roof comes later."

Francesca picked up a bag of hard candy and said, "What about these?"

Chase smiled and said, "Once the whole house is up and secure, we put frosting on the bottom of the candies and lay them on the roof like decorations."

As the three women quietly built their gingerbread house, Nonna surprised her when she said, "Thank you for coming into our home, Chase."

Chase leaned across the table to give the old woman a hug and replied, "Next to Gavin, your family is the best thing that has ever happened to me."

With the gingerbread house complete, the three of them shared a pot of hot chocolate, then Chase yawned and said, "I think I'm going to nap for a little while."

Nonna said, with a smile, "We big fans of the naps in this house."

As Chase reached her bedroom door, she paused and looked back at Francesca and Nonna still finishing their cocoa, and thought, "They've been through so much this year. I wish I could do something to bring them joy this Christmas."

It took Chase less than two minutes to drift off into a deep sleep.

On the second floor of the library, Gavin and Gio were going through a stack of books on eighteenth-century artists. Gavin took a piece of paper from his pocket and read the name of the artist who created the painting that drew Scooter's ire.

"Alexander Lido Francis Johnson," Gavin said. "That's our guy."

"He's not in this one," Gio said, closing a large book, tossing it aside before grabbing another.

After a sifting through a half-dozen books on artists, Gavin said, "Hold up, ladies and gents, I think we have a winner."

He was looking at the table of contents in the front of the book and had his pointer finger directly on Alexander's long name.

"I found you," Gavin said. "Page two-forty-two."

Gio moved closer as Gavin leafed through the large book as quickly as possible. Moving fifty pages at a time it didn't take long to reach the two hundreds and eventually stop on the precise page.

"Alexander Lido Francis Johnson," Gavin read aloud. "Born in 1742 and raised in the West Indies on Nassau Island, Bahamas."

Gavin looked up at Gio and said, "This guy is older than America."

Gavin continued skimming the page, reading again, "His works in oil-base paints primarily focused on architecture and contemporary scenes of everyday life."

Gio said, "That painting your dog barked at was an ordinary street scene, remember?"

"I do," Gavin said, reading further. "While underappreciated during his time, Johnson was one of the premiere artists to emerge from the West Indies in the eighteenth century."

Gavin turned the page to continue reading and found a small sketch of the artist as an old man. He was standing in front of his easel, a distinguished stone structure he was painting appearing behind him.

"This looks familiar," Gavin said to Gio, as he pointed to the building. "Where is this?"

Giovanni looked closely at the sketch and said, "That's the Temple of Venus. It's right near the Colosseum."

Gavin's gaze then drifted up and fixed closely on the artist's face. Alexander's eyes were looking straight out of the book as if he could see Gavin watching him.

"What's wrong?" Gio asked sincerely, after noticing Gavin seemed frozen.

"This man," Gavin replied.

Gio then, "What about him?"

Gavin stood up and stepped back from the book, looking around the room and trying to make sense of what he had just seen.

"What's wrong?" the concerned boy asked.

Gavin returned to the table and the still open book, pointed, and said, "That's him."

Gio looked from the book up to Gavin, asking, "Who?"

"The man who gave me those four clues to finding romance in Italy. That's him," Gavin answered.

Gio looked at the image closely, then asked, "The one from the Colosseum?"

Gavin could only nod his head up and down, answering, "That's him."

"That's not possible," the teen said. "This man has been dead two hundred years."

Gavin shook his head in disbelief. Stoic. Silent.

Gio, trying to make sense of this, said in a reassuring tone, "He probably just looks like the guy."

Gavin shook his head and said, "I suppose you're right."

Gio looked at Gavin's expression and said, "But you don't believe that."

Gavin suddenly closed the book and started toward the door, calling back to Gio, "I have to go do something. I'll see you later."

Gavin was down the library stairs before Gio could even respond.

The boy, being conscientious, returned the art book to the shelf where they found it, then walked down the stairs to the fiction section, stopping when he saw the name of his father's favorite author on the spine of several books: Dumas.

Gio took down *The Count of Monte Cristo*, found the small card in the back with his father's name printed repeatedly, and touched it with his fingers. He then surprised himself, when he tucked it under his arm and took it down to the main desk to check out the book. Gio had read the novel twice before, but this time it wasn't for him.

The man he wanted to read it was already in the backseat of a cab, weaving in and out of Rome's heavy traffic, trying to get to the Colosseum. It was Gavin, with Jules on the phone, asking for a very big favor.

As the cab parked, Gavin saw the security guard who was friends with Jules, the same one who helped them skip the line on their first visit, waiting by the same gate.

"He got hold of you on the phone?" Gavin asked.

The guard looked around nervously and answered, "He did, but this is a big favor."

Gavin reached for his wallet and the man raised his hand and said, "Jules is my friend. Put your money away.'"

With that the pair entered the Colosseum and snaked their way through several corridors where tourists aren't allowed to go, not stopping until they reached the security command center.

"Do you remember the exact date and time when you were here?" the guard asked.

"December fifth, and it was around two in the afternoon," Gavin replied.

The security guard sidled up to a computer and started typing away. Soon a bank of monitors came alive with black and white images. Gavin realized he was looking at security footage showing the inside of the Colosseum, and the date in the upper right corner revealed it was the day he was there with Chase.

"Here is the area where you talked to me that day," the guard said.

Gavin looked closely and said, "Yes, I recognize it."

"Now, what is it you're looking for specifically?" the man asked.

Gavin leaned closer to the monitors and pointed saying, "Just to the left, off the screen a bit, I was talking to a man. He was older, with an easel; he was painting."

The guard fiddled with more cameras and said, "I don't see him anywhere, sir."

Gavin looked at all the angles and said, "I talked to him for five minutes, so I know he was there."

The guard continued changing cameras, and they saw the same people from multiple angles and several shots of Gavin coming and going, but no artist with an easel.

As Gavin got frustrated, the guard said, "As many cameras as we have, there are a few blind spots. It's possible he was standing in one."

Gavin thought a moment and said, "If that's true, why don't I see him coming or going. The guy had to be eighty-years old. He couldn't move fast, not carrying all that gear."

The guard sighed and said, "I can't help you, sir. The camera shows what it shows."

With that there was a knock on the door and another guard ducked his head in and said in Italian, "Supervisor is coming, wrap it up."

The guard apologized to Gavin but told him it was time to go.

Outside, Gavin looked up at the impressive Colosseum and said under his breath, "I don't know what to believe, Alexander, but thank you for your help."

As Gavin stood on the corner, trying to hail a cab, Chase sat up sharply in her bed in the apartment and called out, "Bees."

Scooter hopped up from the floor and barked, then licked Chase's face to wake her.

When Chase's eyes focused, she realized where she was and put her hands on Scooter's head, giving him a gentle kiss back.

"I'm okay, buddy, mommy just had a strange dream."

There was a loud knock on the bedroom door, and Francesca poked her head in asking, "You alright hon? I heard you call out."

Chase got up from the sheets and answered, "Yes, I'm fine. I just need a pen and paper."

Francesca replied, "What for?"

Chase looked at her friend and said, "I just saw something, and I want to write it down before I forget."

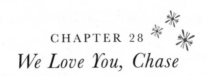

CHAPTER 28

We Love You, Chase

When Gavin returned from the Colosseum, he found Chase curled up on a small couch just off the kitchen, scribbling away on a large pad.

"Working on your next novel?" he asked jokingly.

Chase didn't look up. She just kept writing notes and replied, "I've had a strange day since you left."

Gavin took a seat opposite the couch and answered, "That makes two of us."

Chase looked up to be certain Gavin was okay, then said, "You go first."

"I found a book in the library with an image of the artist Alexander Lido Francis Johnson," he said.

"The one who painted the artwork that Scooter barked at?" Chase asked.

"Exactly. And guess who he is the spitting image of?" Gavin replied.

Chase was clueless, shaking her head indicating she couldn't hazard a guess.

"The old man I met the third day we were in Rome, at the Colosseum," Gavin said.

Chase's face went blank with confusion, then she said, "Okay, so they look alike. What am I missing?"

Gavin put his face in his hands and let out a sigh, saying, "I'd swear it's the same guy."

Chase grinned and said, "But that's not possible."

Gavin stood up and shot back, "Oh, are we suddenly only believing things that are possible? Because I remember a certain girl back in America who saw lots of things that didn't seem possible."

Chase got up and put her arms around Gavin, saying, "You're right. I'm sorry. But Gav, a lot of old men look similar."

"It wasn't just how he looked," Gavin replied. "The man at the Colosseum told me he was from the Bahamas and this Alexander Johnson is also from there."

Chase thought about that and replied, "Maybe a great-great-grandson. Same look, both artists."

Gavin considered the coincidence, then answered, "You're probably right. It just freaked me out."

"I get it," Chase said, reassuring him.

"So?" Gavin asked. "What was strange about your day?"

It was Chase who let out a deep breath now, saying, "I had another dream."

Gavin looked at the note pad on the couch and said, "You wrote it down?"

Chase retrieved the pad and answered, "I did, best as I could remember."

"So?" Gavin asked.

"At first I was in a green field. It felt like summer, and there was a windmill," Chase said.

Gavin took his seat again and replied, "Go on."

"I saw a young man, late teens. He had a stick and was playing fetch with a beautiful German Shepherd," Chase explained.

Gavin listened for more.

"He didn't notice me, so I watched them play for a while and saw he had a shirt on that said St. Stephen's Academy," Chase continued.

"Did you speak to him?" Gavin asked.

"No, I don't think he could see me, but the dog did," Chase replied.

Gavin asked, "What do you mean the dog did?"

"The pup ran after the stick, stopped, and looked right at me," Chase answered.

"Then what happened?" Gavin asked.

"Nothing," she replied, "The guy yelled *Come on, Max*, and the dog ran back to him and then they were gone."

Gavin, curious, asked, "And that was it?"

"No," Chase answered. "There was more."

Chase sat next to Gavin and said, "Remember my previous dreams where I was on a beach. The first one, when I saw writing in the sand—"

Gavin interrupted, "And the second one; you heard a sheet flapping in the wind like laundry."

Chase smiled, "That's right. Only it wasn't laundry."

"It wasn't?" Gavin asked.

"No," she answered. "In this dream I was back on the beach, but the mist lifted, and I could see what was making that noise. It wasn't a sheet, it was a flag, up on a pole on the hill."

"What kind of flag? Italy? America?" Gavin asked.

"I didn't recognize it," Chase answered. "It was all white with a single red stripe through it."

Gavin thought about that image for a second, then said, "That's not the flag for Japan, right?"

"No," Chase answered quickly. "That one is all white with a large red dot in the middle."

"Yeah, you're right," Gavin replied, and then asked, "And that was it? Dream over?"

"No, I was looking at the flag flapping in the wind and felt something crawling on my arm," Chase continued.

Gavin looked down at Chase's arm and asked, "What was it?"

Chase raised the white pad up, turned it over and in big letters it said BEES.

"Bees? Did they sting you?" Gavin asked.

"No," Chase said, shaking her head. "They just startled me, and then I woke up."

Gavin rose again and looked out the window at the street below, finally saying, "So a kid and his dog by a windmill and a weird flag and some harmless bees."

Chase caught Gavin's eyes and the hint of disbelief that was there, saying, "I know, strange, right?"

Gavin said, "Given your track record I'm sure it all means something, but I have no clue what."

"Me neither," Chase answered, adding, "Maybe we don't tell everyone in the house about it. Our wedding is in two days, and I'd rather focus on that."

"Sounds like a plan," Gavin replied with a smile.

It was just after three in the afternoon when Chase and Gavin emerged from the room, finding a small crowd waiting in the kitchen.

"What's up?" Chase asked.

Francesca, Nonna, Riley, and Tessa were all smiling, standing side by side like soldiers ready for battle.

Riley, in that charming Irish brogue, said, "What's up, my American girl, is you get married in two days and we're taking you right now to get a dress."

Chase motioned toward the back bedroom and said, "I have a nice white dress that I can throw on—"

"THROW ON," Nonna shouted at her. "NO, NO, NO, you must have special dress, Chase Harrington."

Chase could see there was no arguing with her new friends, so she said, "Okay, but not too expensive."

Francesca grabbed Chase's jacket off the hanger by the door, tossed it to her, and said, "We'll just see about that."

As the door opened and the women went to leave, Jules and Gio both came into the apartment, laughing.

"What's up, boys?" Francesca asked them.

Gio said, "This is for you," tossing the book he borrowed from the library to Gavin: *The Count of Monte Cristo.*

"Thanks," Gavin replied.

Jules then announced, "We know you ladies are going dress shopping, so we have to go do manly things."

Francesca folded her arms and said, "Define manly! Need I remind you your nephew is sixteen."

Jules, looking slightly offended, scoffed, "We're not going bar hopping, silly. I thought the guys would like to see the coolest thing in all of Italy, the very thing that inspired King Arthur."

Gavin smiled and said, "King Arthur, really?"

Jules handed Gavin his coat and said, "Yes, but they close at six, so let's go."

Ten seconds later the apartment was empty, with Scooter and Giuseppe standing in the kitchen, wondering where everyone went.

A short cab ride took the ladies to a bridal shop called Pronovias, just a stone's throw from the famous Trevi Fountain. There was a three-week waiting list for brides to get into Pronovias, but Tessa knew the manager, and she agreed to give Chase a private showing.

Chase was drop dead beautiful, but never carried herself that way. Always going light on the makeup, Chase liked to keep her look simple and wholesome, the girl down the hall who was friends with everyone. That was Chase.

So, when she stepped into the bridal store and said, "Show me simple and elegant," it only took the manager one attempt to find her dream dress.

"This little work of art is by Azazie," the bridal manager began. "A crepe trumpet gown with V-neck front and keyhole back, very modest."

Nonna touched Chase's arm and said, "Modesty suits you, dear."

As Chase cradled the lovely white dress in her arms, the manager added, "Fine lace details on the sides, form fitting to your hips and zips in the back."

Chase tried the gown on, emerged from the fitting room, and said to the others, "I love it."

The women all applauded, Riley moving closer to give Chase a kiss on the cheek, whispering, "You're *beor*, my love. That means gorgeous."

Chase turned to the manager and said, "I'll take it."

As she reached for her purse, Francesca put her hand on Chase's and said, "We want to treat you to this."

All eyes went to the manager, as she tapped away on the computer and said, "WOW."

Tessa bit her lip and asked, "Wow good or wow bad?"

The manager smiled, "Wow good, that dress is just four hundred euros."

Tessa, Riley, Francesca, and Nonna all said in unison, "A hundred each," before taking out cash and credit cards to complete the transaction.

"You guys didn't have to do this," Chase said, getting emotional at their display of kindness.

"We love you, Chase," Francesca said, the other women smiling in agreement.

A three-hour car ride away, Jules, Gavin, and Gio ran up to the gates of the Abbey of San Galgano. The tours had just stopped for the day and a pair of security guards were approaching the large wrought iron gate with keys in hand.

"WE HAVE TO SEE THE SWORD," Jules shouted at the guards, out of breath.

As the guard began to say something in Italian that sounded a lot like *take a hike,* Jules said in English, "He's getting married in two days, this was my gift."

One guard looked at the other and the two started arguing in Italian.

Jules could see one guard was sympathetic while the other was not, so he added, "We're also here for the boy. Please, he already lost his father this year. Don't add to his disappointment."

The one guard looked to the other and they both opened the gate.

"*Presto, presto,*" the grumpy guard said sharply.

Jules laughed and said to Gavin, "That means hurry it up."

The Abbey was empty, so the three had no issue running quickly to a sacred spot in a small chapel inside.

When they arrived, Gavin, also out of breath, asked, "What could possibly be worth all this running?"

Jules pointed and said, "That."

It was a display, kept safe under glass, showing the handle of a sword that was protruding out of a stone.

"What in God's name?" Gavin asked.

Gio lit up immediately. "We studied this in school. That's the sword of Saint Galgano."

Gavin asked, "Who?"

"He's a saint from the twelfth century," Gio explained. "He grew up very rich in a castle and after a life of sin was told to renounce his terrible ways."

"What did he do?" Gavin asked.

Jules then picked up the story, saying, "He said giving up his wealth would be as difficult as plunging his sword through a stone."

Gavin looked down at the sword handle sticking out, saying, "So he did?"

Jules smiled and answered, "That's what the legend says, and once he put the sword in that stone, he lived a life of virtue."

Gio jumped back into the conversation, adding, "You've heard stories about Excalibur, King Arthur, and the boy who could pull a sword from a stone?"

Gavin answered, "Yes, I've seen movies about that."

Gio pointed down at the sword and said, "That's the real sword that inspired it all."

"Wow," Gavin exclaimed. "That's so cool."

Suddenly they heard a man clear his throat, and the three of them looked over to see the guard waiting with his arms folded and foot tapping.

The guard then said in English, "Unless one of you is going to pull the sword from the stone and become king, you have to go. NOW."

"Can we try?" Gio asked, only half kidding.

"*Andiamo*," the guard said.

"That means *let's go*," Jules said to Gavin.

Outside of the Abbey and back on the street where Jules parked the car, Gavin asked, "Why did you want me to see that?"

Jules rested his hands on the roof of the car and looked across at Gavin and Gio and said, "Most men get a bachelor party where they act foolish and sometimes do things they wish to forget."

"Right," Gavin replied.

Jules smiled warmly and added, "I wanted to show you what a man is capable of, if his heart is pure, and he puts the right things first."

Gio then asked, "You want him to be a saint, like Galgano, Uncle Jules?"

"No, Gio," Gavin answered. "He's talking about Chase and how lucky I am. Aren't you?"

Jules nodded and said, "Sì."

Gavin could see Jules had grown fond of Chase in their nearly a month in Rome, so he replied, with sincerity in his voice, "I know I'm blessed, and I'll never forget it."

Jules bowed his head, letting Gavin know he believed him.

When the three of them got back to the apartment in Rome, Gavin gave Chase a big hug and asked, "Did we find a dress?"

Chase looked over at Nonna and Francesca, who were smiling, then answered, "We did."

Chase then asked, "And what did you find?"

Gavin looked at Gio and the teen surprised Chase when he answered, "Knighthood."

Chase smiled, looking over to Gavin for further explanation, when he replied, "He's not far off."

Chase then said, "One more day and then we get married."

Gavin responded, "Can you believe it?"

Chase took a deep breath and said, "So much has happened in these three weeks. You think we're done with the surprises?"

"Do you mean, do I think we'll relax tomorrow, then get married the day after, and live happily ever after?" Gavin replied.

Chase put her hands on his strong shoulders and said, "Yeah. Can we pull that off, cowboy?"

Gavin hugged her tight and said, "If a man can plunge a sword into a stone, I think we can."

Chase cocked her head and said, "A what into a what?"

Gavin chuckled and answered, "I'll tell you about it at breakfast."

What Chase and Gavin didn't know, couldn't know, was that the day before their wedding would be anything but quiet. Someone was coming who they never expected to see again.

CHAPTER 29
Her Name Was Taylor

No one was able to sleep late on the morning of December 23 because of the noise trucks make when they shift into reverse. That loud beeping sound pierced the air shortly before eight a.m., as a large vehicle backed up and unloaded a snow-white wooden arbor outside of Nonna's building.

"What's this now?" Chase asked, seeing the item being carried by two men into the secret garden.

Riley and Tessa, both sporting jeans and sweatshirts for a morning of pre-wedding labor, answered in unison, "It's for your vows."

The arbor was eight feet high and created an archway wherever it stood. In Chase's case, the workers placed it in the center of the stone patio at the base of the large red heart.

A separate truck, from one of Rome's most expensive florists, arrived not long afterward, and a half-dozen workers emerged and began the task of unloading three hundred white and pink roses along with bundles of baby's breath. For the next hour they would meticulously clip and attach the roses to the arbor, creating what could only be described as a gateway to heaven.

"Who paid for all of this?" Chase asked.

Riley smiled and said, "Your fiancé, of course."

Gavin and Chase would stand beneath the arbor the following day, embraced by hundreds of roses, the stone heart at their feet and water flowing down from the majestic fountain. It would surely be the prettiest place in all of Italy.

Once the floral gateway was set, everyone retired to the apartment above for a slice of homemade spinach and cheese quiche and pitchers of ice-cold mimosa.

When brunch was complete, Gavin and Chase were brought back downstairs for two surprises. The first was Father Leo and his brother, Levi.

"I know the wedding isn't until tomorrow," Levi explained, "but it's too far a journey to risk something going wrong."

"So, you came in a day early?" Gavin asked.

"I did," Levi replied.

Then, pointing at Chase and Gavin, Levi added, "And we should probably have a quick rehearsal today anyway."

Levi then sat with Chase and Gavin on a chilly stone bench, asking questions about how they met or a favorite memory; searching for little anecdotes he could sprinkle into his sermon at the wedding.

"You two have had some amazing adventures," Levi observed.

Gavin answered, "You got that right, padre."

"Oh, I'm not a padre. That's Leo," Levi reminded them. "I'm a brother. Brother Levi."

"Sorry," Gavin replied. "I get you and Leo mixed up sometimes."

"How is the chess game going, by the way?" Chase asked, referring to the months-long game the two brothers were engaged in.

Levi answered, "I would have won around months ago if he didn't cheat so much."

"I heard that," Father Leo called from across the garden.

The priest approached and said, "Funny how I'm only accused of cheating when he's losing."

Levi smiled and said, "I'm teasing. To answer your question honestly, Chase, not so good. I brought my queen out too early."

The monk looked at Gavin and said, "You have to protect your queen, you know what I mean, Gavin?"

Gavin, still holding Chase's hand, gave Levi a wink and answered, "I do."

Levi stood now, saying, "Looks like we're all set. I'll be here tomorrow, Christmas Eve, for the nuptials at noon."

"We can't wait," Chase responded.

Levi then said to his brother, "To the trees, then?"

"Yes," Leo answered, "To the trees we go."

Gavin, curious, asked, "What about trees?"

Father Leo replied, "I have to stop by a tree lot and pick up a half-dozen Christmas trees to decorate the church."

Gavin just nodded, understanding.

Levi then said, "Hey, you're big and strong, do you have plans right now?"

Leo echoed the thought, saying to Gavin, "We could use another set of hands."

Gavin looked at Chase for approval and she said enthusiastically, "Go, have fun."

After giving Chase a kiss on the cheek, he turned to go, when Francesca called out, "Hold up, this is goodbye until tomorrow."

Gavin stopped, confused, and said, "I'm sorry, what?"

Chase was equally lost, asking, "What do you mean?"

Riley and Tessa stepped closer to the group, as Francesca said to Chase and Gavin, "You two can't wake up, separated by a wall, twenty feet from each other on your wedding day."

Riley added, "Plus, how are you going to get ready and not have Gavin see you in the dress before the ceremony?"

Tessa then said to Chase, "You want it to be a surprise!"

Chase looked at Gavin and shrugged her shoulders, then asked, "So how do we not see each other before?"

Francesca handed Chase a brochure with a beautiful hotel on the cover and Chase read it out loud, "Rome Cavalieri, Waldorf Astoria hotel."

Chase looked at the women, all grinning ear to ear, saying, "Wait, am I staying here?"

Riley answered, "Check-in is at three, they have a fine restaurant, a spa, and an indoor pool if you fancy a swim."

Tessa leaned in and whispered in Chase's ear, "Just don't steal the plush robe they put in your room. They tend to notice those things and charge your credit card. Trust me, I know."

Chase grinned at Tessa and said, "Good tip."

Levi then asked his brother and Gavin, "Are we going, gentlemen?"

"Yes," Gavin answered, turning his attention back to Chase, saying, "So, until tomorrow, my sweet."

Chase took his hands in hers and said, "Love you."

Gavin answered, "Me too."

He then pointed to the lovely stone patio and arbor and said, "Meet you by the heart at noon?"

Chase smiled and answered, "Wouldn't miss it for the world."

With that, Gavin, Leo, and Levi were off to collect evergreens for the church, and Chase started walking back up to the apartment to relax. That's when her second surprise of the day arrived.

"Miss Harrington?" a young man's voice called out.

Chase was in front of the apartment building, about to go up, when she turned to see who was calling her.

"Flavio," she replied, "What are you doing here?"

The boy, nicely dressed in white button-down shirt and slacks, was standing by the curb, his hands folded neatly in front of him.

"I know you must be busy with your wedding tomorrow, but I was wondering if you had a moment to talk," the teen said. "It's just a moment, I promise."

"Of course," Chase answered. "What do you want to talk about?"

"Not me," Flavio answered.

He then pointed across the street to a small café with outdoor seating, and said, "My parents. My dad."

Chase's eyes scanned the street and fell upon the same special van, with the wheelchair lift, that was in Venice the day she and Gavin visited the Bridge of Sighs. It was the day she met Flavio's parents, Rico and Rosa.

"Are they at the café?" Chase asked Flavio.

He nodded silently.

Chase crossed the street and realized Flavio wasn't following, so she turned back to find out why.

"He said *alone*," Flavio called out respectfully, taking a seat on the front steps of Chase's building to wait.

Chase just nodded and continued toward the café to find the couple.

They weren't eating. Rico's ALS had progressed to a point where swallowing was getting more difficult, so his devoted wife, Rosa, took care of his nourishment in the privacy of their home. Instead, both sat with a warm cup of tea, waiting for Chase's arrival.

As Chase approached, she saw Rosa's eyes immediately go to the lapel on her jacket and realized she was still wearing the Christmas pin that was given to her as a gift.

"Yes, I am wearing it," Chase said, unsolicited. "I love it."

"I'm so glad," Rosa answered. "I'm sorry to ambush you this way, the day before your wedding."

"It's alright," Chase answered. "I'm happy to see you again."

Chase pointed back toward the building where Flavio was sitting, and said, "You should be so proud of him."

Rosa smiled, "We are. He's a good boy."

Chase stood in front of the couple, not certain what to say, so Rosa answered the obvious question.

"We're here, Chase, because after you met our son and helped him, we made a few calls to people we know in America," Rosa explained.

"Calls?" Chase asked.

"Yes, we were curious about the nice couple who drove across Italy, only to give away their gondola ride to a pair of perfect strangers," Rosa answered.

"It was our pleasure, Rosa," Chase said.

Rosa continued, "My brother works in publishing, so we were surprised to hear you were a writer."

Chase took a seat now at the table, answering, "Yes, I am."

Rosa touched Rico's sleeve and said, "It's hard now for Rico to read, but he loves books on tape."

"Does he?" Chase answered.

Rico nodded his head yes and answered, "Sì."

Rosa then said, "And we downloaded your book, *Manchester Christmas*, and listened to it together."

Chase smiled at them, "That's nice."

Rosa's face took on a serious composure now, as she said, "We assumed you took poetic license with the things you said happened to you at that church in Vermont."

Chase just listened, as Rosa continued, "So I had my brother, the publisher, call some compatriots in the publishing world in America. Do you know what they said?"

Chase answered, "No."

"They said it was all true," Rosa answered.

Chase looked down, not sure how to react, when Rosa added, "They said you're not some mystic or psychic or even very religious."

Chase responded, "That's true."

"But," Rosa said, "everyone believes you saw things and you helped other people with what you saw."

Chase nodded now, feeling proud and a bit uncomfortable at the same time.

"That's why we're here, Chase," Rosa said.

The woman then let go of her husband's hand and lovingly touched Chase's, adding, "Rico has a question for you. Just one question. And please understand, Chase, he traveled a very long way to ask it."

Chase looked at the man in the wheelchair, his body more frail and thinner than it was only two weeks prior when she met him in Venice.

As Chase was about to ask Rico what he wanted to know, Rosa suddenly stood up and said, "He had one condition for me. He wanted to ask it alone."

With that, Rosa stepped between two tables and very nimbly crossed the street to join her son on the chilly front steps to Chase's building.

Chase looked into Rico's sad eyes and said, "Ask me anything."

Across town a red pick-up truck with a half-dozen fir Christmas trees was bouncing along the streets of Rome on the way to the Santa Maria church.

"So, are you nervous about tomorrow?" Father Leo asked.

"Not even a little," Gavin replied. "I adore her, can't wait to be her husband."

"That's the spirit," Levi said from the front seat, sitting next to his brother.

Leo then asked Gavin, "Do you need help with anything?"

"No, we're all good," Gavin answered.

"You sure? You seem jumpy," Leo replied.

"Nope. Don't need help at all," Gavin assured them.

Gavin was fibbing. He did need help answering a question that had been bothering him since the day before, when he visited the library. Part of him wanted to call into the front seat, *Do you two believe in ghosts? Because a painter from the eighteenth century talked to me in the Colosseum the other day.*

Gavin certainly didn't know either man well enough to pose that question, even in jest, so he pivoted to Chase's strange dream.

"Hey, guys. Is either of you good at deciphering dreams?" Gavin asked.

"Why?" Levi asked. "Do you have zombies chasing you in your sleep?"

Gavin laughed, "Not me, I was talking about Chase."

"Chase has zombies chasing her?" Leo then asked.

"No, nothing like that," Gavin replied.

He then leaned up on the seat and said, "She had two weird dreams that made no sense."

"What were they?" Levi asked.

Gavin then said, "In the first one, she saw a boy, late teens, playing with a German shepherd by a windmill. Does that ring a bell to either of you?"

Levi looked at Leo and said, "Do they even have windmills in Italy?"

"I don't know," Leo answered. "Sounds more like Holland."

Levi continued, "You're right, with the wooden shoes. Did the kid playing with the dog have wooden shoes on?"

Gavin shrugged, "I have no idea. I don't think so. She would have mentioned that."

Leo laughed and said, "Ignore him. What was the other dream?"

Gavin thought a moment, then replied, "She was on a beach, with a heavy mist, and when the fog cleared, she saw a white flag with a red line through it."

Leo looked at Levi and said, "A red line? Is there any flag like that?"

"Not that I've ever seen," Levi answered.

Father Leo looked back at Gavin and said, "Sorry, looks like we're zero for two, as you Americans say in sports."

Gavin sat back to make himself more comfortable, answering, "No worries, just silly dreams, I guess."

As the drive continued, Gavin looked out the window at the magnificent architecture rolling by.

The brothers decided to use the silence to catch up on things.

"Did I tell you? I solved the case of the kid always being at church," Leo said to Levi.

"Tell me," Levi replied.

"Turns out Flavio, that's his name, Flavio. Turns out his father is very sick," the priest explained.

"Told ya," Levi replied. "We all end up talking to God when the world is collapsing."

"It wasn't just that, Mister know-it-all," Leo chided back. "There's more."

When he had secured Levi's undivided attention, Leo then said, "Turns out, Flavio's boss at work was up to no good and may have played a role in three men's deaths."

Levi's eyes shot open. "You're kidding!"

"Nope. All true. Tell him, Gavin," the priest said to his backseat passenger.

Gavin, only half listening, answered, "Yes, it's true. The kid knew some things and turned out to be a hero or as much a hero as you can be when people died."

"Amazing," Levi answered.

Then the priest asked, "So, I've solved my little puzzle at church. How about you?"

Levi paused, then said, "You mean Tommaso? No, not really."

As the truck pulled into the parking lot at church, Leo shut off the ignition and said, "I think that's the first thing you've ever really told me about him. His name."

Levi could see his brother wanted more and said, "Leo, there's nothing to know, really. He showed up with a TBI, and we were tasked with helping him recover. We did."

Leo then asked, "Is he planning to stay?"

Levi got out of the truck and started untying the trees in the back and answered, "I honestly don't know. He doesn't say much. I do know he's no fan of the sea."

Leo laughed and said, "He hates the water, but he lives on an island. That makes perfect sense."

"Who are we talking about?" Gavin finally asked the two brothers.

"Tommaso, one of the other men at the hermitage," Levi answered.

"The what?" Gavin asked, confused.

"The place you visited on Elba, when we met," Levi explained.

Then he continued, "Remember you helped them fix the wall? There were three men. The younger one was Tommaso."

"Oh, right," Gavin said. "The one with the old compass."

Levi nodded, "That's the one. Anyway, let's get these trees in before my old fingers freeze off."

As the three of them carried the trees into the church, Gavin said, "Last question. What's a TBI?"

Father Leo answered, "Traumatic Brain Injury."

Gavin finished placing the trees near the altar and said to Brother Levi, "Noon tomorrow, then?"

Levi reached out to give Gavin a firm handshake and answered, "Noon it is."

Back at the café, Chase took a seat next to Rico, and saw he had a white envelope in his lap. He raised it up carefully and placed it gently in Chase's hands.

"For you," he managed to say through labored speech.

Chase opened the envelope and found a single-page letter folded in three, with words typed out in several short paragraphs.

Chase saw her name at the very top of the letter, just as Rico said, "Read. Out loud."

Chase did as she was asked, reading—*Dear Chase, my speech is so slow, that if I were to talk, it might take us a week to finish a conversation and we don't want you missing your wedding tomorrow.*

Chase smiled at the good humor, looking up to find Rico was managing a small smile as well.

She returned to the letter—*In your book, Manchester Christmas, you say a kind man died and you saw him greeted in heaven by his daughter.*

Chase stopped reading again, looked at Rico and said, "Taylor. Her name was Taylor."

Back to the letter—*As you know, with my illness I am facing a dark fate, but it would comfort me to know the answer to one question, perhaps only you can answer, is there a heaven?*

Chase looked up at Rico again, but he motioned with his hand for her to keep reading.

So, Chase continued—*If you made that part of the book up, about seeing heaven in the church windows, I won't tell anyone. I just want the truth. The thing is, Chase, I am scared. I've lived a virtuous life, but I'm scared for what comes next. I worry it could be eternal darkness.*

Chase looked Rico in the eyes, and he nodded, affirming his fear. He then pointed back to the letter in her hands, urging her to finish what she started.

Chase read the final sentence—*Faith is believing when you can't see. I so want to believe there is more. Can you help me?*

The letter wasn't signed. Chase's eyes just hung on those last four words: *Can you help me?*

After folding the letter and returning it to the envelope, Chase took Rico's hand and said, "Many people don't believe me, but I saw what I saw in those church windows."

Rico nodded his head, telling Chase he believed her.

Chase then said, "And things have happened since with dreams, games, God Winks, call them whatever you want, but they all allowed me to help others."

Rico nodded again, waiting for more.

"Can I tell you for certain that there is a heaven?" Chase asked. "No, I cannot."

Chase tilted her head closer, pointing her finger toward the street and houses around them.

"But I know in my heart, Rico," Chase continued, "this is not all there is. This is not the end of our story."

Rico looked somewhat relieved with Chase's answer and reached his hand over to squeeze hers, struggling to say, "Thank you."

A moment later, Rosa returned, adjusted the blanket on Rico's lap in the wheelchair, and said, "We appreciate you talking to us."

Chase let out a deep breath and said, "I'm not sure I helped, but I'm glad you came."

Rosa reached over to touch the pin on the lapel of Chase's jacket and said, "A wedding tomorrow, then Christmas day."

"Indeed," Chase answered. "Thank you again for this lovely pin."

Rosa returned to Rico's side and said, "You're most welcome. It's important we have things to remind us of what matters—pins, rings, watches, medals. Isn't that right, sweetie?"

With that, Rosa reached into the front of Rico's shirt and pulled out a small medal that was dangling from a silver chain, laying it gently on his chest.

"There you are, my love," she said.

The sunlight flashed off the silver medal, catching Chase's eye. She leaned in closer to see what Rico was wearing around his neck and noticed that on the front of the medal was the image of a man with his hands raised in the air, praying.

"That's very pretty," Chase said to Rosa.

Chase paused then, as a memory stirred.

She looked back at the medal a second time and said, "Gavin has one like that from when he was a kid, Saint Francis I think, the patron saint of animals."

Rosa reached over to touch Rico's medal and said, "This is Saint Stephen. I'm not sure who he's a patron saint to. It was a gift from Rico's mother when he graduated from prep school."

Rosa hugged Rico then and said, "A long time ago, huh, sweetheart?"

Rico smiled and nodded in agreement.

Rosa put both hands on Rico's shoulders and said to Chase, "You know what the worst thing about this awful disease is? He's still in there as sharp as can be. It's the muscles that fail you."

Chase wasn't listening though. She was staring at the medal still hanging off the chain, resting on Rico's chest.

"They say they are inching closer to a cure for ALS, but if you look at the funding," Rosa continued, until Chase cut her off.

"Did you say a graduation gift?" Chase asked abruptly.

Rosa snapped out of her lecture on ALS, and replied, "I'm sorry, what?"

"The medal he's wearing, you said it was a gift?" Chase repeated.

Rosa rubbed Rico's shoulder again, "Yes, from his mom at graduation."

Chase then, her face much more animated, "From what school?"

Rosa touched the medal. "Saint Stephen's. It was a college prep school."

Chase was quiet again, thinking, as Rosa added, "That's why she got him this particular medal, because he went to Saint Stephen's Academy."

Chase remembered her dream, only the day before, and collapsed back into a chair at the table opposite Rico and Rosa.

"Are you alright dear?" Rosa asked.

Chase tapped the table, not speaking, just thinking.

"Chase?" Rosa asking again. "Are you okay?"

Chase's eyes rose from the empty cups of tea on the table, up to Rosa's, as she asked, "If there any possibility Rico had a dog back when he was a student at Saint Stephen's?"

Rosa shrugged, "I didn't know him then."

Rico's eyes seemed to come more alive, as Chase asked him now, "Rico, did you have a dog?"

He struggled to speak slowly, Rosa putting her ear right next to his mouth.

Finally, she nodded and answered, "He did. A German shepherd."

Chase was frantic now. Seeing the waiter walking by, she jumped up and said, "Do you have a pen and paper? I need it now!"

The young man was startled by Chase, responding, "Sì, *prendala*. TAKE IT," as he hastily handed her a notepad along with his pen.

"What is it, Chase?" Rosa asked.

Chase ignored the question and wrote something down in large block letters, then turned the paper over so no one could see.

"Ask him what his dog's name was," Chase said to Rosa.

"I don't understand, Chase," Rosa began to say.

"ASK HIM, PLEASE," Chase insisted.

Again, Rosa leaned in and put her ear to Rico's mouth. Chase heard some faint mumbling, then Rosa raised her face up to meet Chase's eyes and said, "Max. The dog's name was Max."

Chase suddenly laughed and looked off, her eyes filling with tears.

"What?" Rosa asked.

Rico seemed to know what was happening, even if Rosa didn't. He slowly raised his arm and pointed to the scrap of paper face down on the table. Rosa reached across and turned it over to reveal three large letters in black ink: M A X.

Rosa stared at the dog's name in disbelief, then looked at Chase and asked, "How did you know that?"

Chase was looking off at the busy street, overcome with emotion. Shaking her head in disbelief, she could only harbor one thought: *It was happening again.*

"Chase?" Rosa called a second time. "How did you know?"

Chase turned to the couple and answered, "I had a dream yesterday of a boy playing by a windmill with a dog. He was wearing a shirt that said Saint Stephen's on the front. When he went to leave, he called his dog and the dog's name was—"

"Max," Rico answered, finding the strength to say it out loud.

"That's right," Chase answered.

"I'm confused," Rosa said. "Why are you dreaming these things?"

"I don't know, Rosa, but I have a question," Chase replied.

She looked at Rico now. "Was the big windmill at your school, St. Stephen's, or was it someplace else?"

Rosa leaned in, yet again, and Rico mumbled slowly.

She looked to Chase and said, "The windmill was in Tuscany, where he spent summers with his grandparents. He loved it there."

Chase took Rico by the hand now, then asked, "And the dog, Max, was he your favorite?"

Rico looked Chase in the eye and slowly answered, "Best . . . dog . . . ever."

Rosa paused, thinking, then asked, "Why are you seeing things from the past?"

Chase looked from Rico over to Rosa and answered, "I don't see the past. The things I see . . . they're always the future."

Rosa hung on that statement for a moment and said, "But that makes no sense, Chase, he's not a boy anymore. That can't be his future."

Chase's eyes were back on Rico's, and she saw a sudden connection. It's as if they were having a conversation without a need for words. An understanding of what was really happening here.

"What?" Rosa asked. "Just say it."

"Did you know the question Rico came here to ask me today?" Chase inquired.

Rosa shook her head, "No. He had a nurse type the letter for him. Why?"

"Rico asked me if there's a heaven," Chase said.

Chase looked from Rico back to Rosa now, adding, "What if that's what I saw in the dream."

She continued then, "What if in heaven, we get to relive the most wonderful moments of our life. No illness, no wheelchairs, young, healthy, just love and perfect memories."

Rico nodded his head in agreement, causing Chase to rise from her chair and go to his side, saying, "I had no idea you'd come here today, and yet, I dreamt that. You, Max, all of it, not twenty-four hours ago. Your heaven."

Rosa went to Rico's side as well, taking his hand.

As she put her head down on his shoulder, Rosa said, "I just don't want to lose him."

Chase saw the love and devotion in her and said, "You won't. Like that kiss under the bridge, your love will never sunset."

Rosa wiped the tears from her face, looked down at her wrinkled hand, and asked, "Do you think when I join him someday, I'll get to be young and beautiful again too?"

Chase could feel her own eyes filling with tears, when Rico said slowly, "You're . . . beautiful . . . now."

As the couple held each other in a loving embrace, Chase silently rose and walked across the street to her friends in a waiting car. Her destination was the Waldorf Astoria, but her heart would stay with Rico and Rosa.

Flavio gave Chase a wave goodbye, rose from the steps of the building where he'd been waiting, and saw a teenage boy turn the corner and come his way.

"Gio, right? You live with Gavin and Chase?" Flavio asked him.

"Sì," Gio answered in Italian. "*Posso aiutarti?*", which means *May I help you?*

Flavio reached into his back pocket and produced a small piece of blue construction paper, folded in two.

"Can you give this to Gavin, *per favore*?" he asked.

Gio took the note and said in English, "Sure."

What Gio didn't realize was, he'd just been handed the missing piece to a puzzle Gavin and Chase had been working on since the day they landed in Italy. A puzzle neither knew existed. Until now.

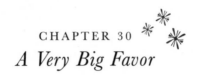

CHAPTER 30

A Very Big Favor

It was just shy of ten p.m. the night before the wedding, and Gavin was restless. It wasn't about taking Chase's hand in marriage the following day at noon—for that he was excited. This was something else. He felt like a man who had looked at an image and felt down to his bones that something was off about it. He was missing something, and it was driving him crazy.

To take his mind off this uneasy feeling, Gavin picked up the book that Gio had grabbed at the library, *The Count of Monte Cristo*. He took a seat in the home's small den, positioning himself in the chair next to the light. Once comfortable, he cracked open the novel and began his search for the famous swashbuckling count.

Gavin quickly noticed what Gio had warned him about: his late father liked to underline important passages in the story. There were so many ink lines, Gavin was amazed the library hadn't taken the book out of circulation and charged Gio's father for the damage. Perhaps because Matteo was the only person borrowing the book again and again, they let the infraction slide.

After reading the same paragraph three times and not comprehending a single word, Gavin closed the book and put it on the table to his right, just as Gio entered the room.

"Did you start it?" Gio asked, seeing the book resting there.

"Just now," Gavin replied. "Haven't really sunk my teeth into it yet."

Gio smiled and said, "I think you'll like it. Anyway, I'll see you at the wedding tomorrow. I'm going to grab a snack, then head to bed."

As the boy turned to go, Gavin called after him, "Hold up, I wanted to ask you something."

Gio turned and waited.

"Did you study flags in school?" Gavin asked.

"Like flags of different countries?" Gio replied.

"Exactly. Did you?" Gavin asked again.

Gio thought a moment, then answered, "Two years ago. Why?"

Gavin was bothered by Chase's strange dream. He knew in the past when odd things happened to Chase, there was always a reason behind it. On the car ride to the fancy hotel, Chase called Gavin and told him about Rico's connection to her dream about the boy, the dog, and the windmill. Still, this business with the strange flag whipping in the wind was a loose end Gavin couldn't abide.

"Gavin?" Gio called out. "Are you listening?"

Gavin snapped his mind back to Gio and said, "Sorry, I was wondering if you know of any flag that is all white with a single red stripe."

Gio ran through the dozens of flags he'd memorized for school two years prior, then answered, "Sorry, it doesn't sound familiar."

Gavin took a deep breath and said, "Okay. Good night then."

"Can I ask why?" Gio said.

"Doesn't matter, buddy," Gavin replied, "See you in the morning."

"Good night," Gio responded, starting toward the door again.

Then the boy stopped and said, "Actually. I think I do remember a flag that was white with a red line through it. For some reason, I'm thinking it was French."

"French?" Gavin replied, "I've seen France's flag. That's not it."

Gio scrunched his face a bit and said, "You're right, it's not. Maybe Napoleon then?"

The boy lingered, then added, "It was a long time ago and I might be misremembering. Sorry I wasn't more help."

With that Gio walked into the kitchen to see if there were any more pastries left on the counter by the fridge.

Gavin pondered Gio's information a moment, then opened his laptop computer and pulled up the Google search engine. In the empty box he typed "Flag France Napoleon" and up popped dozens of images of

France's blue, white, and red flag, with the thick white stripe always in the middle.

"That doesn't look anything like the one Chase saw in her dream," Gavin said to himself.

He shut the laptop and said out loud, "This is silly. I should be getting some rest."

Before he could rise from the couch, Scooter got up from his spot in the corner and walked over to Gavin, resting his head directly on his lap.

"You miss mommy?" Gavin asked the pup as he scratched his head.

The dog kept his chin pressed down on Gavin's lap, his nose touching the computer.

It was then Gavin remembered something else from Chase's dream. Bees. She said after seeing the flag she saw bees crawling on her arm.

Gavin looked at Scooter and said, "Should we? Yeah, I think we should."

With that Gavin reopened the laptop, pulled up the Google box, and typed in "France, Red, White, Bees." When he clicked "search" he immediately sighed, because the screen was filled with photographs of bees, tablecloths with bees, and other odd things.

Gavin thought a moment longer, then cleared the search box and wrote "Flag, Red, White, Bees." Again, he got an array of nonsense and lots of bee images.

Scooter barked, causing Gavin to jump, so he said, "Hang on, I'm trying here."

Gavin remembered what Gio had said moments ago and tried one last thing, typing "Flag, Red, White, Bees, Napoleon." When he hit the "enter" button on the keyboard, his eyes flew open with what appeared. Across the screen, dozens of flags, all white with a single red stripe going left to right and inside the stripe, three golden bees. Never two or four bees, always three.

Gavin stared at the image for a minute, then clicked several of the links, explaining the history of the flag and how it was connected to Napoleon. He then saw there was only one place on earth that flag flew two hundred years ago and still flew there proudly today.

Gavin took the phone from his pocket and quickly snapped a photograph of the flag. He texted it to Chase with the question, "Is this the flag from your dream?"

He wasn't even sure she was still awake, not knowing what fun the girls may have been having on the night before her wedding.

Gavin could see Chase had read his text message, and two seconds later his phone rang.

"It is, that's the flag, how did you find it?" Chase asked excitedly.

"Long story," Gavin answered. "Did you have a nice evening, I miss you."

"I did," she replied. "Miss you too sweetie. Hey, Gavin?"

"Yes hon," he responded.

"What does that flag mean?" she asked.

Gavin paused, then said, "I don't know yet, maybe nothing. I have to go, love you."

Chase rolled her eyes, hating it when Gavin kept secrets, but managed an exasperated, "Love you too," in response.

Gio ducked his head around the corner and said, "One pastry left, you want it?"

Gavin answered, "There were a half-dozen on that plate earlier."

Gio smiled, saying, "And now there's not. Last chance for the last one."

"Toss it," Gavin said, catching the pastry in mid-air before giving it a bite.

Gio then slapped himself on the forehead and said, "I almost forgot. That kid who's a little older than me was here earlier with his parents."

Gavin was confused, asking, "Who?"

Gio, more insistent, "The one who told the truth about the boat company where he worked."

"OH, FLAVIO!" Gavin answered. "Yes, what about him?"

Gio reached into the back pocket of his jeans and slid out the still folded piece of blue construction paper.

"He asked me to give this to you," Gio said.

"What does it say?" Gavin asked before taking it.

Gio shrugged his shoulders, "Beats me. It sounded private, so I didn't open it."

"Thanks, pal," Gavin said, taking the note.

He opened it up and Gio could see Gavin's eyes dancing left to right and back again as he read it. Then a strange look came over Gavin's face. He appeared upset and somewhat excited at the same time.

"Everything okay?" Gio asked.

"I don't know," Gavin answered, "I just . . . don't know."

Gavin sat with his arms wrapped around his knees for the longest time, just thinking. He turned his head and looked over at the novel, *The Count of Monte Cristo*, still sitting harmlessly on the end table, and snatched it up. Gavin began thumbing through the pages again, not reading, but searching for something.

He stared off at nothing, Gio still standing there watching it all in silence.

Gavin put the book down again, took out his wallet, and quickly searched through several business cards in the side compartment.

As he was about to dial his phone he said, "Gio, do you mind stepping out? I have to make a private call."

Gio replied, "Sure, I wanted some milk anyway."

Once the teen was clear of the room, Gavin held the phone to his ear and said, "Detective Bianco, I'm so sorry to bother you this late. It's Gavin Bennett, the American."

There was the faint sound of a man's voice on the other end of the phone when Gavin replied, "Yes, that's correct. Sir, I'm calling because I have a quick question about the investigation of the boating accident."

In the kitchen, Nonna was at the fridge getting a glass of apple juice, when Gio moved in close and gave her a hug.

"Who ate all my pastries?" the older woman asked.

Gio smiled and said, "Probably the dogs."

"Ah, ha," Nonna said, not buying a second of it.

Back in the other room, Gavin hung up the phone, opened his laptop again and started typing something in the search bar. A moment later Nonna stepped in to wish Gavin a good night's sleep before his big day.

She spied over his shoulder and said, "Web MD! Are you feeling okay?"

Gavin was scrolling through a dozen article headings when Nonna called his name louder this time: "GAVIN? Are you sick?"

He finally looked up and realized someone was in the room, saying, "Sick? Me? No. I'm fine. Goodnight, Nonna."

She leaned in and for the first time since Gavin came to Italy, Nonna gave him a hug as if he were part of her family.

As she broke the embrace, Gavin asked, "Wow, what was that for?"

Nonna looked toward the kitchen, then back to Gavin answering, "For being so kind to Giovanni and my daughter-in-law. And me. We love you, Gavin."

Gavin felt himself getting misty-eyed, as he replied in a slightly cracked voice, "Chase and I love all of you too."

Gavin's eyes returned to his computer screen, and he finished reading something. He then shut the laptop and placed the novel Gio had given him and the piece of paper from Flavio into a neat little pile on top. He folded both hands on all of it, as if praying, his eyes far away in thought.

He then suddenly raised his phone, looked at the time and said, "I hope he's still awake."

Gavin dialed another number, waited, and on the fifth ring, a groggy male voice answered, "Who died?"

"Hello?" Gavin replied. "Father Leo, is that you?"

The priest at Santa Maria church had been in bed asleep for more than an hour when Gavin's call shook him awake.

"Yes, it's me," Leo replied.

"What did you mean, who died?" Gavin asked.

The priest turned his bedside lamp on and sat up, answering, "Habits of the trade, my son. Whenever someone calls a priest at this unholy hour, it's usually because someone died or is very sick."

Gavin nodded and said, "Well, everyone is fine. I'm sorry to wake you."

"Well, now that you did, what do you need?" Leo asked.

Gavin, still holding the blue construction paper from Flavio in his hand, looked down at what the teen had written and said, "What I need is a very big favor."

"Okay," the priest answered.

"And I have to tell you up front, padre," Gavin continued, "it probably won't make sense, but you have to trust me, it's important."

The priest listened to Gavin's request, then said, "You're right, I don't understand, but I can tell from your voice this is important to you."

"It is, father," Gavin answered. "And isn't faith believing, even when we don't have complete understanding?"

Father Leo rubbed the sleep from his eyes, smiled, and asked, "You shopping for a job with the clergy, son?"

"No sir," Gavin answered calmly. "Just appealing to your better angels."

After the phone call, Gavin fell into a deep sleep. It wasn't that his mind was finally at rest, it was sheer exhaustion that overtook him in the dark of night. Good thing too, because in just a few hours the farmer from Manchester, Vermont, had a date with destiny on a stone altar that love built.

CHAPTER 31

A Day for Heroes

Chase's friends in Italy wanted to make her wedding day perfect, so they left nothing to chance. Tessa arranged for Rome's most sought-after makeup artist to arrive at Chase's suite at the Waldorf shortly before ten a.m.

Room service brought a pitcher of mimosas and a sterling silver tray of assorted bagels. Even Siena, the woman Chase helped save her candy shop, took part, hiring a young lady who played violin, to fill the suite with beautiful music as Chase got ready.

The dress fit perfectly, and she truly did look like Cinderella going to the ball. All she needed was proper transportation, and the ladies took care of that too. After they coaxed her out onto the balcony, Chase saw a golden horse-drawn carriage waiting on the cobblestone street below.

"You're kidding," Chase said, shocked.

Riley took Tessa's hand in hers and said to Chase, "We all chipped in."

"Thank you for letting me be part of this," Siena said thoughtfully to the other women.

Francesca smiled at Siena and replied, "Of course you're part of it."

Francesca then looked directly into Chase's eyes and said, "You touched so many people in your short time in Italy, we all had to play a role in this special day."

Riley approached Chase then, her fist closed around something, reaching out to hand it to the bride.

"What's this?" Chased asked.

"What is it you Americans say?" Riley answered. "You need something borrowed and something blue?"

Riley opened her fist and placed in Chase's open palm, her grandmother's brooch. The very one that the antique dealer had given back to Riley as a gift. It was pearl with gold trim around a small blue, sapphire stone.

"This is borrowed and blue," Riley said.

"Thank you," Chase replied, pinning it to the underside of her dress. "I'm honored to wear it and promise to give it back right after."

Chase was an only child, and she had always been curious about what it would have been like to have a sister. From that moment on, she never wondered again.

Across town, Gavin was struggling with a black tie that matched with his Armani suit.

"Need help?" a man's voice asked.

It was his driver and friend, Jules, looking sharp in his own suit, standing at the open bedroom door.

"I've spent my entire life avoiding situations where I wear a tie, but today is the exception," Gavin said.

With that, he completed the knot and slid the tie up into place.

As Gavin walked into the kitchen, Nonna, looking gorgeous in a sparkling blue dress, stared at him, and said, "Bello."

Jules nudged Gavin, translating, "She says you're handsome."

"Grazie, Nonna, you look pretty bello yourself," he replied.

Jules corrected him: "*Bello* is for boys. She's *bellissima*—that means beautiful."

Gavin gave Nonna a hug and said, "Bellissima then, very bellissima."

Before heading downstairs for the ceremony, Gavin asked, "Where's Gio?"

"Right here," the teen answered, emerging from his mother's room wearing a striking charcoal gray suit.

"Giovanni," Nonna exclaimed, "you look just like your father."

Gio ran his hands down both lapels and said, "I should, Nonna, this is one of his suits."

He adjusted the jacket a bit and added, "A little big, but nothing I can't grow into."

Gavin crossed the kitchen and shook Gio's hand firmly and said, "You look like a man. I'm sure your dad would be proud."

Downstairs, the horse-drawn carriage parked on the side street, giving Chase the shortest walk possible into the secret garden.

"Wait, not yet," Francesca cautioned Chase. "Your man has to get to the altar first."

A knock at the door upstairs told Gavin and the others it was time to come down and pledge eternal love.

Jules looked at Gavin and said, "Remember the sword in the stone. Today is a day for heroes."

Gavin smiled at him and said, "You ever think of writing screenplays? They'd love you in Hollywood."

Jules fussed with his own hair and answered, "I am handsome enough."

Nonna cleared her throat and said, "Do I need to get the broom and swat you both?"

Gio opened the door and said, "Let's go before she does it."

When Gavin reached the garden and took his place under the arbor, he noticed a young woman in a satin dress holding a violin, and a beautiful white piano with an equally attractive young man sitting at the keys.

"Hello," Gavin said to the young lady. "And you are?"

"My name is Ivana," she answered. "I was playing for your bride this morning at the hotel and now I'm here."

The girl then pointed to the young man at the piano, and said, "That's my brother, Simone."

Gavin waved and said, "Welcome to you both."

Gavin looked around the garden to see if there were any other surprises, and off to the left, flush against the building, was a twelve-foot by twelve-foot projection screen. It was blank and dark.

Brother Levi emerged from a side door, approached Gavin, and said, "Nervous?"

Gavin gave him a confident smile and said, "Never. Not for this. Not for her."

With that, Ivana looked to the garden entrance and whispered to Gavin, "Here we go."

Ivana nodded to her brother, and he began to play a familiar piece on the piano. It was Johann Pachelbel's famous "Canon in D," a very popular instrumental that brides world-round march to on their wedding days.

There were no chairs or pews, this not being a church, so the half-dozen or so in attendance stood on each side of the aisle and turned in unison to watch Chase make her grand entrance. Since Chase's family was back home in Seattle, it was Giovanni—Gio—with his arm extended, walking Chase toward the arbor and her love-struck fiancé.

Gavin was not one to cry, even at sappy movies, but seeing Chase with her auburn hair up, her eyes shining, and that stunning white dress, he was overcome with emotions too powerful to tame.

He cleared his throat and swallowed hard, but never broke eye contact with his bride-to-be. The piano and violin unison playing was as magnificent in its simplicity and beauty as any twenty-piece orchestra might be.

When Gio handed Chase off to Gavin, the two locked hands and turned to Levi, ready to take their sacred vows. Levi raised his right hand, signaling for the music to stop.

"Ladies and gentlemen, we gather here in the eyes of God to wed these two beautiful souls," Levi began.

Then he shocked Chase and Gavin when he said, "You know what? I'm sorry, I never do this, stop a ceremony once it has started, but something is wrong."

Gavin looked at Chase, wondering if she knew what was happening or if this was joke. She looked confused and alarmed as well.

Brother Levi then said, "It's tradition, especially in America, to give anyone at the wedding a chance to protest if something doesn't feel right."

Levi scanned the small crowd and said, "Is there anyone who has a problem with this marriage proceeding?"

Chase and Gavin both turned around and looked at their friends, completely lost, when Jules raised his hand and said very seriously, "Um, yeah. I do."

Francesca, Riley, Tessa, Siena, Nonna, and especially Gio all seemed stunned when Jules started walking toward the couple waiting under the arbor.

When Jules reached the front, next to Levi, he said, "My problem with this wedding is, your families aren't here to witness it."

Chase leaned in and said, "I told you we plan to do a big ceremony and party in the spring back home."

Jules answered, "Right, you did say that. BUT this is the actual ceremony and when it's done, you two will be legally married, correct?"

Gavin looked at Jules, getting a bit angry at the interruption, and answered, "YES, what's your point?"

Jules smiled at the couple and then reached inside of his jacket, producing a small black remote.

He pointed it at the large blank projection screen against the wall and said, "My point is . . ."

With that he pushed the button, and the screen lit up, revealing six different Zoom screens all lined up.

Jules then said, "Your family and those who love you should be with you when you say *I do.*"

Chase looked more closely at the screen and said, "Oh my God, there's my mom and your dad."

Gavin pointed at the screen, now saying, "And some of my friends from Manchester and all your friends from New York City."

Suddenly all the people important to Chase and Gavin were waving and shouting from the screen, "HELLO!"

"We love you, Chase," one woman called out.

"Love you too, Mom," Chase answered.

An older man with a barn behind him said, "Proud of you, son."

Gavin, getting choked up again, replied, "Thanks, Dad."

Chase then saw her friend Raylan, from the Furrever Java café in Manhattan, asking him, "You still adopting out dogs, Ray Ray?"

He smiled back through the screen, "You know it. How's Scooter?"

Chase laughed, "He's great, thanks."

Levi then said, "I know you two would like to catch up with everyone, but we have some business to take care of first."

Chase looked at Gavin, then back at the large screen and said, "You're right. Hey everyone, we're going to get married now."

Gavin looked from the screen filled with faces he loved, over to Jules, and said, "Nice touch, my man."

Jules nodded back, saying, "I figured it's only six hours ahead here, so they could all get up early and watch."

The ceremony was simple but sweet. Brother Levi shared the story of how Gavin and Chase met, and reminded them from the Bible that love is patient and kind. And when it came time for the actual vows, Gio had another surprise.

"We worked on this for a week," Gio said, before whistling.

Suddenly, Chase's dog, Scooter, and Gio's pup, Giuseppe, both appeared wearing bows on their dog collars, and walked up the aisle carrying boxes in their teeth.

"I'm guessing those are the wedding bands?" Levi asked.

Chase got down on one knee and gave Scooter and Giuseppe a kiss on the nose, before taking the small boxes, opening them to reveal the rings.

After blessing the wedding bands and each putting one on the other, Levi asked Chase and Gavin, "Is there anything you two want to share or say to each other?"

Chase, being a writer, thought about penning some poetic prose that would be so romantic and moving, their children's children would recite them a century from now. Instead, she and Gavin chose to share the same loving phrase that came often when they parted.

Chase looked at Gavin and said, "I love you now."

To which he replied, "I love you always."

Levi then said, "You may kiss the bride."

As they broke from their perfect kiss, Gavin and Chase hugged their friends and looked over to the big screen, watching the people they loved in America crying and blowing kisses.

Chase and Gavin felt so blessed in this moment, from all the gifts they'd received. What neither realized, what nobody realized, was that the greatest gift of all was waiting two blocks away at the very spot where love began.

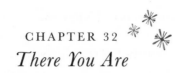

CHAPTER 32

There You Are

Verdile's restaurant had reserved the largest and most sharply dressed table for the eleven wedding guests who slowly made their way down the stone walk, cars honking and people cheering, every time someone saw Chase in her gown.

Rose petals were laid from the curb to just inside the front door, another nice touch courtesy of Riley and Tessa.

After sitting at the long table, just to the side of the well-appointed bar with the famous bell that waiters rang on special occasions, Chase and Gavin raised a glass of red wine to toast their good fortune.

Gavin took an index card from his breast pocket and, to everyone's surprise, read in Italian, "*Dio ci benedica tutti.* Which means *May God bless us all.*"

After the toast, as everyone engaged in joyous dialogue, Chase noticed Francesca's conflicted expression as she looked around the restaurant. Chase knew this had to be hard for her, being back for a wedding reception, knowing Verdile's was where Matteo had proposed marriage and given Francesca that special kiss.

"You okay?" Gavin asked Chase, seeing she was worried about her friend.

She looked into Gavin's hopeful eyes and her mood instantly changed, answering, "Yes, my husband, I'm very happy."

Gavin kissed her deeply and Gio leapt up and ran behind the bar, asking an employee, "*Posso?*—May I?"

When the bartender smiled and stepped aside, Gio yanked the rope side to side, ringing the loud brass bell, causing every head to turn.

Chase and Gavin ended the kiss with giggles, both thinking that they had seen people tap spoons on glassware at weddings, urging the newlyweds to kiss, but the bell was positively rambunctious.

Food began to arrive and there were endless and exotic drinks; everything about the wedding and reception was perfect. Then it happened.

Gavin's phone, sitting dark and harmless on the table, let out a "ding" indicating he had a text message.

"Another congratulations?" Chase asked, as Gavin retrieved his phone.

Gavin looked down at the screen, then immediately over to the restaurant's front door, catching the eyes of Father Leo, who was waiting just outside the glass on the sidewalk.

He gave Chase a quick peck on the lips and said, "No, sweetheart, something much better, I hope and pray."

Gavin rose and dashed to the door, opening it quickly and closing it behind him, talking to the priest just outside.

Chase continued watching them, unsure what was happening, then realized there was another man standing with Father Leo who she didn't recognize. He was dressed like Brother Levi, in a long baggy brown robe, his hair short, his demeanor calm.

Chase saw Gavin take a very deep breath before opening the door, letting both men into the restaurant. Father Leo acted normal, smiling and waving to people he knew, but the other man stood silent, his eyes, at first distant, coming more alive with each passing second.

The man slowly looked around Verdile's, so intense, it was as if he were trying to memorize every inch of the restaurant.

Music was playing from speakers in the ceiling above and the hum of the crowd sounded like waves on the ocean at night. Brother Levi was joking with Gio about how many rolls one boy could eat before exploding, and then, as he laughed, Levi's eyes drifted toward the door, and he saw the unexpected guest.

Levi rose and approached Gavin, his brother, Leo, and the man he'd grown fond of in recent months.

"Tommaso? What are you doing here?" Levi asked.

Tommaso didn't answer, his gaze resting now on the beautiful woman with dark hair, sitting next to a handsome teenage boy. His eyes were fixed on Francesca and Gio.

Levi looked to his brother now and asked, "Did you bring him here? Why?"

Father Leo looked at Gavin for help, then Gavin answered, "I asked him to."

Levi then stepped into Tommaso's view and shook his hand. "It's good to see you off the island finally."

Yet again, Tommaso was silent, shifting his head to the right so he could see around Levi's face and look back at the wedding table and the woman with her child.

At that very moment, Francesca raised up her white ceramic cup of espresso to take a sip, her eyes drifting off in the distance and locking on the man who was staring at her from just inside the front door.

Francesca's eyes met Tommaso's and time stopped.

The cup fell from her hands and landed on a plate, breaking into several pieces.

The breaking glass was loud enough to startle those around her, everyone looking to see if Francesca was alright.

She stood up now, still staring at Tommaso, and he back at her.

Chase saw her face and stood up herself, turning to see what had Francesca so alarmed.

"Tommaso?" Levi said again to no avail.

Gavin looked from Tommaso's face, over to Francesca's, and then back to Levi and Leo's, shocking them when he said, "His name isn't Tommaso."

Francesca slowly started walking toward the three men, her feet barely able to move. Chase, watching this, instinctively motioned to the bartender, pointing at the music coming from the ceiling and then drawing her finger across her throat, asking him to shut it off.

Suddenly, the music stopped, and the roar of the crowd died down instantly, everyone wondering what was happening.

Francesca inched her way to Tommaso and brought herself face to face with him. Her eyes, at first a sea of confusion, filled with tears and she began to tremble.

Chase joined her, then leaned into Gavin's ear and whispered, "Who is this man?"

Gavin pulled Chase to the side and in a low voice, only she could hear, explained.

"Your dream, about the white flag with a red stripe," he started.

"What about it?" Chase answered.

"There is no flag like that, but then I remembered the bees, on your arm." Gavin continued.

"What about them?" Chase replied.

"There once was a flag that was white with a red stripe and on the stripe were three golden bees," Gavin continued.

Chase just waited for more.

"Napoleon flew it when he was placed in exile on the island of Elba," Gavin said.

"Elba?" Chase asked, still confused.

"Yes," Gavin answered. "Then there's the book, *The Count of Monte Cristo.*"

"What about it?" Chase asked.

"Francesca's husband Matteo took it out of the library all the time," Gavin explained. "Underlining favorite words and passages."

Chase shook her head, lost again.

"The hero in the book goes to the island of Elba," Gavin said. "And every time there is a reference to Elba in the Count of Monte Cristo, Matteo underlined it."

Chase looked at Francesca, still looking at this man and said to Gavin, "I don't understand what any of this has to do with—"

Gavin then pulled the note that Flavio had sent him and handed it to Chase, "This is from Flavio, the boy at the shipping company. Read it."

There was an overhead light casting a spotlight down, as Chase opened the folded construction paper and read.

Dear Gavin,

I've kept one secret from you and even now I'm not sure I should be telling you this because I would never want to raise false hope. The three men on the boat died that day, of that I'm certain, their bodies lost to the sea. But there is one thing the police didn't know.

On the top deck of the ship there were six life jackets clipped to a cable line. They are there just in case the crew encounters rough water. When Crane Shipping recovered the wreckage of the boat, the cable line was still intact, and the life vests still attached. Except one. One was missing. It likely became unclipped in the storm and drifted away. Unless.

I hope I did the right thing telling you this.

Your friend,

Flavio

Chase's mind was swimming with possibilities as Gavin continued. "When I went to the island of Elba to meet Levi, I also met several monks. One of them was this man, Tommaso."

Chase looked at the man staring at Francesca, repeating the name, "Tommaso?"

"Yes," Gavin continued. "After reading Flavio's note I called that detective, Bianco, and asked him the names of the two crewmen who died with Matteo on the boat?"

Chase starting to catch up now: "And?"

"Their first names were Paulo and Tommaso," Gavin replied.

Chase looked back at the man again and said, "So he's?"

"Listen," Gavin replied. "I learned this man became a houseguest at the monk's retreat after suffering a traumatic brain injury. He was found wandering the island of Elba with a head wound within days of the boat disaster."

"Wait, wait, this is going too fast," Chase said.

She continued asking, "So the boat hits the storm, this Tommaso puts on a life vest and somehow gets hurt but survives. How?"

Gavin then, "I looked at the map, and where that boat capsized, the nearest island is Elba. Someone in a vest could have very easily drifted there, especially if they were clinging to some piece of wreckage."

Chase thought a moment and then asked, "But what does this have to do with Francesca or the flag and book?"

Gavin smiled at Chase now, indicating there was one last piece to the puzzle.

"What? Tell me before I burst," she said.

"Tommaso Michele Coppola was the worker on the ship, date of birth: December 26, 1962," Gavin said.

Chase quickly looked at the man in front of Francesca, then back to Gavin and said, "That would make Tommaso sixty years old. This man is forty at best."

"One last thing and then I'm done," Gavin said, taking Chase's hand.

"Flavio told me it was unseasonably chilly the night of the storm and that the men on board were known to loan out their warm jackets to any passengers they might be transporting," Gavin explained.

Levi walked over to join Chase and Gavin now, asking in an insistent voice, "What in God's name is going on?"

Chase turned to Levi and asked, "When this man came to live with you, did he tell you his name was Tommaso?"

Levi scratched his head and said, "No, he was suffering memory loss and needed bed rest. He told us his name later."

"Tommaso?" Gavin asked the monk, "He said to you, 'My name is Tommaso'?"

Levi looked over at the man he had grown fond of these past six months and replied, "Now that I think on it, no. He was wearing a work jacket with his name stitched right over his heart, right here, Tommaso."

Gavin then said to Chase, "The book, your dream, the storm, the brain injury, it all pointed to Elba and this man."

Chase brought both hands to her face now, realizing the truth.

Francesca saw the scar over the man's left eye, understanding he must have suffered a terrible blow to the head somehow.

She looked him in the eyes and said, "Do you know who I am?"

The man looked around and realized everyone was watching him now, and that made him anxious.

"Don't look at them, look at me," Francesca insisted.

Levi instructed from the side, "Look at her, Tommaso, please."

The man looked from Levi back to Francesca now, as she said, "Your name isn't Tommaso, it's Matteo."

Hearing the word from his wife's lips seemed to break a wall of thick ice around his brain, images starting to flash into his mind. Soon, Gio and Nonna were standing at Francesca's side, the man realizing that both were crying as they looked at him.

The man looked to the boy and a tear fell down his right cheek. Then to his mother, who was so overwhelmed she could barely stand. His eyes then returned to Francesca's and something in them changed. His lost and distant look was replaced by one of love and familiarity.

Francesca saw it instantly, causing her to say, "There you are."

Matteo slowly raised his hand and took his index finger, gently moving a single strain of hair off Francesca's forehead. He then traced the finger down her nose, resting it on her lips.

"Francesca," he softly said to her.

Nonna gasped and started to cry, Gio taking her arm to steady her.

Instead of a kiss, Matteo fell forward into Francesca's arms and wrapped his wife in a hug. As tears streamed down his face, he broke the embrace and open his arms to his son and mother.

"How is this possible?" Francesca asked Gavin.

"We all lose our way sometimes," Gavin answered.

Francesca looked to Chase, and as she wiped tears from her face, Chase said, "It's a long story, but it has a happy ending."

Gio saw the brown robe his father was in and asked, "What is he wearing?"

Levi answered the boy, "Your dad was with us for a time, healing. That's why he looks like that."

Chase looked over at Father Leo, and said, "I heard a story once about a man who had to become something he wasn't, going into another world to save others. Helping them find their way."

The priest smiled at the memory of his talk with Chase, then said, "That too had a happy ending."

Matteo then said, "Finding your way."

"What are you saying, sweetheart?" Francesca asked.

Matteo reached into the pocket on his robe and withdrew his clenched fist.

"Perhaps this helped me," he said, handing something to Gio.

The boy took it and smiled. It was the compass Matteo had repaired back on the island of Elba.

"Merry Christmas," Matteo said to his son.

Brother Levi took Matteo by the hand then and said, "I feel like I should give you a winnowing oar."

Matteo answered, "I guess my name isn't Odysseus after all."

Matteo looked around then and realized Chase was in a wedding dress and the others were all dressed up, asking, "Did somebody get married?"

Francesca took Matteo's hand and said, "Yes, dear, this is Chase and Gavin. They are very special to us because they—"

She stopped talking, getting choked up again, before finishing, "They got you home."

"Congratulations," Matteo said to the newlyweds.

Nonna hugged her son and looked at the scar above his eye, asking, "Are you alright?"

He rubbed his forehead and said, "There's a lot I don't remember or know, Mamma, but yes, now, I'm okay."

Francesca returned to her husband's arms and said, "You didn't give me a Christmas gift, and what I want, I want right now."

With that, Francesca moved her lips closer to Matteo's and they gently shared a kiss, to the applause of everyone in the restaurant.

When they broke their embrace, Matteo said, "What's this now?" spotting a dot of red sauce on Francesca's dress.

He then took a dab of club soda on a napkin and began blotting the tiny stain.

As his face was only inches from Francesca's, she could only stare, not believing that all of this was real.

"Clean as a whistle," he said, looking deeply into her eyes, realizing he was back where he belonged.

Suddenly the bell behind the bar began to ring and all eyes turned to Gio, swinging the brown rope side to side, as happy music and laughter filled the air.

A short time later, Chase and Gavin were escorted by horse and carriage to the suite at the Waldorf Astoria to begin the next chapter in their never-ending love story. Francesca, Matteo, and Gio retired to their modest apartment in the Monti neighborhood of Rome to reconnect and begin again.

Nonna, overcome with emotion from having her son back, felt an overwhelming desire to talk to her late husband and share this miracle that could only have happened on Christmas Eve.

Quietly and by herself, she found her way down to Alessandro's secret garden, to share the news about their son's seeming resurrection.

Nonna stood at the center of the heart made of stone, looked up at the flowing fountain, and removed a small letter from her pocket. It was the one Alessandro had written for Nonna, for moments just like this.

Her wrinkled and trembling hands unfolded the letter as her glistening eyes looked down upon his words—

My beautiful Ava,
How do you say goodbye to someone who has been your entire world? The answer is that you don't.
   If you are reading this I am now with God, but this is not goodbye.

*I will make a place for you and will wait for you with an open
and patient heart.*

*In the meantime, on the days when you miss me, go stand at the
center of my heart and look for a sign.*

Until I hold you again, I am yours always,
Alessandro

Nonna looked down and saw her feet resting directly at the center of
the Alessandro's heart.

She then glanced up to the piercing blue sky above and said, "I am
here, my sweet. Send me a sign."

It was then that something inexplicable happened. Nonna heard a
gentle chirp, lowered her gaze to the water fountain in front of her, and
there a large bright red cardinal was perched, not quenching its thirst,
but looking straight at her.

Nonna smiled at the messenger from heaven and said, "*Buon Natale*—
Merry Christmas."

ACKNOWLEDGMENTS

Setting a story in a country you have never visited is a Herculean task that cannot be completed alone. When I put out a *call for help* for information about what life in Italy is like, several people answered the call. Special thanks to Vincent Zandri, Mary Fran Fiorillo, Arista Caffaro, Nick Hargrave, and Alexondra Purnomo for your invaluable insight.

Having an editor who has lived in Italy is also a Godsend, so a VERY special thank you to my editor Robert Edmonson at Paraclete Press for making certain my *Italiano* was *perfetto!!!*

Also, a tip of the hat to the entire support team at Paraclete including, Jennifer Lynch, Rachel McKendree, Danielle Bushnell, and Sister Estelle Cole.

To my family for their continued support and to all of you who purchase these books and continue to encourage my writing.

A heartfelt thank you to Brian Herzlinger and his lovely wife Megan for believing in me and helping us bring the story of Chase and Gavin to the television screen.

Last, but certainly not least, much love also goes to my partner in crime, my sweet wife Courtney, and to all of my furry pack at home.

You make my life a happy place.

God Bless,
John

ABOUT PARACLETE PRESS

Paraclete Press is the publishing arm of the Cape Cod Benedictine community, the Community of Jesus. Presenting a full expression of Christian belief and practice, we reflect the ecumenical charism of the Community and its dedication to sacred music, the fine arts, and the written word.

SCAN
TO
READ
MORE

Learn more about us at our website:

www.paracletepress.com

or phone us toll-free at

1.800.451.5006

YOU MAY ALSO BE INTERESTED IN . . .

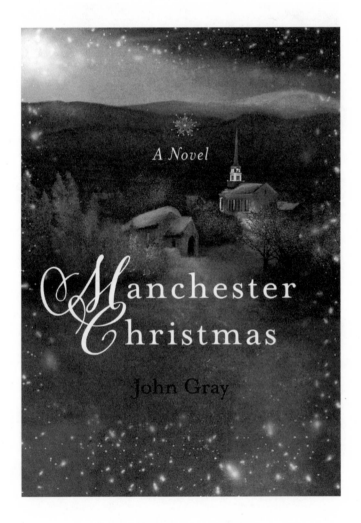

A Novel

Manchester Christmas

John Gray

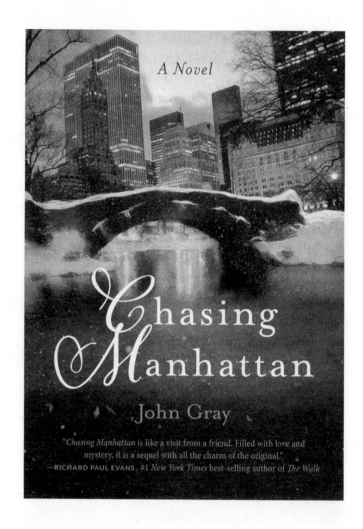

A Novel

Chasing Manhattan

John Gray

"*Chasing Manhattan* is like a visit from a friend. Filled with love and mystery, it is a sequel with all the charm of the original."
—RICHARD PAUL EVANS, #1 *New York Times* best-selling author of *The Walk*

www.paracletepress.com